MIRROR FLOWER, WATER MOON

TOOTH & CLAW
BOOK 5

AMELIA FAULKNER

Ravensword Press

CONTENTS

ONE

The books still glowed.

Nobody seemed to believe him about that, even if they said they did. Randall came the closest to not treating Jay like he'd grown a second head, but even Han only seemed to be humouring him about this.

They'd stuffed the suitcases back into Han's Range Rover after nightfall and driven all the way to the Rotherhithe tunnel just to double back on themselves once they were south of the river to get home, and Jay was eternally grateful that while Han seemed willing to cook his fingers off in the sun in the name of science, he took Ellis' warnings about crossing running water as seriously as Ellis had intended them to be.

Now they filled a spare room in the apartment. Aaron had sifted them into piles based on whether or not they were in English, then Jay had sub-categorised them into glowing and not-glowing. Beyond that, he didn't really know what to do other than start reading, so that's what he did.

There was no master list, no reading order. The books all glowed in different colours, and while some were faint, others were bright as daylight. The ones that didn't glow were still crammed with randomly-gathered information. None were printed or otherwise mass-produced.

Every single book in this stolen collection was hand-written.

"Hey. Did you want dinner?"

Jay gasped in surprise. Han had snuck into the room so quietly that his voice startled Jay. "Don't do that!"

"Mate, if sneaking up on you turns out to be my super power, I'm gonna want a refund on this whole vampirism thing." Han grinned and plopped himself down on the seat next to Jay. "It's late. Have you forgotten to eat again?"

Jay's stomach growled, presumably just in case Jay tried to lie, and he sighed. "Fine. Yes, I may have. I could eat. I mean, I should eat. Fine, let's eat."

Han laughed and leaned over to kiss his cheek. "Nerd."

"Geek." He eyed Han's hands, just to make sure he still had both of them.

Han tutted. He'd seen Jay checking. Of course he had. Goddamn vampire super-senses. There was no evading his notice. "I'm thinking I'll test factor 50 next."

"Oh, just you dare!" Jay smacked his thigh lightly. "You'll make me go grey, and grey is so not me! Where are we eating?"

"Abokado?" Han offered.

Jay checked the time on his phone, then hopped up. "Yeah, we can make it."

Han stood and looked to the books, then tailed Jay to the door.

IT WASN'T the kind of place people went to for a romantic date, but Abokado was just across the street from the glitzy tower block they lived in, and because the area was mostly offices, the fast-food restaurant was pretty quiet in the evening. Jay picked out a small sushi selection while Han nursed a bagel he could pretend to forget to eat, and they tucked themselves into a corner.

"Any progress?" Han murmured.

Jay figured that if they were in danger of being overheard, Han would detect it way before he did, so he parted his chopsticks and picked out a maki roll. "I don't think so. It's all so chaotic. These people needed a good PA."

"You think there's more than just Bryce?" Han frowned at that and set his untouched bagel down.

Jay shrugged. "So many different styles of handwriting, the books are all like different ages and bindings... I think she might've stolen most of them herself. Didn't Ellis say she'd gone around killing other sorcerers for decades? Maybe these are all the things worth pinching off them."

Han propped his elbow on the little table and stared off into space. "Right. And if she was killing them all off, then it's not like you can just find one and ask for their help."

"Yeah," Jay agreed. "Oh my god! What if there are other people out there like me who don't know about any of this because she's killed off anyone who could have taught them?"

Han shrugged at that. "I'd say it's likely. Without numbers to crunch I couldn't give you the statistical likelihood, but it makes sense, doesn't it? Then that would leave a vacuum that would take decades to recover from." He grinned. "Congratulations, you just became Yoda to a whole new generation of Padawans!"

Jay scoffed at him. "Shut up! I don't even know what I'm doing!"

"I wouldn't worry about it. It's not like there's any hurry." Han picked up the bagel again as though this was totally the time he would put it in his mouth. "You can build an index as you go. You love that shit."

"Administration?" Jay raised an eyebrow.

"No." Han laughed. "Organisation."

Jay picked at his sushi and didn't say a damn thing, because Han was right.

HE ATE Han's bagel on their way home while Han talked about further ideas for narrowing down which parts of sunlight were actually harmful, and he almost missed it when Han said, "Phone."

On cue, Jay's phone buzzed in his pocket, so he swallowed his latest mouthful and pulled it out. The caller ID read *Randall*, so he answered.

"Hey hey, Randall! What's up?"

"Hey, Jay. Hey, Han, if he's there."

"He is," Jay confirmed.

"Great." Randall sounded full of false cheer. "Look, I, um. I was talking to Dad earlier about... you know, Bryce and... the books and stuff..."

Jay nodded in sympathy.

Bryce had kidnapped Randall's dad almost twenty years ago. The poor bugger had just gone out to get a newspaper, and so far as Randall knew he never came back. Except it turned out a sorcerer had plucked him off the street and used him as her own personal weapon of mass destruction ever since, and it was only after she kidnapped Ellis that he got rescued.

Jay couldn't even begin to imagine what George Carter's life had been like, or how he'd managed to retain any shred of sanity in all those years, but he must've met pretty much every single sorcerer in the UK... right before he killed them against his will.

"Uh huh," he prompted.

"Anyway, he says there was one she really hated, but never managed to bump off. She wasn't even willing to risk Dad on the job. She just basically ignored the bloke and hoped he never came for her."

Jay stopped walking, but Han grabbed his elbow and started him off again, until they reached the kerb. "You're joking," he breathed. "You mean there's actually one still alive?"

"Yeah." Randall still sounded hesitant.

"And he's a psychopath?" Han offered.

Jay snorted, then repeated for Randall's benefit. "Han wants to know if the guy's a psycho."

"I dunno. But, well... She was a total nutcase, right? And she was too scared of the bloke to even try it." Randall sighed. "Anyway I thought I'd let you know."

"Okay. Thanks for asking him. I really appreciate it. How's he doing? Is he settling in okay?"

"Pretty well, yeah. Mum's, like, helping him catch up on what's gone on in the world, and Kieran's calming down a bit, too."

Jay bit his lip and glanced to Han, unsure whether he should ask the next question, but Han gave him a little nod. "And Ellis?"

Randall sighed into the phone. "I think he needs some kind of help. He doesn't seem to be handling things well. I can't say I blame him, but he's just... in laa-laa land most of the time, you know? Doesn't want to eat, keeps saying he's unravelling, he's getting colder and colder. I'm really worried he's just..." Randall paused. "Fading."

Han opened the door to their building and strode across the vast, marble-lined lobby, and Jay hurried after him. Their goal was to get to the lifts as fast as they could so nobody asked any questions, but living without a reflection was pretty hard, and Jay doubted they could get away with this forever. It was just another thing they needed to find a solution for.

He didn't mind. It was better than the alternative.

Better than Han being dead.

"And of course he can't just see any old psychiatrist," Jay sighed. "How do you talk to them about being tortured by a sorcerer?"

"Yeah," Randall agreed. "Anyway. I'll let you get on. Thought I'd just let you know about this bloke Dad never met." He chuckled briefly.

"Thanks! I don't suppose your dad got an address, did he?"

"Yeah apparently he's out near Aylesbury or somewhere near there."

"That's not actually an address," Jay chuckled.

"You think not," Randall said. "Then you find out who it is."

The lift reached their floor, and Jay followed Han out of it. "Come on, don't keep me in suspense! I'll get wrinkles!"

"All right, all right." Randall sighed. "Apparently it's the Duke of Oxford."

Jay blinked slowly. "Like, an actual duke."

"An actual duke," Randall confirmed.

"Right," he said faintly.

"So, uh. Good luck with that."

"Yeah. Thanks a bunch!"

"You're welcome!"

Jay hung up and stared at Han, then stuffed the last bit of bagel in his mouth and chewed it.

"I just want to get this straight," said Han as he dropped onto the sofa. "Our one lead to someone who could potentially help you sort all these books out is basically untouchable *and* — I reckon this is the important part here — too terrifying for a woman who used a werewolf to murder her enemies to pick a fight with."

Jay swallowed tightly, and winced as the lump of bagel went down uncomfortably.

"Yeah," he croaked. "I think you've pretty much nailed it."

Maybe going solo wasn't such a bad idea.

TWO

HAN PULLED his laptop out and set it up at the dining table. He figured that anyone with a peerage would be eminently findable on the internet, so at the very least they could find out whether this was remotely worth pursuing.

Being a vampire was the weirdest thing. He supposed that, sooner or later, he'd get used to it, but for now he was sorely limited. He couldn't use touch-screens or phones, didn't show up on cameras or in mirrors. All that was bad enough, but he had a business to run, and he'd been forced to start getting to the office before dawn, keeping all his blinds closed, and not leaving until after sunset.

Employees were gonna start to worry whether the company was in trouble at that rate, and those kinds of rumours could turn into self-fulfilling prophecies like wildfire.

It might've been better to let nature take its course, but he'd made his choice, and now he got to deal with the consequences like a real adult.

Jay fetched himself a glass of water from the kitchen then came to sit next to him. "Okay. What've we got?"

Han rested his knee against Jay's and turned the screen toward him. "Duke of Oxford. Three sons. Wife died a few years ago. Oldest son lives in America, youngest is in the RAF, but the middle works right down the road." He jerked his thumb toward the window over his shoulder. "He's a lawyer. Or a trainee lawyer, anyway."

Jay rubbed his knee slowly against Han's as he gulped down water. "You're thinking we can't approach a duke out of nowhere, but we can talk to one of his kids?"

"He's in town, right? We can test whether or not sorcery is inherited. Just walk past the guy carrying one of your glowy books and see if it catches his eye." He grinned. "If not, phase two, we send this duke a letter or something."

"Can you find out where he works?"

"Baby, it's the internet. I can find anything I want."

Jay laughed. "You're so sexy when you're smart."

Han shook his head. "What you're saying is I'm always sexy?"

"Bingo!"

He flashed a sly grin. "So if I'm sexy, does that mean you want to do sexy things?"

He heard the way Jay's pulse sped up, saw the muscles in his irises contract as his pupils dilated. His breath quickened, and the slight shift in posture was like a signal flare to Han's new senses, so he already knew the answer, but waited for Jay to say it.

"Oh, yes!"

Han shut the laptop and bounced out of his chair, then reached toward Jay with hands like claws. "Better run, then, before I catch you."

Jay launched out of his chair, giggling as he ran for the bedroom. "Oh no, the monster's gonna get me! And then he's gonna... Wait, what exactly am I running from, here?"

"The big bad scary vampire?" he offered as he sprinted after Jay.

Jay scoffed and kicked his shoes off. "The really small not remotely terrifying vampire?" he teased.

"Oh, I am totally making you pay for that!" Han shed his own shoes, then peeled off his clothes and scattered them on his way to the bed.

Jay shed clothes just as fast, and threw himself backward onto the bed with a whoop of glee. "My evil plan comes to fruition!"

He shook his head as he climbed onto the bed and straddled Jay's lap so that their cocks lay together, and he idly brushed his fingers over Jay's toned stomach. He watched as skin twitched and contracted under his touch, making tiny translucent hairs raise from the surface. He could see the way that Jay's pulse made the flesh over his ribcage and in his throat fluctuate minutely with every beat of his heart, but it was more than just his sight that had been turned up to eleven.

Beneath his fingers, he could feel each one of those tiny hairs as he ran his hands over them. With a single breath he could smell Jay's arousal, the increased pheromones from the faintest release of sweat. The warmth which radiated from his body now that blood was rushing to his cock was something he could detect from even the least sensitive parts of his own body as it was conducted by the air between them.

There wasn't any rhyme or reason to how a vampire functioned that he could tell. He'd done all kinds of experiments, but none of the physics or biology made any sense, and one of the things he still couldn't figure out was that his body was still capable of arousal, still able to gain and sustain an erection despite his faulty heart no longer beating at all. But he wasn't going to complain about that in the slightest, because the idea of living without *this* was just unacceptable.

"Hey," Jay breathed as he ran his hands over Han's thighs. "What're you thinking?"

"Oh, the usual," he murmured as he leaned forward. "How beautiful you are. How lucky I am. You know, all that stuff."

"Flattery will get you everywhere with me," Jay chuckled, and lifted his head for the incoming kiss.

He settled his lips softly against his husband's and, like always, they fit perfectly. Jay's warmth seeped into his mouth, soon followed by his tongue, and Han drew his hands up to roam freely across Jay's ribs and over his biceps.

"But what're you really thinking?" Jay added once their lips parted ways.

Han laughed at that and dipped his head to Jay's throat to kiss, to lick, to nibble at his tender skin, and Jay moaned softly as his head fell back against the pillows. "I'm thinking sixty-nine."

"Oh, I like that thought!"

"Thought you might." He grinned and rolled aside, then turned around and waited as Jay wriggled himself further down the bed.

Bloody hell, he was absolutely amazing.

Han straddled Jay's head and dropped forward onto all fours, and Jay didn't hesitate in wrapping his lips around the cock which lay across them. The wet heat which enveloped him was mindbogglingly amazing, and it took him a few seconds to remember he had something else to do other than just stay there getting his dick sucked.

He leaned down and took Jay into his own mouth, drawing him in slowly and ensuring his shaft was nice and wet before he started to bob his head, suckling gently, luxuriating in the feel of that gorgeous cock in his mouth every bit as much as he was enjoying Jay working below him.

There was no hurry, no race to climax. There never was with Jay. He would rush around his daily life juggling a hundred tasks at once, but the moment Han got him into bed he was utterly at ease, happy to lay back and let Han take the wheel. They sucked each other with tenderness, with love, gently easing each other into slowly-building pleasure which crept up on him like an old friend. He began to thrust a little into Jay's mouth just as Jay began to thrust into his, and Jay's soft moans were every bit as intoxicating as his mouth and his dick.

Han lightly traced fingers over Jay's thighs, and Jay ran his hands over Han's arse. Warmth turned to heat, and heat turned to pressure, and he could feel the hardening of Jay in his mouth, hear the tightening of his balls.

He moaned gently, a little encouragement, and Jay bucked beneath him. His dick jerked as he came, and Han swallowed as his own orgasm rippled through his body.

Jay was worth the swallow.

They rocked together for long, precious seconds, and then were still. He carefully released Jay and eased his hips back from Jay's mouth, then fell aside and sprawled a leg over Jay's chest as he wrapped an arm over his legs.

"Oh god," Jay whispered. "I love you so much."

Han smiled and kissed Jay's leg. "I love you too, gorgeous."

If they could just stay like this forever, he'd be the happiest man on Earth.

HIS EYES FLICKED open as the alarm went off, and he

reached for his phone out of habit, only remembering once he had it that he needed the stylus that lay next to it.

This needed fixing, fast. Technology use would only increase and get steadily more biometric, and he made his entire fortune out of being able to use that technology.

A tap and a swipe silenced the alarm, and he leaned over to kiss Jay. "Morning, gorgeous."

"Muuhh," Jay managed, but it got stolen by a yawn.

Han slipped out of bed and hurried to the bathroom. He had something to take care of, and it was like a dead weight in his gut until he did, so he closed the door and placed his hands either side of the sink, casting a glance to the empty mirror while he focused on getting his insides to expel what he'd consumed. He kept it as quiet as he could, then brushed his teeth. Sunrise wouldn't be for another hour, but he vastly preferred to take care of these things on his own schedule.

Jay pushed the door open and wandered in, still yawning, his hair adorably mussed. "Wee time," he said as he grabbed Han's bum.

"Urgh, you humans with your bodily functions," he laughed as he ran his hand down Jay's side.

"Yeah, yeah. We're gross. Get out." Jay grinned at him.

Han smirked and left the bathroom so Jay could do the essentials, and wandered out to the lounge to pop his laptop open. There was no getting away from the fact that he could hear everything Jay did in there, but he could at least pretend not to, so he spent his time quickly doing a few more searches on this duke's local son and scribbled down some addresses for Jay. When Jay's footsteps emerged from the bedroom, he closed the laptop and pointed to the notepad.

"Addresses for you," he explained. "The Viscount's office, plus a couple of places he gets spotted."

Jay blinked and looked to the notepad. "You've been stalking?"

"You never need to stalk rich people," he muttered. "Someone else is always doing it and shoving it online."

Another reason to fix the technology problem sooner rather than later.

"I suppose." Jay stretched and stifled another yawn, then broke out one of his dazzling smiles. "Shower?"

"You're on." He led Jay back through to the bathroom. "Are you going to go try and track him down today?"

"I may as well." Jay turned the shower on and waited for it to warm up before he stepped in. "At least do the old walk-by-with-a-book thing. We can always regroup if he doesn't react. You? Day in the office?"

"Of course," Han chuckled as he shut the enclosure door. "Gotta make the money, honey."

"Great, we'll go together, then I'll sneak off out once the world wakes up."

"Okay. And just in case he's actually a terrifying sorcerer himself, be careful, yeah?"

Jay drew a soapy X across his chest. "Cross my heart," he promised.

Han nodded. It'd be hypocritical for him to push harder for Jay to take care of himself, so he just smiled and reached for the shampoo.

But he doubted it'd be easy to sit in his office waiting for Jay to come back knowing the duke was the scariest sorcerer in the country.

THREE

JAY DID his floor-walk through the office once people were actually there, saying hi, chatting with staff, being Han's public face so that Han could hide in his office as long as possible, but once that was done he snuck off outside and wandered through the warren of narrow streets between Blackfriars and Temple. The weather was bitterly cold, but at least there wasn't much wind, and he hunkered down in his coat with his scarf up to his nose, book clutched against his chest with one gloved hand.

He wasn't sure this was the greatest plan ever conceived. Now that he drew nearer to the Viscount's workplace, he began to chew over all the ways it could go horribly wrong. What if the fella saw the book and used some terrifying magical powers to steal it off him? What if he put a curse on Jay and left Jay to die horribly of plague later in the day? Or what if he just didn't take any notice and they had to try and find a way of contacting the duke directly?

He popped out of the tiny one-person-wide alleyway from Middle Temple Lane onto the stretch of road where Fleet

Street became Strand and turned left, searching for a potential waiting spot. The Viscount worked down Devereux Court, and often visited the Royal Courts of Justice which were literally right across the road, so if Jay could camp out somewhere between those two he should be set.

The Royal Courts of Justice themselves were a vast, cathedral-like building, all white gothic stone and pointy spires, but quite conveniently there was a zebra crossing leading across the road right to its huge front doors, so Jay checked what sat on his side of the street with coverage of that crossing.

A coffee shop, a pub, and a sandwich place. He discounted the latter as he didn't spot any tables, and then he discounted the pub for looking like it was a thousand years old with bottle-glass windows and limited visibility.

Decision made, he ducked into the glass-fronted coffee house, bought himself a large, over-priced tea to nurse for as long as he could, then sat at the counter which faced out onto the street so that he could begin his stakeout.

HE'D NURSED his cuppa well into cold, faking sips as often as he took them to eke it out even longer. Resisting the urge to do work on his phone while he waited had been the hardest part, since he needed to keep his eyes on that bloody crossing all day.

What if the guy didn't even go there today?

Jay groaned to himself and caved in to look at his phone, quickly searching for pictures to double-check that he could identify the guy's face, then forced himself to put it away.

This stakeout rubbish wasn't anywhere near as entertaining as it was on telly.

People came and went around him. His bum started to go numb. He texted Han now and then to let him know he hadn't been horribly killed by magic.

Around four in the afternoon, the bright gleam of pale blond hair caught his eye across the street, and he rocked his head back and forth to try and get the crick out of his neck. He squinted as the man he was watching descended the steps outside the courts and approached the zebra crossing. He wove through the arrangement of wrought iron gates and stepped out onto the road.

Jay pushed his tea dregs away and almost fell off his stool, stamping his feet and hopping toward the door while he tried to get his arse working. His muscles tingled as sensation slowly returned, and he shouldered his way outside with the book against his chest.

He eyed the Viscount as they approached each other. The guy was as almost as tall as Jay, maybe an inch shorter at most, and everything about him screamed money, from his flawless haircut to his heavy wool coat. Even his scarf looked the sort of thing that cost well into three figures where most people made do with one that was three quid in Primark.

Where Jay carried a book, the Viscount bore a leather briefcase in his hand, and as Jay lingered by the crossing, eyes so pale he could've mistaken the guy for a vampire swept over him.

Jay swallowed tightly. If this was where he got his arse handed to him, it'd be amazingly anticlimactic.

The Viscount stepped onto the pavement and out of the flow of people, still watching Jay, his ridiculously good-looking features cast in an expression of placid interest. "Is there something I can do for you?"

"Um." Jay looked down to the book and back up, then smiled widely. "Maybe we could talk somewhere?"

Seconds ticked by while he waited for an answer, then the Viscount merely inclined his head. "Follow me."

As Jay scurried down the narrow alley of Devereux Court it occurred to him that it'd be a great place to murder a newbie.

HE WAS LED through a discreet door and up two flights of stairs before the building revealed the modern offices tucked away inside. Jay had to sign in at a reception desk, where he noted the Viscount idly checking his name in the book, and then he was taken to a small office with windows overlooking the pub next door and very little else.

"Take a seat."

Jay closed the door, then scurried to sit at the desk and rested the book in his lap. "I'm so sorry for just, well, totally stalking you, but I didn't know what else to do."

The Viscount shed his scarf and coat, hanging both on a coat stand just inside the door, then he walked around his desk and settled behind it, easily dominating the room both with his size and his confidence. The bloke probably played rugby at Eton if his shoulders were anything to go by.

Jay's gaze was drawn to something behind the tie the Viscount was now removing, though. As the bright splash of blue silk was removed and set on the desk, there seemed to be the faintest green glow behind it, peeking out from under his shirt.

"I presume this is all because you can see it," the Viscount drawled as he undid his top button then tapped at the glow.

Jay nodded quickly. "And most people can't, right?" It was impossible to keep the excitement out of his voice, so he didn't even try.

"Correct. Jay Newfield, is that correct?"

Jay nodded. "Frederick d'Arcy, Viscount d'Arcy?"

"Of course."

Up closer, Frederick's grey eyes were truly eerie. They lacked the faint luminescence of Han's or those of any other vampire Jay had met, but their pale grey was arresting nonetheless.

"How may I help you, Mr. Newfield?" Frederick continued.

Jay sucked in a deep breath. There was little point trying to lie, but he could at least be cautious until he was reasonably sure he wasn't gonna get turned into a frog. "Okay so. It's kind of a long story, I'll try to cut it down to the basics. There was a sorcerer called Bryce. She went around the country killing other sorcerers and stealing their books, like this one." He placed it on the desk. "But apparently the one sorcerer she didn't even attempt to kill was your dad, because he scared the heebie jeebies right out of her."

Frederick's lips twitched faintly. "That makes her wise," he murmured. "How does this lead you to me? Are you intending to finish the job?"

Jay blinked, then laughed weakly. "Oh my goodness no! I just, um. I was sort of hoping it ran in the family so that I didn't have to try to talk to your dad because if he's that scary I don't know if I wanna go there."

"You don't," Frederick agreed.

"But if you can do magic too, then maybe you could help me?" His voice squeaked a little as he lifted it into a question, and he swallowed. Everything about Frederick seemed terrifying, from his physical presence to the way he stared directly into Jay's eyes. "I mean, I have all her books, I just don't know how or where to get started?"

"One would presume that reading some of these books would be the starting point?" Frederick reached across the desk for the one Jay had placed there, and drew it toward himself, then idly opened it and began flicking through the pages. "Ah, of course," he surmised after a moment. "You don't speak the language."

"Right." Jay nodded quickly. He'd brought one of the non-English glowing books on the off-chance that he lost it, figuring at least he couldn't read it anyway. "Can you?"

Frederick seemed to find some amusement in that. "Yes. Benefits of a classical education, dear boy." He closed the book and tapped his fingers on it, then nodded faintly. "All right. I would be happy to assist you, but in doing so I must be perfectly clear up front."

Jay tried not to let any disappointment take hold just yet. "Oh?"

"First, I cannot use magic. I lack the..." Frederick waved his fingers slightly. "Gift, shall we say. I am more than willing to put my linguistic talents to this task, but I'm afraid the magic is all on you."

"Oh!" Jay's gaze fell to the green glow, faint beneath Frederick's shirt. "But—"

"I didn't make this." Frederick tapped the glow. "A friend did. Ironically, to protect me from my father, which I think dovetails quite nicely into my second point. Stay well away from him. He *will* kill you as soon as look at you, of that I have no doubt." He pushed the book back toward Jay. "I would also suggest that you bring your materials to my house for study, until we are able to unearth the spells necessary for you to ward your own home."

Jay felt a little dizzy. This wasn't at all how he thought this meeting could possibly have gone. If Frederick couldn't use magic, he sure seemed to know a lot about it, and Jay sat forward with sudden realisation. "Your friend can do magic though, yes?"

"Correct, but he isn't in this country at present, and he's

unable to fly in on a whim. And he's more of an... acquaintance," he admitted with a faint wince. "Regardless, I suspect that I'm your best bet for the time being, and I certainly wouldn't object to stretching the old linguistic muscles."

Jay nodded quickly. "Okay but I don't think I can pay, if that's what you're thinking?"

Frederick quirked an eyebrow. "I think perhaps you underestimate the value of making a new friend who can use magic. Let's not beat around the bush here. I'm not going to call on you to make predictions about the Lotto or anything so inane, but if I encounter an esoteric threat that seems in accordance with your speciality, I will be calling on you, because I'm ill-equipped to deal with that nonsense."

Jay licked his lips and drew the book into his lap like it could protect him. "Does this happen a lot?"

"Not yet. But I should say that once is too often, don't you think?"

Jay had to admit that there was some pretty infallible logic there. "Then I'd love to, if you don't mind?"

"Not at all. I'm afraid I will be here until quite late, so why don't you pop over later this evening and we can begin?" Frederick took up a fountain pen and scrawled his address on a legal pad without flourish, then tore the sheet off and folded it to pass across the desk. "Say, eight o'clock?"

Jay took the paper and slipped it into the book, then nodded quickly. "Eight," he agreed. "I'll be there. Thank you."

"Oh, don't thank me yet, Mr. Newfield," Frederick chuckled. "I'm afraid I can be quite the taskmaster."

Jay beamed at that as he rose from his seat. "Good. Because I like to work hard and get things done." He offered his hand across the desk. "Here's to a productive relationship."

Frederick stood and took his hand, then gave it a single, firm shake. "Wonderful," he murmured.

Jay saw himself out, pausing at reception to sign out in the ledger there, then he hurried off toward Jade Enterprises with a spring in his step.

This was all going swimmingly.

FOUR

"WHAT WE'RE THINKING IS the pay-for-play market is reaching saturation, so we need to start investigating other models."

"In-app purchases are still where it's at."

"Nobody likes subscriptions."

Han was only really half-listening as the meeting in his office continued around him. His contact lenses were irritating him, and it was like his eyes just refused to get used to them no matter how long they stayed in, so every now and then he got distracted into blinking like he was trying to communicate a secret message to a spy across the room.

"What do you think, Han?"

He shrugged like he'd been paying attention as Susie looked his way. "I think the moment we stop innovating is the moment we start dying. This industry is fast and we need to be able to pivot whenever it moves. Investigating alternative income streams is never a bad idea. I say we go ahead on that."

She seemed satisfied with his answer, so it looked like he'd managed to pull that one off nicely.

"I mean, what're the percentages on in-app purchases anyway?" Ian tapped his pen against his notepad. "It's only around five percent of users, isn't it?"

"Right," Han agreed. "But it's virtually impossible to monetise the other ninety five percent, and that five percent is still thirty seven billion dollars globally. The aim should be to increase our tiny nibble of that pie into a way bigger bite, rather than trying to incentivise non-buyers into spending. They're not interested in converting."

Ian looked a little disgruntled at that, but he didn't argue.

"I think we *can* convert some," Dave interjected, "if we go hard on the game theory. Casuals are great, but if we target some hardcore players who obsess over being the best we can lure them into making a few purchases to get there. It works well enough for the console market."

"Totally different market," Susie countered. "They pay up front *and* make in-game purchases."

"Okay." Han put his hands on the meeting table. "We're starting to go in circles. Susie, start investigating potential alternative revenue models. We can't choose if we don't know the options."

"All right." Everyone shuffled to their feet and gathered up their things, then filed out of the office as Han returned to his desk. Ian closed the door after himself, but he knew it'd open again soon, because he heard Jay enter the office and walk through it saying hi to everyone.

It was a huge relief that Jay wasn't dead or kidnapped or otherwise not coming back, that was for sure, especially since Randall's dad had only gone to get a newspaper one day and a sorcerer kidnapped him.

Jay breezed into his office with pink cheeks and the faint odour of fresh sweat. "Oh my god it was brilliant he's not a sorcerer but he knows about magic and he can read the books and he's offered to help can you drop me over there this evening?"

Han laughed and took his contacts out, dropping them into a clean pot and filling it with saline from his desk drawer. "Went well, yeah?"

Jay dropped into a chair and put his feet up on the desk. "I'm so excited! He asked if I could go 'round his at eight." He flipped open the book in his lap, then opened a sheaf of paper folded into it. "Egerton Crescent. SW3."

"Just outside Ellis' territory?" Han pursed his lips. "Do we know who it belongs to?"

Jay bit his lip. "No," he admitted. "I'll ask Ellis." He pulled his phone to speed-type a text, and it was done in moments.

"With any luck whoever it is won't notice me if I just, like, drive in and out," Han mused. "I could probably decamp to Ellis' place and wait for you there. How long do you think you'll be?"

"No idea, sweetie. There are so many books. Where do we even start?" He sighed. "Once we find some like protective spells though I think we can do it at home. He's only suggested his place because he has all that protection in place already."

"But..?" Han blinked a few times, and the irritation disappeared like it had never happened.

"But he's not a sorcerer himself. He didn't cast the wards. Lay them. Put them there..." Jay waved his hands fussily. "Whatever the terminology is. So he can't just come to ours and do it for us. I think we'll probably look for that kind of spell first, so we can protect the flat, then take it from there. Is that okay?"

Han chuckled at him. "Is it okay if you do what's necessary to learn to do this thing that — to our knowledge — only you can do? Yes, babe, it's totally fine."

Jay scrunched up his nose with his laugh. "You're the best!"

"Yes, I am!"

HAN FOLLOWED the satnav's instructions to Egerton Crescent and pulled up outside the house Jay pointed to.

It was massive. Four storeys above ground and a basement level behind iron railings, it was part of what could only loosely be described as a terrace. The entire crescent was a single arc of pure white building, interspersed with windows and a front door every few feet. The higher storeys had wrought iron lined balconies, most with carefully cultivated potted conifers on them.

When everyone even had the same tree cut to the same shape and height, there was some next-level rich person bullshit going on. It kind of looked like the house Ellis' wanted to be when it grew up.

Jay let out a low whistle as he leaned forward to peer up at the house. "I should see if he needs any paintings. I know a good art dealer that could help."

Han snorted in agreement. "Right? Ellis would have a field day if you can turn this guy into a customer." He closed his eyes and rubbed them, but it just made the contacts itch more. "Okay, let's get you unloaded so I can take these stupid things out sooner."

"I think it could be the healing," Jay mused as he unbuckled his seatbelt. "I mean, normally you'd get used to contact lenses after a few days' wear, right? You stop being so sensitive to them. But I think you're healing even the slightest bit of irritation, so you're always fresh to them, like you've just put them in that very second." Jay clicked his tongue and looked apologetic. "I think it might just be one of those things that can't be fixed, sweetie."

"I'll add it to the list," he grumbled. "Want to go make sure he's still up for it before we offload everything?"

"Oh! Yes!" Jay leaned over and kissed his cheek quickly, then slipped out of the car and hurried up the marble steps.

Han got out and went around to the boot, popping the glass up and the loading shelf down in readiness.

They'd only loaded around half of the suitcases. If the Viscount turned out to be a book thief himself at least Jay would still be left with far more material than he knew what to do with.

It was a risk, trusting this total stranger who by his own admission couldn't even use magic, but what else where they to do? Han was used to hiring translators, but they all spoke modern languages, and he wasn't sure how much material he could pass off as in-game shots for something that wouldn't be released for a while.

A guy with bright red curly hair opened the door, and Han made like he wasn't eavesdropping, even though it was impossible not to.

"Hi. I had an appointment with Viscount d'Arcy?" Jay said.

"Jay Newfield?" The redhead had the faintest twinge of an American accent, as though he'd been born there then raised in the UK.

"Right!"

"Michael Brennan. Do you need help bringing anything inside?"

"If you wouldn't mind?" Jay laughed warmly. "There's a lot of it."

"No problem."

They came around to the back of the car, so Han began to unload suitcases, lining them up on the pavement. When

Brennan approached, he offered his hand. "Han Xie," he said. "I'm just the driver."

Michael shook his hand and smiled, and Jay laughed. "Oh my god, Han! This is my *husband*," he explained as he grabbed a couple of handles.

Michael just chuckled at that. "Don't worry. I'm often relegated to driver, too," he said as he winked at Han. "Will you be joining us?"

"No. I have a friend who lives nearby, so I'm going to stop by and visit. Jay can call me when he wants a lift home again."

"All right."

Between the three of them they managed to get the suitcases up the steps and into the house's hallway in a single trip.

Han's flat was huge. It was in a prime location overlooking the Thames, and before he'd been turned it was just a short walk across Blackfriars Bridge to get to work. But he suspected the cost of that flat didn't hold a candle to the value of this house.

Still, maybe one day he could afford something similar.

He smiled to himself at the thought, then gave Jay a hug. "Okay. I'll see you later, baby. Enjoy yourselves."

Jay squeezed him and leaned down for a kiss. "It's gonna be great!"

"If you say so."

IT WAS ONLY a couple of miles through zig-zagging streets to reach Ellis' house in Pimlico. He stowed it in the house's parking bay, and since he only needed the parking permit if he intended to stay all day he grabbed his briefcase and locked the car as he left it. He wouldn't be coming back to it until it was time to leave.

He hopped up the steps and pressed the doorbell, then said, "It's me. Han."

It was a dicey proposition, being a vampire on someone else's territory, but it was dicier still being a vampire who didn't legally exist. Despite the fact that Ellis was now a Councillor himself, it wasn't enough for him to turn people willy-nilly, and he hadn't sought permission before he turned Han. There hadn't been time. Han's heart was on the brink of failure.

The doctors had told him he could have months. Turned out he'd had weeks.

He heard the footsteps from inside the house as they approached the door, and the heartbeat which came with them, so when Randall answered the door, it was hardly a surprise.

"Randall!" Han grinned and gave him a one-armed hug. "How're you doing?"

"Not bad. Just a bit, you know." Randall squeezed him just as tightly, then ushered him inside. "Harried. No Jay?"

"No, he'd found someone to help him translate Bryce's books—"

He stopped at the sound of laughter from deeper inside the house. It was the kind of laugh that made people uncomfortable to hear, and Han frowned faintly at it.

"I think he's still a bit amused that she's dead," Randall sighed, and the guilt in his dark eyes was clear as day.

"You did the right thing," Han murmured. "C'mon. Where is he? The office?" He made his way toward the laughter as it began to die down, and Randall hurried after him.

To say that the sight which greeted him was unnerving would be a serious understatement. Ellis was wearing crumpled clothes without any socks, which wouldn't be too shocking if it weren't for his usually impeccable presentation. He was scrunched up in the chair behind his battle-scarred desk, arms around his knees, and his skin was deathly white, almost grey.

Worst were his eyes. Whatever Bryce did to him had turned them blood-red, yet they still had the luminescence of a vampire's eyes which was all the more obvious to Han now that his senses were sharpened to a knife's edge.

Tiberius was curled around Ellis' feet without his harness on, and while Han was no animal expert, it seemed pretty clear that even the dog was worried.

Whatever was going on here, it was clear that Ellis' condition wasn't improving.

Han moved further into the room, circling the desk entirely to place his hand against Ellis' forehead, and he gasped at the temperature difference. Through various experiments, he had noted that unless recently fed, he would default to ambient temperature at all times, but Ellis was noticeably colder than Han was.

"He won't eat," Randall fretted by the other chair in the room, a far less comfortable thing of wood which faced the desk. "Says he isn't hungry."

Han swore softly and ran his hands through his hair. "Ellis? What're you doing, mate? You trying to lose weight?"

Ellis snorted at him, and Han heard something else from him, just for a second, and he tilted his head in confusion.

It sounded an awful lot like a single heartbeat.

"No need," Ellis said, sounding the kind of cheerful that people put on when their life was falling apart. "It'll come off sooner or later."

Han exchanged a look with Randall, who shook his head helplessly, so he turned to Ellis again. "You need to eat."

"I don't think I can."

"Of course you can. Come on, damn well eat something!"

Ellis ran a hand through his hair, pushing it back from his forehead, and whole clumps of it came out between his fingers, turning to dust the moment they parted ways with his scalp. "Oh," was all he said.

"Oh my god." Randall rushed around to grip Ellis' shoulders. "El? Are you okay?"

Han frowned as Ellis dropped his hands.

"I'm areet," Ellis murmured.

Han leaned in to get a closer look, but he wasn't sure he needed to. It was pretty clear to him that the hairs had come loose far too easily, and when he reached up to pluck another few strands away, they fell apart with hardly any effort at all.

"I'm not convinced," he said quietly.

Ellis seemed to be falling apart very literally.

FIVE

Jay had packed an entire bag full of organising supplies, and began to collate notes to document which books contained what material. To differentiate between all the books without anything printed on the cover, he used a simple index card with a code handwritten on it and placed it inside the front covers. The code was very basic, consisting of a few letters to denote the language, and then a couple of letters for the colour of the book and the colour of any magical glow, then a number. It should help make each book more findable later on, once his reference document was complete.

Frederick seemed impressed by his sort-fu, and the Viscount was every bit as finicky and detail-oriented as Jay. Michael appeared to be Frederick's partner, though they didn't go in for much in the way of PDAs, and he was excellent at keeping them supplied with tea, bringing and returning books, and otherwise running around doing any necessary minor tasks without getting underfoot.

"I believe," Frederick said as they paused for tea again, "that the different colours mean different creators." He picked up the last book that had been indexed and peered at the card. "You say this is dark red?"

Jay looked to it, then nodded. The dull glow was visible across the room. "Yeah."

Frederick nodded and set it back down. "While I don't doubt that, over time, surely there must be a sorcerer whose magic matches the shade of a previous sorcerer's, the human eye can only determine so much, so I would suggest that once we have catalogued everything you then check books which colour-match — if any arise — to see whether they have the same author. If the handwriting differs, then we have proof that you cannot rely on the colour alone to identify a spell's origin."

Jay gulped down a few mouthfuls of his tea. "That makes sense. Urgh, what I really need is a spell that lets me read all these."

"I'm sure there is one," Frederick chuckled. "It's just a case of whether that spell exists among these materials. I would suggest that your priority should be a spell which allows you to see or otherwise detect magic, as well as warding your own property."

Jay propped his elbows on the desk at that, and curled his fingers around his cup. It was bone china, effortlessly delicate and beautiful, faintly translucent. "I can see your glowy thing —" he gestured to Frederick's chest.

"Can you see the wards?"

Jay blinked and looked around the room quickly. "Are they in here?"

"Every room."

"Then you have a point," Jay admitted. It felt a bit weird knowing there was invisible magic around him. He'd assumed he'd be able to see it all, since the books glowed, along with Frederick's pendant, but he'd been so eager to get started on the books that he hadn't thought about the wards Frederick claimed to have.

"My understanding is that it's rather rare for a sorcerer to be able to see other sorcerers' wards," Frederick explained. "My acquaintance is able to do so because he bears a particular heritage, but others have expressed surprise to him that he had such ability."

Jay blinked. "So he knows others?"

"All in America, alas," Frederick said. "We shall have to make do."

"We can do it," Jay grinned. "We're making awesome progress!"

THEY WORKED UNTIL MIDNIGHT, and then straight on past it to almost one in the morning, and it was only when Jay began to yawn in earnest that he realised he might have to call it a night soon.

Michael looked just as shattered, and Frederick had finally developed a little darkness under his eyes, so Jay sat back and stretched. "I don't think I can go any longer," he admitted in an apologetic tone.

"Mm," Frederick agreed. "As much as I would like to push on, I do need to be at the office in—" he checked a clock "—around six hours." He paused to look at the multitude of books spread around the room, all in neat little piles. "Would you like to leave these here, or shall we begin to pack them?"

Jay bit his thumbnail a second as he tried to make up his mind, but the thought of interfering with the current organisation in his state of exhaustion seemed like an incredible amount of effort when they'd have to do it for goodness knew how many nights until he learned to ward his own home.

He shook his head. "I don't mind leaving them here, if you're sure you're all right with that?"

"I don't mind in the slightest. Between the physical and esoteric security surrounding this house, it should be the safest spot in the country for them." Frederick hid his hand behind his mouth, and his eyes fluttered with a yawn. "That and I'm not a great fan of double-handling."

Jay bit his lip, then nodded and pulled his phone to text Han. "Thank you. Shall I come over same time tomorrow? Er... Today?"

"That would be excellent. And I shall have keys cut for you so that you won't need us to be here."

Jay blinked at him. "You sure you trust me enough to give me the keys to your fancy house?" he blurted. He was too tired for filters.

Frederick laughed. "Dear boy, I'm doing my best to give you access to potentially unlimited magical power. If I can't trust you now, how am I going to trust you once you're a fully-fledged sorcerer?"

He paused to digest Frederick's words, then nodded, feeling suddenly sombre.

"Fair point," he murmured.

HE EASED into the passenger seat and frowned at the look of concern which creased Han's features.

"What's wrong, sweetie?"

"It's Ellis," Han said, his voice quiet. He pulled away and drove along the crescent quietly, only speaking again after a minute. "He's eating so little that I don't think he's healing any more. A whole clump of his hair just fell out and turned to ash, and all he'd done was run his hands through it. I think he's falling apart."

Jay gasped in horror. He'd spent hours fussing around with books, and in the meantime Ellis was falling to pieces.

"In more ways than one," Han muttered as he steered the car south. "He's kinda unhinged. I think he needs proper help. Assuming we can even get him to eat anything."

Jay bit his lip as the car glided through the dark streets.

Ellis had only really described his treatment at Bryce's hands as 'torture'. He wouldn't expand on it, but when Han and Jay had arrived at the warehouse she's kept him at, there was dried blood all over the floor, as well as matted into Ellis' hair and clothes. To say he was a wreck was a complete understatement, but beyond that, Jay knew nothing about what had gone on, and now that he worked back at Jade Enterprises with Han he didn't get to see either Ellis or Randall anywhere near as often as he used to.

But he knew people who did.

Mind made up, Jay looked to Han. "Okay. Let's go home. I can't do anything on zero sleep. Do you need me at work first thing?"

Han glanced to him, then shook his head. "Other than to grab your arse? No."

"Right." His brain was already spinning out various permutations of ideas, forming the embryonic stages of a plan, so he waited another couple of miles for them to take some kind of shape. "Then I'll go talk to Christy about this, then see if I can get hold of Randall. In the evening I can have a word with Barb and see if she knows anyone who could help."

Han gnawed at his lip a moment, then sighed. "What if this is just... a vampire thing?"

He looked across again. "How?"

"You know. Jiangshi begin to rot as they age. Maybe that has some basis in reality."

Jay frowned. "I dunno. Aaron doesn't look rotten and he's like forty or fifty or something. And Barb's from the Eighties. None of her bits have dropped off." He paused, then added , "None of you's gonna fall off, sweetie. No matter what your mum might say."

"Oh my god, I'm not telling mum I'm a vampire!" Han snorted at him. "She'd mourn me for the rest of her life!"

"And throw grains of rice at you?"

"More likely she'd just hit me with a broom," Han grumbled.

"Is this some traditional Chinese method of repelling vampires?" Jay laughed.

"Yep."

"Oh, we so have to tell your mum!"

Jay could see the struggle on Han's face. The strain of trying not to laugh.

"We really don't," Han insisted.

"Do."

"Not."

"Do."

"Nope."

They bickered the rest of the way to Rotherhithe, and Jay began to feel like maybe his plan would yield results.

Yeah. He could juggle a hundred suppliers at once, all while booking taxis and holding staff meetings. He could figure out how to save Ellis' arse.

And then he'd learn magic, and be even more awesome.

There was no way the plan could fail.

SIX

HAN TURNED his alarm off quickly, but as ever it didn't stop Jay from stirring, so he leaned over and kissed him quickly. "Go back to sleep," he whispered.

Jay's eyes fluttered half-open, and he gave a crooked smile. "Bite me."

"I mean, if that's what you want." He leaned in to gnaw playfully on Jay's shoulder, tickling him with his tongue.

Jay laughed and squirmed under him, raising a hand to slap his shoulder. "All right, all right! Stop!"

Han chuckled and poked him square in the chest. "Told you go to back to sleep."

"You're such a bumhole," Jay chuckled as he snatched the sheets and dragged them up over his head. "I'm a burrito. Burritos don't like bumholes."

"Burritos are very tasty, though..." He leaned back over to gum at Jay's shoulder through the sheets, and if Jay's giggling were to be believed he'd hit the right spot. "God, yeah, that's delicious!"

"Go to work," Jay snorted, muffled by sheets.

"Fine, fine. I'll have burrito later."

———

IT WAS LESS than half a mile down Blackfriars Road to Southwark station, and the road wasn't too busy so early in the day. Han made sure he had plenty of time until sunrise just in case there were problems with the tube, but there were always other Londoners up and about, even in this relatively sparsely populated area.

Maybe he should sell the flat and move north of the river, though. The Thames was beautiful to look at, but apparently it'd be hugely detrimental to his mental health to go over it at all, so if a move could save him this farting about, maybe it'd be worth the effort.

He entered the station, swiped his Oyster card, and hurried down the escalators on the left hand side.

The platform wasn't all that busy either. Han found a spot to stand which would be near the tail-end of the train when it arrived, and tucked his hands into his pockets.

This really was a lot of messing around. Despite Southwark and Blackfriars being so close, there was no direct tube line between them. Han had to get on the Jubilee line to Westminster, then switch to the Circle or District line to Blackfriars. Fifteen minutes of travel to cross a body of water.

His desire to move house grew just that little bit stronger.

———

WHEN HE FINALLY REACHED BLACKFRIARS, he checked his phone before sprinting up steps, just to be absolutely sure he wasn't about to get a dose of sunburn. All his experimentation suggested he should survive a few minutes of weak spring sunshine first thing in the morning, but he really didn't fancy it.

His phone insisted he had a good three quarters of an hour of safety net left, so he jogged up the escalator and out through the ticket barriers, then set off on his way to the office.

He was maybe fifty feet from the door when he saw the vampire coming toward him.

Han slowed himself down as casually as he could, but on the inside he was about as close to panic as he could possibly get without screaming. He was used to staying calm in the face of rude suppliers or angry customers, but none of those were likely to actually kill him.

Bloody hell, what was it Ellis had tried to drum into him about territory rights? Could Han kill this guy for being here? Or was Han on someone else's turf all along?

And then there was the whole unsanctioned thing...

Han just put his hands in his pockets again and watched the stranger come closer. The bloke was taller than he was, but Jay would say that just about everyone was, and he'd formed a kind of shorty solidarity with Randall over it.

He was a white guy, which Han found the least surprising thing ever. From all accounts, London's vampires were a bigoted bunch, having had their attitudes frozen sometime last century. They tended to turn men, and white ones at that, and Barb was the only woman any of them knew of. Han could bet his arse that there wasn't a single other ethnically Chinese vampire in the damn city.

Bollocks. When he put it like that, he really was a fucking signal flare of youth and inexperience, wasn't he? He couldn't stand out more if he had a flashing neon sign over his head.

There was no way this could go well.

"I wondered if one day you might show your face without

your protective meat shield," the stranger said, finally stopping two feet in front of Han.

Han did his best not to respond. Not physically. Even moving his hands would make sound which might make the other vampire think that an attack was imminent, so he resisted the urge to ball his fingers into fists in his pockets. Instead he ran his gaze over the stranger while he tried to think up a diplomatic response.

The guy had pale, ice-blue eyes, which seemed to be what happened to any blue-eyed human being when they were turned. Jay had assured him that his own had become amber, almost golden, which is why he tortured his poor eyeballs with coloured contact lenses all the damn time. Staff would notice if the boss turned up to work with glowy gold eyes one day, just like Han had noticed once Ellis' eyes changed colour. It was impossible to miss.

"Well," he eventually said. "Now you have your answer."

They stood facing each other. Unmoving. Unbreathing. Han sure as hell wasn't going to make the first move, and unless this guy had sunlight protection equally close by, Han could stand here the longest.

"You're on my territory." Finally the words came, forced with great irritation. "The laws give me free reign to deal with you as I see fit."

Han kept his face neutral. He shrugged faintly. "They do," he agreed.

"I could kill you for this!"

"Sure." Han made a show of glancing around, then smiled warmly. If he pretended he had the upper hand, maybe he'd be believed.

It was a ballsy move, but what choice did he have?

"Street looks clear," he added as he turned back to face the other vampire. "You want to do this, or do you fancy behaving like an adult instead?"

"How dare you come onto *my* territory and lecture me!"

Han shrugged again. "Look, here's the problem. What's your name, by the way? I'm Han." He whipped a hand from his pocket and offered it.

His opponent sneered at him and didn't answer.

"Great, anyway." He put his hand away again. "Here's the problem, Gary. I feel like you're a Gary. You remind me of a Gary I knew once—"

"The name is Richard," the vampire spat.

"—Gary," Han continued blithely, "the thing is that I work here. This is my job. I can't help that—"

"—Then find another job!" Richard cut in.

"No can do, Gary. See, it's not easy to get to the interviews when you burn to a crisp in sunlight. So are we going to have a problem here, or are you going to maybe consider that we could reach a deal whereby I get to go to my job, and you get to not murder me whenever you fancy it?"

Richard stepped closer, and leaned in until their noses almost touched. He had a few inches on Han, that was for sure, but Han was well used to being around taller people, and especially those who felt their height was some advantage.

"That deal doesn't sound like I get anything out of it," he hissed.

Han laughed in his face. "What? You get the pleasure of not having to kill me. Isn't that enough? A little fragrance clings to the hand which gives flowers."

If Richard was alive, Han had no doubt he'd be bright red by now. "Do you know who I am?"

"No." Han didn't hesitate. "And that means you aren't on the Council, and you're not a Vassal. You aren't even a Constable. You are every bit as much of a nobody as I am, which means you are every bit as disposable as I am." He finally raised an eyebrow. "Are you going to let me pass, or are you going to do something stupid? Because sunrise is coming, and I'm barely five feet from shelter. How far do you have to go to be safe, Gary?"

He was damn well playing with fire here, relying on his poker face which had served him well in business negotiations but had never been tested in a dust-off with another vampire. The fact was that he didn't know a damn thing about Richard, from how old he was to what his power might be, and he sure as hell didn't know what his own power was or how to use it. If Richard's abilities were remotely martial in nature, Han would be screwed.

Richard obviously knew Han worked here, too. He must have a perch somewhere nearby, somewhere to observe from where Han wouldn't have picked out the person without a pulse with the vampire's eyes. He implied he had seen Han come and go with Jay several times, but he wasn't willing to break the laws and talk to Han about this with Jay present.

Han didn't have a scrap of information, and all he could hope was that Richard didn't want to leap into the fray with just as little information as Han had.

He was, as it turned out, wrong.

Richard lunged for him, crossing the remaining few inches too quickly for Han to dodge. He head-butted Han and then blinked out of existence.

Han reeled back a couple of steps, but the pain had already receded.

Where the hell had Richard gone?

He whirled, straining to look around quickly, to listen, to try and figure out whether Richard had teleported away or turned invisible or was otherwise using some kind of superpower to attack him while Han couldn't see him, but he saw nothing. Heard nothing. Nothing other than the empty little street, the distant people and traffic.

No.

Wait.

He heard the faintest *shh* of clothing, right in front of him, and then a sharp, stabbing pain in his chest. He looked down, startled, in time to see wood sinking through his shirt.

Motherfucker was invisible, Han realised.

He was invisible, and his stake wasn't.

Han tried to back up, to get away from the wood before it reached his heart, to grab it and stop it pushing in further, but it came with him, it just kept coming, and panic began to mount.

Bollocking hell. He was going to get killed and Jay wouldn't even know.

In a last-ditch effort he heaved against the stake, but then he felt a scratch deep inside his chest, like something vital had been hit, and his body ceased to exist.

And all he heard was Richard's startled words.

"What the fuck?!"

SEVEN

Jay rolled onto his side and checked the time on his phone, then almost leaped out of bed until he remembered Han had sneaked off and Jay was *supposed* to be having a lie-in.

Problem was that he was so used to being up before sunrise that his brain didn't seem to want him to get that lie-in, so he slid out of bed and headed for the bathroom, tapping out a text as he went.

Hey Randall. Are you awake?

He had time to shower before Randall answered.

Yeah. What's up?

Can you talk?

His phone rang seconds later, so Jay abandoned brushing his teeth to answer it. "Hey Randall! I take that as a yes?"

Randall chuckled. "Yeah, I'm free. Just taking Tiberius out for a walk before I go meet my first client of the day. What can I do for you?"

"I'm just going to put you on speaker. Hang on." Jay thumbed his phone as he left the bathroom, then put it on a chest of drawers so he could dry himself off and get dressed. "Han says he stopped by last night."

"Yeah."

He sucked his lip briefly, then sighed. "He says Ellis' mental health isn't doing so great."

Randall was quiet so long that Jay managed to get his boxers and both socks on while he waited.

"He has nightmares," Randall whispered so faintly that Jay's heart went out to him. "I think he's scared of me."

"Oh, sweetie, no! Why would you think that?"

"Because Charles made me attack him, and... And I don't think he's been okay since then, and that was before what Bryce did..."

Jay frowned to himself as he joined the dots.

Ellis and Randall lived in the house which had belonged to some super powerful old vampire called Charles. Charles had been trying to kill Ellis for ages and finally decided to try it directly instead of using patsies, but in the end it was Charles who got killed, and Ellis used antiques in his house to repay his dad's loan.

The antique they couldn't sell was a beautiful old desk on the ground floor. It was marred by deep scars across its beautifully polished surface, and even if it got restored, the value was forever wiped off it, so Ellis decided to keep it.

Those deep scars were long and ran in parallel lines.

Like claw-marks.

"Sweetie, it wasn't you," he breathed. "Charles was mind-control central. You didn't have a choice and you can't blame yourself."

"But—"

"No," he said, more firmly. "I know you, Randall. You can't beat yourself up over that. If Ellis is having nightmares, that's totally understandable, but it's not your fault. It's Charles'."

Randall said nothing to that.

"So what're we going to do about it?" Jay prompted.

"I dunno," Randall choked out. "God, Jay, what do I do?"

"Well for a start we need to get him to eat." He sucked on his teeth as he pulled a shirt on and buttoned it quickly. "We can't just force blood into him, can we?"

"No, I don't think it works like that. He's gotta take it from the source."

"Right," Jay agreed. "And if he's refusing to pull his fangs out, I don't know if either of us cutting ourselves will do the job. Not that I am racing to the knife, believe me."

"I could try it." Randall sounded doubtful at best.

"I don't think taking a sharp knife to your own body is as easy as it looks in films," Jay sighed. "Anyway, if Ellis is so hungry he's starting to fall apart, what if he loses control?" He hesitated, then bit his thumbnail. "When we went over to that warehouse to collect all of Bryce's books, weren't there markings all over the floor?"

"Yeah," Randall said slowly. "She'd warded the place against vampires. We had to damage the markings before Barb and Aaron could get inside, or before we could get Ellis out of where she'd put him. Dad said just breaking any of the lines in the sigils was enough to do it."

He hopped as he pulled his trousers up. "And she was specifically kidnapping vampires."

"Looking for what made them immortal."

"Okay. I think I've got an idea."

"What?" Randall sounded like he'd perked up.

"Nothing concrete yet, but she knew how to handle vampires. She was trying to figure out something specific about them. So maybe somewhere in all these books is a lot of information about vampires. And if we can find that—"

"—we might find something that'll help! You're a genius!"

Jay laughed. "You know, I think you're right! Okay, I'm going to bury myself in some books and see what I can find. I'll text you later if I come up with anything."

"Thanks. Honestly, just for trying. It means a lot."

"Hey, don't get mushy on me. Speak later."

Jay hung up and trotted back into the bathroom to finish brushing his teeth, then he hurried through to the remainder of the books and went straight for the English-language pile which wasn't glowing.

It was time to put his speed-reading skills to use.

HE FLIPPED through book after book, refusing to let himself get distracted by pictures or by any mentions of boggarts or pixies, werewolves or gods. Jay was laser-focused on the word *vampire* and any possible permutations he could think of, though really the only one that came to mind was *vampyre*, and he figured someone would only have written that if they came from the Nineties.

When he hit one, he just set it aside and kept going. He had to hope he hadn't taken anything relevant over to Frederick's, but if he had he'd be able to get to it this evening. He'd just need to explain that his priorities had shifted.

Jay bit his lip.

If he did that, it meant telling Frederick that vampires existed, that he knew one, and all kinds of other admissions.

But on the other hand, Frederick was reading through spell books which might have all kinds of other information stowed away between their pages. Simply by dint of being able to read them, Frederick might already have been exposed to things Jay didn't even know about yet.

Bugger. He hadn't considered that at all. He'd been too

fixated on finding translation help that he hadn't paused to consider that in doing so he'd be giving away several lifetimes' worth of information that might not really be his to give.

Still, he couldn't worry about it now. That cat was so far out of the bag it had long since disappeared, and Jay was going to need all the help he could get before Ellis let his own head fall off.

Jay had to find a way to get Ellis to eat. And if Bryce was as obsessive about picking vampires apart as she'd seemed to be, maybe she had enough notes on vampire physiology to help get Ellis over that hurdle. Then Jay could worry about the bigger picture.

He pored over the books he'd found. There was so much information that it was hard to skip over it and try and find the one thing he needed right now. He found whole treatises about the whole 'infliction' process — whoever had written this book didn't see it as a 'turning' at all — that he had to zoom past to try and get to information about blood. Then he called Randall.

"Hey," Randall said.

"Hey. Okay, I think I have something." Jay sat on the floor with one book in his lap, resting between the knees of his crossed legs. "Are you free?"

"Yeah. What is it?"

"So it looks like vampirism is like this magical state," Jay said as he skimmed back and forth through the pages, just in case he'd missed something. "It's like a spell that converts a living creature into pure magic. It's hugely complicated. I don't think it occurs naturally. Like, I think someone must've made this at some point. Anyway, the point is that once they're converted, they need this specific mixture of fuel to maintain that state."

"Blood," Randall surmised.

"Nailed it in one! Don't ask me why. But more than that I think the blood's just a carrier. We're getting into some very unscientific woo-woo stuff here, so bear with me, but frankly considering you guys exist I think you can give me a little leeway."

Randall chuckled at him.

"I think the reason it doesn't work when the blood's already outside of a body is that the vampire's actually feeding on the target's life force, or whatever you want to call it. I mean, a living body is made up of billions of other living things. Not just its own cells, but bacteria and..." he waved a hand. "Things. And it's surprisingly hard to differentiate between alive and dead when it comes to human beings. Like, we can't define death as a stopped heart, right? People come back from that." Jay bit his lip. He'd *seen* Han come back from a heart attack. "Even brain death is super complicated. But something marks the line between alive and dead, and I think it's the presence of that life force or whatever it is that is what vampires need to feed on. Then it gets converted into their new state, into magic, and they can use it."

"So we're back to the knife plan?" Randall asked.

"Looks that way. For now. But actually you don't need to go that far. Maybe a pinprick would do."

"Are you sure?"

Jay shrugged toward the phone. "Hey, if someone's so dehydrated they're almost dead, you don't give them two litres of water. You dab little droplets on their lips and they get absorbed through the skin. So if you just prick a finger and, er, shove it in his mouth, maybe it'll have the same effect. Just don't whip your dick out if he starts sucking."

He heard Randall gasp. "Jay! Oh my god!"

Jay laughed and closed the book. "Unless you like that sort of thing. I wouldn't dream of prying into your personal life. Well, I would, but I'm not going to. Let me know how it goes, okay? Maybe don't do it until after sunset, just in case he goes a bit loopy and tries to run outside."

"Why would he do that?" Randall just sounded even more stressed, the poor thing.

"Honestly? I don't know. I'm just over-cautious. Play it safe, and let me know how it goes. I'm going to keep reading, then pop over to see Barb later and see if she has any ideas."

Randall huffed. "All right. Thanks, Jay. I'll try it."

"Catch you later, sweetie."

He hung up and switched back to the book about how the 'infliction' worked and began to skim-read it in case there was anything immediately valuable in it.

And once the gallery was open, he could go over and chat to Christy about Ellis' mental state. There wasn't any need to trouble Randall with that part of his day's plans. Nobody wanted to hear 'I'm gonna discuss your boyfriend's mental health with his employee,' but if anyone had noticed specific details it'd be Christy. Randall was too close, to emotionally attached, but Christy was hyper-vigilant, highly excited that her boss was a vampire and eager to pay attention to every little thing about him.

With any luck, her new obsession could hold some clues on how to help get to the bottom of this mess.

EIGHT

Was this what being staked was like?

Han felt like he didn't exist. Like he could feel the tiniest gaps in bricks in the wall and every speck of dirt in the spaces between slabs on the pavement, yet he couldn't feel his actual body. He'd lost it somehow, and it was deeply unsettling.

Richard appeared, but he seemed so small now.

Small, and terrified.

The stake was in his hand, held like a shield, and Han could see it from so many angles, from below and above, from each and every side.

He tried to move away from the other vampire, and flowed like water over new sections of wall, new areas of pavement. His all-encompassing view of Richard shifted, and Richard let out a little scream.

No, this couldn't be what being staked was like, because Richard still held the stake, and Han was getting away from him.

Han reached for Richard, partly to see if he even could, and he saw darkness approach, creeping toward Richard across the pavement like spilled oil.

Richard dropped the stake and ran for his life, screaming as he went.

Han coiled around the stake, drawing it into the darkness, and flowed toward the front door of his office, then pondered what the hell to do about getting inside before someone saw him and, well, ran screaming for the hills the way Richard had.

Bloody hell. This was no good. He needed his damn body back, and fast!

He tried to reach for the door handle, but more darkness just spread across it.

Hands. You need hands.

What the hell was he supposed to do? If this was his so-called power, what even was it? Had he turned into some kind of fluid?

One unaffected by gravity?

No, now wasn't the time to try and apply scientific method to that question. First he needed arms and legs and all those other things that let him walk around in polite society.

He tried to remember what having those things felt like. It seemed like it'd be obvious since he was pretty used to them, but it took a surprising amount of effort to imagine fingers and toes, eyes and hair.

Han took a breath and stepped forward once he was reasonably sure he had a grasp of self, and he landed a foot unsteadily against the ground. As he glanced back, he saw darkness recede, like the shadows of the building had become just a little less black, and suddenly he was whole again.

He wasn't going to take that for granted, though, and he hurried inside to the safety of his office before he could do it again.

Whatever *it* was.

HAN MIGHT HAVE SPENT way too long searching the internet to try and find lists of what vampires were supposed to be able to do, but the trouble with that was that such lists included whatever the list-writer could think up, with no actual data. He couldn't resent that, he supposed, if vampires were supposed to be some great secret, but it didn't help him any.

He didn't want to practice whatever it was either. What if someone came into his office? What if he couldn't get back into his own body quickly enough?

So instead he fussed with the internet, and pretended to work, but the urge to practice, to try and pin down what exactly he'd done and how to replicate it, was too damn strong.

Jay wouldn't mind this kind of experimentation, right? Han wasn't going to harm himself, expose himself to the sun, or do anything else dangerous. And if this ability could save him from a stake to the heart, then surely it was worth getting on top of.

He talked himself into it with ease and headed to his door to lock it, then he double-checked all the blinds were closed.

How was he supposed to replicate it? That was the question. He wasn't even sure what *it* was, and he couldn't exactly check a mirror to find out. He paced the office a while, then decided it had to be kind of like riding a bike, right? You tried it, you fell off a few times, but you learned to pay attention to your body. You learned what balance was and how to maintain it.

He'd done this once, so all he had to do was learn what it felt like.

Han closed his eyes and put himself back on the pavement, recalling the sensation of Richard's stake penetrating his skin and burrowing toward his heart. There had been a moment, when the wood reached the point where it was about to win, when he had seemed to just... fall apart, so he clung to that feeling, tried to immerse himself in it.

It returned.

He couldn't be sure at first whether he was just imagining it really well, but when he tried to open his eyes, he didn't have any, and he saw his office from such a wide angle that the office was suddenly small to him. Cramped, like he filled more than half of it.

Han laughed, but stopped when the sound reverberated around the room as though a thousand mouths had uttered it. It wasn't a natural sound, and he would've been even more afraid of it if he hadn't known that he was the one who had made it.

But if he could see the room from so many angles, surely some of those angles could see himself?

He shifted across floor and walls, spreading across ceiling and carpet alike, until he could see himself. Or, at least, the inky black shadow which he had become.

That was exactly what it looked like. The darkest shadows cast by the strongest light, except the light in here was just from energy-efficient bulbs. He tried pulling himself from one part of the room and spreading to the other, and that water-like flow sensation rippled through him.

He was a shadow.

A moving, conscious shadow.

And he'd been able to pick up the stake like this earlier.

Han reached out and moved things around. Blackness coiled around his chair and nudged it. It spread to his desk and moved his phone, pen, notepads, laptop. He withdrew the chair into the shadow completely and spat it out on the other side of the room, passing it along within himself like it was somehow still a three-dimensional object.

Hell, if this was his power, he wasn't going to complain. It was *awesome*.

HE SHIFTED BACK and forth a few times, doing his best to get to grips with what it took to do so, before he started experimenting with whether he could just transform parts of himself or whether it was an all or nothing affair, but once he'd turned his hand to shadow and back a couple of times his gums began to itch.

All this shapeshifting was making him hungry.

Han frowned at that and stopped immediately. Did it somehow cost him energy to shift back and forth? That made a certain sort of sense — as much as anything about being a vampire did — but it also meant he had to reign it in a bit. It would still be a while before he saw Jay, and if Jay wasn't in the mood for being nibbled Han would have to wait even longer.

A knock at the door roused him from his thoughts, and he hurried across to unlock it. "Hey." He smiled to Steve. "Sorry, long conference call. What's up?"

"I figured it was something like that, but I thought you'd like to see this." Steve stepped in carrying his laptop, and headed for the little meeting table in the corner of the room, so Han tailed and sat with him. "This is the weirdest thing,"

Steve added as he popped the screen up and tapped the trackpad.

Han stared at the screen. It took two seconds to identify the patch of street outside their front door.

Shit, Steve had been reviewing security footage. Or someone in his team had, and brought it to him.

He leaned forward, half in curiosity and half in dread, as the footage showed absolutely nothing.

And then a wooden stake appeared in mid-air.

It wasn't all that clear from the footage that it was either wood or a stake. The footage was grainy from low-light. It just looked like a line of pixels that could've been some kind of blip if they weren't there for several seconds, moving around before they disappeared altogether.

"Huh," Han breathed.

"Weird, right?" Steve frowned. "Maybe it's time to get better cameras. These run at a really high ISO at night."

"Yeah." Han poked at the screen like he could maybe rub the specks of dirt away. "Yeah, that's definitely a... thing. Are we sure there wasn't a bug walking across the lens or something?"

"Maybe. But I'd still recommend the upgrade."

Han nodded slowly. "Okay. Put in a requisition order. I don't want us to get caught with our knickers down if this is some kind of penetration test."

"Exactly what I thought!" Steve beamed cheerily. "Anyway. Sorry to interrupt your day. I'll get out of your hair."

"No, no problem. Thanks. I look forward to spending lots of money on new cameras," he said dryly.

Steve laughed as he took his laptop and left, and Han remained at the meeting table, rubbing his jaw.

Shit. This raised all kinds of questions, but also posed all kinds of problems. London was the city of CCTV, and if things vampires had in their hands showed up on film even though everything else about them was invisible, it meant he couldn't walk and text at the same time, or more and more people would start scratching their heads.

This technology problem *really* needed to be solved.

Fast.

NINE

JAY HEADED over to the gallery mid-afternoon, figuring that would give Christy more than enough time to go through any deliveries and letters that had arrived. It should also mean that he could nip out after and grab a bite to eat then go directly to Barb's house once the sun had set.

He pocketed his wallet after the barriers at Bond Street and strode quickly out of the little shopping centre which his chosen exit led him out through, pausing only to grab a cup of tea from Costa. His stomach grumbled at him as he eyed all the muffins and cakes, but he reminded himself that he was a good boy, and just made do with tea.

He knew better than to drink and walk in London, so he coddled the cup as he sauntered down Davies Street toward Claridge's, weaving between other pedestrians as a matter of course.

It was a delicate negotiation, one which not all people instinctively understood the nuances of. The Londoners knew this dance, and they knew how to discern which way to pass an oncoming stranger. They knew that if both parties just stepped slightly aside, neither had to be the one to do all the hard work, and everything flowed beautifully. But this well-oiled machine would be disrupted by tourists, children, dog-walkers, or those who just paid full attention to their phones, and Jay gave his best passive-aggressive huffs to those who refused to participate in the efficiency.

It was bloody cold out. Despite Spring technically being just around the corner, Winter showed no intention of pissing off, and while that meant the streets were a little easier to move along, it also meant the gallery was likely suffering. Very few people wanted to buy art when the weather was awful. Sunshine brought out the customers in all areas of retail, but especially when it came to laying down thousands of pounds in a single transaction.

He darted down Brook's Mews with Claridge's to his left and hurried to the gallery's front door, then eased it open and headed into the glorious warmth inside. He paused to listen for potential customers, then drifted toward the stairs, looking around to make doubly sure that there weren't any here.

Sadly, there definitely weren't.

He hopped up stairs two at a time, and called out, "Christy? Are you home?"

"Hi, Jay!" Her voice came from the office, and she sounded chirpy. "What brings you here?"

He headed in and grinned to her, putting his drink down on her desk so he could shrug his coat and scarf off and hang them by the door. "Well, I thought you'd be lonely."

"So you brought me a cup of tea?" She laughed.

"No, that's mine. You've got a kettle."

"So you could've had tea here."

He clicked his tongue. "Busted. My hands were cold." He grinned and dropped into the seat facing her desk. "How's it going? No problems?"

She pushed her keyboard aside and hopped up to go put the kettle on. "If only someone had told me this job was long, boring hours without a single customer," she teased.

"But then why would you take the job?" He popped the lid off his cup and took a sip. "You get to play a lot of Minecraft though."

"Minecraft is like so over," she said as she dropped a teabag into a mug. "Didn't you even bring a cookie or something?"

"Honestly, do you want me to go get you something, or are you just boredom eating?"

She gave him the side-eye and a firm frown. "Fine. Maybe. You've got a point. I should get a treadmill up here or something."

"I used to read books." He wasn't unsympathetic to her plight. "You don't even have to do it on your phone, you can install the app on the PC."

"I suppose." She stirred her tea, then brought it over and sat back down. Her hazel eyes fixed on him. "What can I do for you?"

"When was the last time you saw Ellis?"

Christy pursed her lips and looked toward the ceiling, then nodded to herself. "A few days after his brother finalised the house business and all the auctions."

Jay frowned. "He hasn't come to work since then?"

"No. I've had to close the gallery when I leave."

"Wow, that must be awesome for business."

"Right?" she agreed with a small huff. "I'm happy to work later, but I still don't want to be wandering down that mews after ten."

"I don't blame you." Jay swallowed some tea. "He might have made enough from all the auctions to coast for a bit, but he's got contractual obligations to fulfil, and he doesn't need to let people think the place has closed down. Those kinds of rumours can kill a business."

"Urgh." She blew on her own tea a while before she took a sip. "I don't think he really knows how bad it is. Or even how much time he's letting go by."

"Yeah? What makes you say that?"

Christy shifted in her chair and glanced away. "I think he might not be... you know. Okay. After all the things that happened." Jay just looked at her, so she continued. "He just doesn't seem... *serious*. I mean, I know, he jokes around a lot, but now he doesn't even seem able to focus on a conversation or subject. He zones out, then cracks a joke about something totally unrelated."

Jay nodded to himself. Han had said pretty much the same thing, but it wasn't getting him any closer to a solution, or even how to find a solution.

"He needs help," Christy said bluntly, finally meeting his eye.

"Yeah." Jay downed the rest of his tea, then tossed the cup in a recycling bin as he got up. "Okay. Thanks, Christy. I'm gonna see if I can find that help."

"Oh, in the glowing books?" She smiled hopefully.

"God, no." He backed toward the door. "From a chocolatier."

She looked less inspired by that. "Oh. Well. Okay. I guess."

He headed for the stairs and had to admit that maybe the glowing books would have been a cooler solution, but he needed something faster than that.

HE PAUSED to grab and eat a couple of onigiri on the way to Barb's, then stuck his nose into her shop to see if she was there yet, but the staff said she wasn't in until later, so he popped next door and tapped on it.

"It's Jay," he said quietly.

He heard her boots clatter down the stairs, and she opened the door, eyeing him like she still hadn't decided whether or not to eat him yet. "Hey there, tall, pale, and gorgeous. Come on up."

He shut the door after himself and hurried up the stairs to her poky little flat. "Sorry to bug you. Have you got a minute?"

She snorted and dropped down onto her velour sofa. She spread her arms across the back and crossed her legs, then grinned. "I got all the minutes in the world for you, Jay. Whatcha need?"

He paced a little. There wasn't room to pace a lot. "You did that thing a couple of months back where you all sat down and went through the entire census to figure out which vampires Bryce had taken and who she might take next, yes?"

"Yeah. Admin. Just what I signed up for!" She laughed. "What about it?"

"So you got to eyeball the list of every vampire in town. And what their power is."

Her laugh faded, and she leaned forward, elbows on her knees. "Okay, I'm hooked. Yes, I did. Where's this going?"

He gnawed his lip briefly. "I know Charles was the mind control guy, but is there anyone else who can work as, like, a psychiatrist? Or even just a mood stabiliser? Ellis really isn't holding up well, he's not eating, he's literally falling apart, and he's not even taking any of it seriously. If there's anyone that can even just, like, help him a tiny bit..." He tailed off, sitting in the armchair and facing her fully. "Anyone at all."

Barb bounced her foot up and down as she looked at him, her eyes narrowed for a good few seconds. "Honestly," she sighed, "it's like two hundred people or whatever, and I got to see like a quarter of it. But if anyone knows, it's Aaron. He's had like decades with that info."

Jay sighed. "Sod. How do I find him?"

"Don't worry about it. I'll talk to him. That way you're not —" She broke off a split second before Jay's phone buzzed.

He drew it out and chuckled. "Han does that as well. Knows when a phone's about to go off."

"It's easy in a quiet location," she said as he checked and found a new text from Han. "We can hear the screen power up."

"No way!" He opened the message and read it quickly, then tapped out a reply. Han was asking where he was, so he sent *Barb's.*

"Yes way," she said. "It's getting harder though. Really new screens are super quiet. And if a phone's on *do not disturb* it doesn't light the screen up when a new message comes in."

"Put phone on DND," he laughed. "Got it."

Han's next message read: *Are you ok?*

Sure, he tapped back. *Are you?*

Got staked, found out what power is, need to experiment more. Also could do with eating.

"What the fuck!" Jay leaped out of his chair and almost called Han, but remembered at the last second it was pointless, so he speed-typed his response.

What the actual fuck you can't drop that on me who staked you why what is going on where's the bastard now argh!

Barb had taken the opportunity to take out her own phone and tap away at it with a stylus, but now she watched Jay, her blonde eyebrows high. "What's going on?"

"Apparently Han got staked! He's okay — I mean, he's texting me — but oh my god." Jay hurried toward the door. "I gotta go. I'm sorry to bust in on you like I did."

Barb hopped up and raced him to the door, putting her hand on it to stop him. "Wait. Hold your horses, cowboy."

Jay bit his lip and looked her straight in the eye, but he didn't speak. For all his urgency, she had a reason to stop him, so he waited to find out what it was.

"He's texting you," she said softly. "Which means he's not staked now."

"Right," Jay nodded tightly.

"So, I'll talk to Aaron for you, okay?" She raised her chin. "We'll see if we can figure out between us who might get Ellis to eat something, or psychoanalyse him, or whatever. We'll work it out. Then I'll let you know." She pulled a business card out of her jacket pocket and handed it to him. "Text me so I've got your number."

Jay took it and snapped a photo of it just in case he lost it.

Barb was absolutely right. Running around in a panic wasn't his default state, and it led to inefficiency, his least favourite thing. He'd coped with a hell of a lot these past few years, from Ellis getting turned, to Han's cardiomyopathy, to Randall being a werewolf, and he'd always done his best to take it all in his stride. It was harder when Han's life was in danger, but damn it Jay prided himself on his ability to keep all his plates spinning without his hair getting ruffled, and whatever had happened today with Han wouldn't be solved by Jay running around like his hair was on fire.

He let out a slow breath, and nodded to her, then smiled a little. "Thanks. Good luck with the revolution!"

Barb laughed. "Thanks. And no problem. Now go get your man." She opened the door with a flourish.

"You bet I will!"

TEN

HAN JOGGED UP TO ST. Paul's as soon as the sun was low enough to let him, tapping out messages to Jay only when he was sure Richard wasn't about to try and stake him again.

The inability to just make a call was getting increasingly irritating, especially after Jay's last — and somewhat garbled — set of questions. How could he answer without it taking half an hour to type it all out?

Instead he sent *I'm jumping on the Central Line. Meet you at Oxford Circus. Exit 8.*

You better, was Jay's swift reply.

Han pocketed his phone and jogged through the maze of pubs which ran along the north side of St. Paul's Cathedral itself until he reached the station entrance, then darted down the stairs and through the barriers. He didn't begin to relax until he was on the platform, and even then he wasn't completely satisfied he was safe. Once he was on the train itself he was much happier about the situation.

Nobody would be daft enough to try and stake him on a packed train, surely.

HE MADE it to Oxford Circus without incident, which made it a hundred percent less likely that Jay would yell at him, and he navigated the maze of exits and the powerful flow of bodies travelling into the station instead of out of it.

Exit 8 was a little thing tucked down a short corridor, and it led straight up onto Argyll Street rather than spitting him out onto the chaos of the main intersection. He hopped out of the tiny exit and smiled as he saw Jay waiting right next to the doorway.

Jay wasn't smiling.

Han hooked his arm around his husband's and drew him south toward Liberty, sticking to the pedestrianised centre of Argyll Street. "Sorry," he said once they were away from the station. "So much happened, I figured by the time I'd typed it all out I could be here and telling you face to face."

"What happened?" Jay hunkered down a little to bring his head closer to Han's level.

"So apparently my office is in this bloke's territory," Han muttered. "He's been watching us come and go for God knows how long but he wasn't going to start anything with witnesses around, including you. This morning he comes at me, gives it the old 'you're on my turf I'm allowed to kill you' stuff, then goes at me with a wooden stake."

Jay gasped in horror, his eyes wide. "What did you do?"

"Well the problem is it turns out he can go invisible," Han groused, "so actually what I did was stand there like an idiot wondering where he'd gone, right up until he pulled a stake out and stuck it in me."

"But—"

Han held a hand up briefly and gave Jay a reassuring smile. "At which point my super awesome cool powers kick in which apparently make it impossible for me to get staked."

Jay blinked rapidly. He glanced around them, then leaned in again. "What is it?"

"Honestly I'm not sure. I seem to be able to just—" Han waved his hand vaguely, like he could possibly mime what the hell had happened. "I need your help to figure out what, to be honest, 'cause I *seem* to turn into this living shadow or pool of liquid or something, but I can't really, uh, touch myself to work it out."

Jay stumbled to a halt, which pulled Han to a stop, too.

"That's..." Jay's mouth kept moving, but words weren't coming out. "Awesome?" He sounded doubtful. "Weird? Weirdly awesome?"

"Gotta test and find out," Han agreed.

"I know you too well." Jay pursed his lips. "You've been testing already."

"For most of the day," Han agreed. "And it's left me a bit peckish."

"Which makes sense. I've been reading," Jay added, "and the short of it is that vampires undergo this one-way conversion process that transforms them pretty literally into pure magic. Everything you do consumes just a smidge of energy to fuel that magic, so if you've been totally shapeshifting from one thing to another and back all day that's probably burned through a lot of your juice. I don't think Ellis' thing consumes anywhere near that much energy. All his power happens inside his own head, but if you're, like, turning from one thing into another thing, that's got to be way more intensive, right?"

"Sure," Han chuckled. "Why not?"

Jay eyed him, then sighed. "You're right. Magic and logic don't necessarily seem to be BFFs."

"Right. But I think in this instance you might be onto

something." He squeezed Jay's arm and started walking again. "What else've you got?"

"Well, Barb's gonna rope Aaron into trying to find someone who can help Ellis out. Randall's going to give him a bit of blood this evening to see if that gives us more time. I haven't got over to Frederick's yet, but I was going to ask him to help figure out Bryce's stuff on vampires, since that was her specific area of research."

Han ran his fingers over Jay's arm while they walked, and considered his words. The idea of just coming right out and talking about vampires to a stranger made his eye twitch, but Jay would have considered all his options already. If this was the decision he'd reached, he'd weighed all the pros and cons and felt the risk was worth the potential payoff.

"If you're a hundred percent," he said.

"No?" Jay smiled. "But the sooner we get a solution, the less Ellis has to suffer."

Han couldn't refute that kind of thinking. "Okay. I'd better head home."

Jay shook his head. "Nope. Not if traveling alone gets you attacked by vampires. Either I walk you home, or you come with me."

He laughed and leaned in closer. "My big, sexy hero," he cooed.

"My delicate little flower," Jay laughed.

"Okay, fine. Let's go meet your mentor. And promise to never call me that again."

"I never make a promise I know I'll break!"

Han snorted at that. "Do you want to walk it, or get the tube?"

"Rush hour?" Jay squinted. "May as well walk it."

Han was inclined to agree, so he pulled his phone and put it to work on calculating their route.

———

THEY CUT across a corner of Hyde Park, strolling at a leisurely pace. It was only a couple of miles' walk to the Viscount's house, and in the cold, bitter weather, most people scurried down to the tube for warmth, so the walk was nice and peaceful, and this was Ellis' territory. There shouldn't be another vampire for the entire journey.

"You said you were hungry?" Jay murmured once they were safely out of earshot of other pedestrians.

"It can wait." Han smiled, though. "Thank you."

"Okay, well, I mean, if you want a quick nibble..." Jay made a great show of looking around like they were in a panto. "I don't think anyone'll notice," he stage-whispered.

"You want me to ravage you in public?" Han faked a gasp. "You pervert!"

"I'm just saying." Jay raised his hands.

"What'm I supposed to do? Climb you like a tree?" He grinned up at his husband. "Yell 'timber!' as I drag you to the ground?"

Jay's cheeks pinked, and he laughed. "Okay, so maybe we leave it for later. Then you can drag me to the floor all you want."

Han nodded in agreement. "Too right I will."

———

HE WAITED behind Jay on the steps as Jay used the huge iron knocker. Just one step below emphasised their height difference, and Han briefly considered pretending to be a small child who had wandered here by mistake.

He heard the knock reverberate down a hallway the other side of the door, and then footsteps approached. With his back to the barely-used road, he could focus his hearing on the house, and it didn't take much effort to pick out two heartbeats among the plumbing and wiring sounds. No pets in the house, then. Or vermin.

He glanced briefly to the small, private park across the road. Surely a mouse would sneak into a huge property so close to food if there weren't a cat or dog around to stop it?

The door opened, and Han turned back toward it to find the lanky redhead who had helped them unload the car yesterday.

"Michael!" Jay shook his hand enthusiastically. "I'm early. Is that okay?"

Michael smiled widely. "It's absolutely fine. Come on in!"

"Is it okay if Han joins us?"

Michael looked to Han, and nodded. "Sure. Come on. Can I get either of you some tea? Have you eaten?"

Han tailed them into the vast hallway, and he closed the door as he looked around.

This place was properly Georgian, with a checkerboard floor and high ceilings. As he nudged his shoes off and padded after the other two, he noted that there were no plants in here either. In fact, there was no clutter at all. The furniture was modern, graceful, and he was sure he could smell the faintest trace of paint, as though there had been some redecoration recently.

"I haven't eaten," Jay said as he shrugged his coat off and hung it on a hook, "and I'd love tea, if you don't mind?"

"I'm not hungry," Han chimed in, "but I wouldn't say no to tea."

"I'll bring it through." Michael gestured toward a door, but continued on down the hall.

"Thanks!" Jay grinned to Han, then led him into a huge

sitting room, where the Viscount was mid-way through rising from his seat. "Oh, wow!" Jay added.

All the books they'd brought over yesterday were arranged in neat piles on the floor with little notes poking out of each and every one. D'Arcy's desk held a couple more piles, and a huge ledger which looked like it was made for accountants from the Seventies.

"Michael and I decided to spend the day completing the task," d'Arcy said as he approached. He had that properly snobby drawl to his English which indelibly marked him out as the product of money. "I decided to call in sick so that we could get it done. Hello," he added, looking Han in the eye as he offered his hand. "Frederick."

Han's hand was dwarfed by the Viscount's every bit as much as the man towered over him, and the hand was hot to the touch. "Han," he replied. "Jay's husband."

"A pleasure," Frederick replied. "Please, make yourself comfortable."

Han tipped his head faintly. Frederick's pulse had lifted ever so faintly, then settled again. His pupils had dilated, but otherwise he seemed unruffled by... well... whatever seemed to have momentarily ruffled him. As Han removed his jacket and loosened his tie he realised they'd just spent an hour walking here in the near-freezing cold, and he was hungry.

God, his hand had probably felt like ice. No wonder Frederick's hand felt so hot. It probably gave Frederick a moment's discomfort, in which case the Viscount seemed amazingly in control of his outward expression.

"Thank you," Han finally said as he went to hang his jacket next to Jay's coat.

"You really didn't need to take time off," Jay gushed as he hurried to the ledger and began to skim through it. "Oh my god, you've done all of them in a day?"

"I had Michael's aid," Frederick said. "But it does allow you to get on with the task of prioritising your studies." He returned to the desk to stand by Jay's side. "What intrigues me is that she spent quite a lot of time studying vampires."

"Vampires," Jay echoed, and Han could hear and see every little thing which made Jay such a poor liar. His pulse raced and his eyes widened. Tension mounted in his shoulders, and the smile he plastered on was patently false. "Ha. How weird is that?"

Frederick simply raised an eyebrow, then turned that raised eyebrow meaningfully on Han. Then he patiently looked to Jay again.

Han heard Jay swallow, so he decided to save them all the time.

"Yes," he sighed. "That's me. The vampire in the room."

ELEVEN

JAY'S HEART seemed to want to fight its way right up through his throat and into his mouth, and he swallowed again.

What the hell was Han doing?

How did Frederick know?

Shit, Ellis was going to kill him! Purely metaphorically.

"I've been reading highly intensive research notes about vampire physiology all day," Frederick said dryly, "and your husband's hand is considerably colder than yours. As vampires who have not recently fed tend to settle at ambient temperature, and you have both been outside, the fact that Han is several degrees cooler implies that he either has a critical circulation problem, or he's a vampire. And he isn't undertaking any effort to mitigate a circulation problem. He is neither hugging the radiators nor is he wearing thicker clothing for the weather. In short, Jay, your husband is very bad at disguising what he is." Frederick looked to Han again. "Though I'm curious. Are you wearing coloured contact lenses?"

Jay turned to watch as Han blinked and sat down on a sofa. "I am, yes."

"It's a good disguise," Frederick said. "For those you don't offer a hand to."

"Lesson learned," Han replied, far more steadily than Jay felt right now.

Michael entered the room, bearing a tea tray with teapot, cups, milk jug, and sugar cubes all neatly arranged on it. He set it down on the desk and began to pour the tea. "This is awkward," he chuckled.

"Yeah, just a bit," Jay tried to keep the squeak out of his voice, but failed, and he was saved by Han's glance toward Jay's phone a split second before it buzzed. "Excuse me."

He stepped away from the desk and checked the message. It was from Randall.

Success. No attack. Still says he isn't hungry.

Jay thumbed out his response and sent it. *Great! We'll be over later!*

"Problem?" Frederick murmured.

Jay bit his lip and weighed the phone in his hand. He glanced to Han, who only shrugged at him, then looked to Frederick again. "We have a friend. A vampire. He's not well."

"I'm not surprised." Frederick crossed to one of the larger piles and plucked a book from the top. "This is, I would say, the work of your sorcerer, Bryce. She's spent decades pulling vampires to pieces for research and documenting her results." He handed the book over, and Jay took it. "This is the last of her journals. She's barely a third of the way through and then her notes just end midway through an experiment, so my guess is that said experiment is your friend?"

He flicked through the meticulously hand-written pages until he reached the end of Bryce's notes, and skimmed over them. There was a whole lot of jargon, talk of threads and weaves, and the more he read the more he realised that they referred to Ellis' body.

Ellis was nothing more than a tightly-woven bundle of magical threads to her, and she'd pulled on them, picking them apart, tugging and testing and cutting her way through to try and find the one she wanted.

"Oh my god," he breathed.

"So far as I understand it, from these notes," Frederick murmured as he moved to add a little milk to his cup, "she spent her time abducting vampires and quite literally picking them apart to try and find the thread — as she put it — which made them immortal. As with any sweater, the moment you begin pulling on these things, the whole thing eventually unravels."

Jay felt sick. He scoured the last page of notes, but it didn't offer up anything. There was talk of how Ellis had to be some great elder vampire for all the power contained in his tapestry, and her luck was tremendous in finding such a great 'subject', but there was nothing about unravelling.

"She must have been going senile," he whispered. "Ellis isn't an elder. He's barely a couple of years old."

"Are you certain?" Frederick set his tea on a coaster, then carried the tray over to Han.

Han murmured thanks and poured himself a cup, but didn't add either milk or sugar, and he cradled the cup in his hands as Frederick brought the tray back to the table.

"A hundred percent," Jay insisted. "We both knew him before he got turned."

Han nodded in agreement. "Even though I didn't know what it was," he chimed in, "the change was extremely noticeable."

Frederick nodded and moved to sit in an armchair with his tea, and Michael perched on the arm of his chair with his own cup. "Well, regardless of the cause of her confusion, prior experimentation suggests that once she has begun pulling her subjects to pieces, they will unravel of their own accord within a few weeks. Once she discovered that, she did her best to perform her experiments at speed, which may explain why she tested so many of her subjects to destruction in such short timeframes."

The sick feeling didn't go away. "A few weeks?" he echoed.

Oh shit.

Ellis kept saying he was unravelling.

Jay put the book shakily on the table and dropped a sugar cube into the remaining cup, then he tipped some milk in and stirred it.

"I would say," Frederick murmured, "that you may well have a new priority."

"Yeah," Jay said thickly.

Assuming it could even be done.

"I'll order pizza," Michael declared.

THEY PORED over Bryce's notes together. As she'd written them in English, they were able to divide the books up between all four of them and sit in a huddle as they cross-referenced notes and identified various spells she had used in her experimentation.

The trouble was, Bryce had only jotted down any spells she had amended, which meant other spells had to be buried in the rest of her library somewhere, and Frederick was sure that they weren't in the ones he had, which meant Jay would need to bring the remaining half over to be categorised.

He had, though, found a spell which Bryce had modified from simply viewing magic to specifically enable her to see these threads she worked with, so he set that book aside for now and referred to the ledger to find the spell it was originally based on.

It was a start.

If he was able to maintain both spells concurrently, it should enable him to see both the wards on Frederick's house and the very stuff that Han was made of, and if he could see the latter it meant he'd be better able to figure out how screwed Ellis was.

Both these things required he actually did magic, and that in itself seemed an enormous ask, considering he'd never actually done any before. He might look like a total lemon.

But if it worked... God, the possibilities were truly limitless if it worked.

He bit his lip, then sat back in his seat and eyed the pizza boxes which were mostly empty now. He debated whether he really wanted another — cold — slice, but ultimately he figured he was just trying to delay looking like a twit in front of his husband and two virtual strangers.

"Okay," he sighed. "I think I'm ready to give this a try."

Han raised his head and blinked a few times. His contacts were probably bothering him, Jay noted. "Magic?"

Frederick stifled a yawn, and stretched slowly. "What do you need?"

"I think something I can write on and stand in."

"We have Sharpies," Michael said as he eased to his feet. "I'll go get one."

"And something big enough to stand in," Frederick mused. "You're slim, but I don't think a sheet of A4 will cut it."

"And you don't want to be drawing on the floor with Sharpies," Han said.

Jay's eye turned to the pizza boxes again.

"I think I've got something," he breathed.

ALTHOUGH BRYCE HAD WRITTEN out both spells, they were both in Latin, and so Frederick walked him through the pronunciation of the first one several times as Jay practiced the unfamiliar words.

"Okay," he said. "I think I'm ready to try it."

He'd already transcribed the circles and sigils from Bryce's notes onto the inner lid of one of the pizza boxes, and he took his notes, the book, and the box lid out to the hallway, where the tile flooring would provide a less malleable surface to stand on. He didn't know whether crinkling the circle over carpet would cause the spell to fail, but it was better to eliminate it right from the start.

The rest of them followed him and crowded the sitting room's doorway like spectators waiting in the wings by a stage.

"I'm probably not going to set anything on fire," Jay teased.

"You'd better not," Han snorted.

"Probably." He grinned as he dropped the box lid to the floor, then he stepped onto it, looking around himself to make sure he was completely inside the circle. "Okay. Here we go!"

Everyone fell silent.

Jay held the book in his left hand and his page of pronunciation notes in the right, and ran through it once more in his head to be sure he knew what he was doing, and then he took a breath.

The world seemed to pause.

"Revela oculos meos," he began.

It was as though the universe held its breath. As he continued to speak, unhurried, taking care to ensure each word was accurate, he felt an increase in tension which didn't come from inside him. The very air seemed to hold still, until he breathed the last words of the spell.

A soft, pinkish flare curled from his lips and disappeared into the air, and the world sprang back into motion.

And the walls around him were coated in a faint, green glow.

"Oh my god!"

"What?" Han sprang toward him. "Are you okay?"

"Did it work?" Frederick asked more calmly.

"I think it worked!" Jay squealed and snapped the book shut, then squeezed past them into the sitting room.

The windows had a green sheen across them which glowed faintly. The walls, too, were bathed in it, though it didn't seem to cover the internal walls. Jay hurried through to the kitchen at the back of the house, and the windows which separated house from garden were also tinged in green.

"Oh my god, this is amazing! I can see them!" He reached out and ran his hand over the glass, but it was just cold, smooth glass. He felt nothing unusual about it. "I can see the wards!"

"Really?" Han stepped in beside him and looked up at the windows. "What do they look like?"

"Just like—" Jay waved his hand. "This green glow. All across the walls and windows. Oh, wow, I should totally run around checking stuff out now!" He turned, and Frederick's talisman was virtually a signal flare. "Wow," he added.

Frederick blinked at him.

"Yeah there's no way your tie would've hidden that from me," Jay added. He put a hand in front of the talisman, not touching Frederick's shirt, but the glow still poked out from around his palm. "It's like a beacon."

Frederick's nose crinkled. "I'm not especially fond of wearing beacons," he murmured.

"I guess it's that or be targeted by magic you can't see, though, right?" Jay shrugged. "There's the trade-off."

"I concur."

Jay licked his lips, then nodded. "Okay. Let me see if I can do the next one."

They parted out of his way and he scooped up the second pizza box lid, placing it beside the first. With the two side by side he could just about make out the differences — a slightly changed sigil here and there, or a totally different one in two places — but at a glance he wouldn't have known which was which if he hadn't written *1* and *2* in the corners of the box lids.

He stepped onto it, turned his page of notes over, flipped to another page in the book, then began over.

The spell also began the same way, with only a few changes in the middle. Frederick had walked him through the English meaning of it, and whereas the last spell was more *open my eyes to the magic all around me*, this one was all *show me the vampire stuff*, more or less.

Another faint wisp of pink that dissolved into thin air and suddenly it was Han who was the beacon.

Jay gasped at the sight. Where Michael and Frederick looked unchanged, Han was now a bright red bundle of string, like a ball of elastic bands in the shape of a person. Jay hopped off his pizza box lid and approached his husband, reaching out to trail fingers over his shirt.

Threads softly buckled under his touch.

"Oh my god! This is so weird!" He grabbed Han's hand and could see most of the threads disappear up his sleeves, but others wrapped out and around the cotton of his shirt. "It's like your clothes are part of you!"

"That doesn't seem to make a whole lot of sense," Han said.

"Yeah. But whatever magic makes you kind of extrudes out

around what you're wearing, too." He looked up to meet Han's eyes, but even they were part of the mesh now. "This isn't the most flattering look," he added with an apologetic smile.

Han just laughed and raised Jay's hand to kiss, then let go of it. "If it helps diagnose the problem, it can be as unflattering as it wants."

Jay nodded, then looked to the front door, which still glowed green. "Okay," he breathed. "Both spells are still going. Oh my god, it's actually working! I can do magic!" The well of excitement burst, and he balled his hands into fists, waving them in front of himself like a T-Rex at a party. "I can do magic!" he squealed.

Han laughed and backed away. "Okay. Do you want to go eyeball Ellis and see if you can figure out where the problem is and how long we've got?"

Jay nodded quickly, and watched as Han picked his jacket up. It was incredibly fascinating how the material wasn't consumed by Han's magic until he slipped his arms into it, at which point the mesh suddenly extruded around it, drawing it in.

He tore his gaze away and looked to Freddy. "Thank you so much. For everything. I know we've literally only just started, but I couldn't have got even this far without your help."

Freddy inclined his head. "Think nothing of it. There's a lot more work ahead. But if you don't mind, Michael and I would rather head to bed right now. That and I'm not sure that your friend would appreciate total strangers visiting him in the middle of the night. It sounds as though he has enough on his plate already."

"Of course! Absolutely!" Jay shook Frederick's hand, then Michael's, and grabbed his coat while Han slipped his shoes back on.

It was time to see Ellis.

TWELVE

Jay took two steps outside the house and stopped before he even reached the pavement.

There was a vampire across the road, and with the mass of red obscuring everything but the general shape he had no idea who it was. All he knew was that it was there.

Han bumped into his back with a soft *oof*. "What?"

"Who's that?"

Han stepped down to stand beside him. "Where?"

Jay blinked.

The vampire started walking toward them.

"Right there," Jay hissed. "Coming toward us."

Han sucked in a breath. "I don't see anyone." He grabbed Jay's elbow. "The bloke who went for me this morning can turn invisible, though. I hear footsteps... Clothes..."

"Invisible vampires?" Frederick drawled from the doorway. "How tiresome." Then he lifted his voice a little. "Bugger off. We don't want whatever you're selling."

"How long have you been there?" Jay watched the mass of threads as it stepped up onto the pavement.

"Long enough." The vampire answered. "The Council is going to want to hear about this."

Han let out a soft hiss and took a step forward, but Jay grabbed his shoulder.

"You followed us?" Jay grinned. "Which means you're now the one on someone else's territory."

The vampire stopped on the pavement. Jay wished he could make out the guy's expression.

"Devitt is dead," the vampire said cautiously.

"But O'Neill has Devitt's turf now. *Councillor* O'Neill," Jay added, emphasising Ellis' status. "So I just want to get this straight. You crossed however many vampire territories to get here, to then spend all evening trespassing on a Councillor's territory. We crossed Councillor Applegate's territory to get here, too." He rolled his shoulders and slid his hands into his coat pockets. "Seems like you've trespassed on a lot of powerful people's ground to get here tonight, sweetie. Now, you can go running to those very people and explain how you attacked one of their Vassals on their territory, if you fancy?" He gasped, then clapped his hands. "In fact, we're on our way to Councillor O'Neill's house right now! Maybe you should come with us and explain it to him!" Jay flashed his teeth, and added, "I hear he's only killed every single vampire who tried to fuck with him."

The vampire snarled softly. Jay saw him flex his fingers. "That doesn't excuse humans knowing what you know."

"Oh, you didn't hear the part about me being able to do magic?" Jay lifted his eyebrows. "I can see you, no matter how invisible you think you are."

This was all a horrible gamble, and he knew it. The guy had already attacked Han, and while there was some kind of stalemate there this morning, Han was running way lower on energy now. Jay wasn't any kind of fighter — the best he could do was bite someone really hard and hope that was enough to make them let go of him, but that wouldn't work on a vampire — they didn't react to non-lethal pain as badly as the living did.

And then there were Frederick and Michael, and while Frederick was built like a Rugby player, Michael looked every bit as flimsy and squishable as Jay felt.

Despite the four to one ratio, Jay didn't fancy their odds against an invisible vampire who could bite any one of them to inflict instant paralysis.

"I hear O'Neill's blind," the vampire said slowly. One hand moved up toward his chest, and various weaves shifted slightly. It took Jay a second to realise the guy was reaching into his coat. "I'd be doing him a favour."

"Goodness," Frederick gasped. "How staggeringly ableist of you. Aren't you a charmer!"

The vampire darted forward, and a shaft of wood appeared in his hand, separate from the weave of his body.

Han's mesh dropped to the ground like he'd turned to water. One second he was there, a step ahead of Jay, and then the next he was draped over the steps. The pavement. The railings. He was *everywhere,* seeping across the ground and into the road, beneath the other vampire's feet.

And then, with a startled scream, the vampire fell down as though the ground had swallowed him whole.

"Holy shit," Michael breathed.

The mesh of Han spat the wooden stake out, and it clattered across the pavement, then rolled into the gutter.

There was no sign of the vampire.

Han re-formed like he was being sucked up through a straw. The red weave receded across the ground and drew up into a Han-shape until he was all there was to it, and he cleared his throat awkwardly. "So there's that," he murmured.

Jay stared at him. "Oh my god! What the hell did you just do?"

"That's my thing," Han murmured. "What did it look like?"

"Like—" Jay gestured to him, but it was his own pulse which raced like he'd just run a marathon. "I can't really see you right now. I can only see the magic you're made of, and that kind of splooshed all over the place and then he fell into you and now you're here and he isn't." He gasped in horror. "Did you eat him?"

"Ew," Michael said.

"I don't think I did." Han seemed to be patting his chest. "I think he's in here somewhere. I did it earlier with a chair, but I spat it back out again. I didn't know what would happen if I re-formed without throwing him back out, but apparently he's... I don't know. In me?"

"I have a theory," Frederick murmured.

Jay turned to look up at him.

Frederick gestured to Han. "Perhaps you are not merely some sort of..." he hesitated. "Autonomous shadow when in that form. Perhaps you are actually a portal to a pocket realm."

"You've lost me," Han admitted. "Like, another dimension?"

Jay blinked. "That's possible?"

Frederick nodded faintly. "It's not uncommon for sorcerers to carve little pocket realms out to use as personal sanctums. If you are able to take things into yourself and then eject them again at a later stage, you may well be doing exactly that. It's only a theory, of course. I have no way to be certain, and I, ah... I wouldn't suggest you try it with a living creature. Pocket realms don't naturally come with their own supply of fresh air, to my limited knowledge."

It was, Jay figured, the only theory they had right now, and it was a hundred percent better than no theory at all. "I suppose some testing is in order. Thank you, Frederick. Michael." He reached for Han's arm. "Is it okay if we come back tomorrow?"

"Please do. I think it may be time to find out how to ward things against vampires," Frederick said dryly. "No offence, Han."

"None taken. I wouldn't want that arsehole breaking into my house while I was asleep," Han said.

Frederick simply nodded in agreement. "Be careful."

"We will!" Jay finally made it to the bottom of the stairs, and turned toward Pimlico.

It was a half hour walk via Belgravia to reach Ellis' house, and when they got there, Randall let them in.

"All right, Randall?" Jay was grateful that Randall still had a face of his own, unlike Han right now. "Where's his nibs?"

"Through here." Randall led them into the living room, and Tiberius bounced over to greet them, so Jay let the dog slobber on his hands a moment, then he looked toward Ellis.

"Bloody hell," he breathed.

Where Han was bright, Ellis was radiant. If Bryce's determination of a vampire's age was by how blindingly he glowed, he could see how Bryce might have mistaken Ellis for an elder when he gave off three or four times the kilowatts Han did.

Except, unlike Han, Ellis' weave wasn't nice and tight. It was a mess, like a sweater dumped in the corner and slept on by cats for three months.

"Aha, y'areet?" Ellis chuckled. "Everyone's being so polite. It's nice to hear something different, for a change."

Jay approached him and reached out. His fingers seemed to disrupt the weave, sending minuscule ripples across its surface, and the closer Jay looked, the more he could see that several strands across Ellis' body were frayed, or even severed altogether.

"You sound upset," Ellis said softly.

"Upset?" Jay squeaked. "Ha. Upset. Me." He bit his lip and leaned back. "Did you eat?"

"A wee bit. Randall insisted."

"I told him to. Don't be hard on him."

"I'd rather be hard *in* him."

Randall's choked gasp was loud enough that even Jay's regular old human hearing was good enough to catch it, and he couldn't help but laugh softly. "Dirty bastard," he said. "Look, Ellis. You said you were unravelling."

"Aye."

"Can you feel it happening?"

"Oh, aye." Ellis' hand reached for his desk and tapped it briefly, then fell back into his lap. "Snap, snap, snap."

Jay nodded to himself as Ellis poked at his own chest, and one of the threads which had been struggling to hold on gave up and broke apart.

"Snap," Ellis said again.

"Balls. Okay. I'm working fast as I can to fix this, all right? But it might take a while. Do you think you can hang on a bit more?"

"Plenty of time," Ellis chuckled. "No rush!"

Jay eyed the magic which held him together. The fractured threads were few, but those which were fraying were less so. There was no way to know how long Ellis had left, but he was willing to bet it would be less than a month. They'd already eaten into some of his time by not even knowing this was a problem.

"Right," Jay said faintly. "Oh, by the way, Han's your new Vassal."

"I wondered when we were going to get around to that," Han said dryly.

"I have a Vassal?" Ellis laughed. "Hurrah. Why?"

"Because I've been going back and forth across town, and I got noticed," Han said. "So far, it's contained, but..."

"Contained?" Randall cut in. "How?"

"Good question!" Han replied. "You and Ellis will be joint-third to know just as soon as I figure it out."

"Um," Randall said uncertainly. "Okay?"

Jay backed away from Ellis without touching him again, just in case doing so somehow accelerated the rate of decay. "It's a bit complicated," he said, tearing his gaze away and looking to Randall. "Hang on."

He closed his eyes a moment and figured out which of his spells was which, then just... stopped worrying about the second one, trying to figure out how to cancel it, or even if he could.

He felt it lift away into nothing, and when he opened his eyes again, Han had a face, and that face looked confused.

"God, that's so much better," Jay sighed. "Now you all have faces. Magic," he added for Randall's sake. "You had a face anyway. God, this is so confusing! Go on, Han, show him."

Han shifted from confusion to discomfort. "It's not my party trick," he said.

"Shh. Go on."

Han's body darkened and broke apart, like ink dropped in water. The darkness fell and spread across the carpet and up the wall, nothing more than deep shadows cast by the old house's weak lighting.

Jay gasped. "Oh, wow!"

"Shit," Randall breathed. "Han? Are you okay?"

"What am I missing?" Ellis asked.

"It's like Han's just turned into, like, this... *shadow*," Randall explained, sounding lost. "God, it's kind of spooky, actually."

"It's amazing!" Jay enthused. "Oh, wow! Han! You look like... Just like Randall said! Like this huge shadow is just taking up half the room. I bet you could give people a proper fright with that!"

"I suppose," Han said, and his voice seemed to come from everywhere, like wherever the shadow rested was where it came from. It wasn't multiple voices all speaking at once.

It was downright eerie.

"What I mean," Han said, "is this."

Tendrils of shadow flickered across the floor toward the huge, clunky chair which faced Ellis' desk. They coalesced around the base of it, and then the chair fell down, consumed by the darkness.

Not even a ripple remained to show it had been there.

"Fucking hell!" Randall leaped back three feet.

"Five out of ten," Ellis said. "It'd be better if there were an audio described showing."

The chair emerged, whole, from ten feet along the wall, slid out onto the carpet like a child returning a stolen sweetie to a bag. The shadow withdrew from around it.

"Basically," Jay said, sounding every bit as distracted as he felt, "Han's turned into a huge shadow, swallowed your visitor's chair whole, then spat it back out again several feet away."

Ellis tilted his head faintly. "Like, made it disappear?"

"Yeah." Jay nodded weakly. "It's kind of cool... And kind of weird."

"Thanks," Han said, his tone dry. "Hang on."

A panicked wail broke the surface as Han spat out a humanoid figure, which tumbled across the carpet and then skittered to the far wall in blind panic. "Oh, fuck! Fuck! Fuck!"

"All right, Gary," Han said. "Calm down. His name's not Gary," he added. "It's Richard."

Richard screamed weakly as he backed up against the wall, eyes wild, hair and clothes in total disarray. He stared at the shadow, then managed to tear his eyes away to look at the rest of the people who surrounded him.

"Where?" he wheezed.

"Fuckin' 'ell," Randall breathed.

"Oh, you're in my house." Ellis leaned — or more accurately sprawled — across his desk and took his glasses off, setting them down next to one of the scars on the otherwise immaculate surface.

The red glow of his eyes was unmissable.

Richard stared in horror. "O'Neill?" Then he blinked. "Um. Councillor O'Neill?" he corrected quickly.

"Yes." Ellis said it slowly, with a predatory smile. "You seem to have broken into my property, on my territory. I should do something about that." He placed a hand on his desk and leaned on it as he rose to his feet, then stepped around it, fingers trailing along the edge of the wood.

"No! No, I'm sorry! I didn't... Fuck, I didn't know he was your Vassal, Councillor, I swear!" Richard scooted along the wall, but Ellis' face turned toward the sound of movement. "I won't interfere. I promise!"

Ellis stepped free of the desk. He grinned, and Jay caught sight of fangs.

"Han," he breathed.

"Mm?"

"Put Gary back in the box. Fast!"

The shadow swept around the room, and Richard fell into

it with a choked sob, and the moment his mouth passed the threshold he was silent, like he'd never been there.

Jay stepped in front of Ellis and placed a hand against his chest to stop him.

"Ho boy," he murmured as those blood-red eyes failed to focus on him. "We have *got* to talk."

THIRTEEN

HAN PULLED himself back together once Richard was tucked back into whatever the hell dimension Han had put him in.

His gums itched, and he ran his tongue over them to try and soothe it, but the gnawing in his gut combined with it to make him realise just how hungry he was. Maybe seeing Ellis' fangs had made his own try to come out in sympathy.

Jay had his hand on Ellis' chest, which didn't seem massively wise, so Han moved in to stand beside his husband just in case Ellis got fruity.

"What about?" Ellis said.

"Put them away," Jay countered.

Ellis' lip curled, but his fangs slowly receded. "I were only going to put the wind up him," he grumbled.

Jay eyed him like he didn't quite believe it.

"I think the wind was pretty successfully put up him," Han said softly. "Isn't there somewhere safe we can put Gary? Somewhere that is a bit less me?"

"If his name's Richard," Randall said, "why are we calling him Gary?"

"Because he's an arsehole, and I knew an arsehole at school called Gary," he replied.

"The Constabulary has cells dotted around the city," Ellis mused. "You could pop him in one of those?"

Han crinkled his nose. If Richard had been standing around eavesdropping on them all the time they were at Frederick's house, he would've heard some downright juicy things that Han wasn't sure he wanted escaping into the wild. He rubbed his jaw and glanced to Jay, then sighed. "He followed us to where Jay's mentor lives. We did a lot of talking. About magic," he added.

Ellis head tilted in a most unsettling way. That slightly death-dealing look was still in his eyes, like he'd happily reach into Han to pull Richard out for a quick murder if he could. "This seems problematic."

"Yeah," Jay agreed. "That and Frederick realised pretty quickly that Han's a vampire, so there was that whole conversation."

"And Frederick's partner was there," Han continued. "So that's three humans sitting around discussing the existence of vampires, as well as the nature of your current status."

"Ooo. I have status?"

"The unravelling," Jay supplied.

Randall crinkled his nose. "So he knows a Councillor isn't at the top of his game right now, could point to three people who know about vampires but shouldn't, and can turn invisible at the drop of a hat."

"Plus he knows where Frederick lives, and Frederick can't use magic," Jay added.

"Then how's he teaching you?"

"He can read the books I can't, and he's got sorcerers as friends and family. He knows his onions, he just can't chop them himself."

"Which means Richard could just walk right up to that house and go on a killing spree if he felt like it," Han filled in. "And the Council would probably be all for it, because they kill a lot of their problems."

"You should eat him," Ellis said.

Han blinked slowly, then exchanged a look with Jay to make sure he'd heard that right.

Jay looked utterly mortified, so at least Han's hearing was working.

"Um," Randall said.

"I'm not going to eat the bloke, Ellis," he sighed. "That's disgusting. Why would you even say that?"

"You know," Randall said quickly, his heart going ten to the dozen, "maybe El's tired. I know I am. You, Tiberius? Tired? Yeah, you look it! We could, um, continue this tomorrow maybe?"

Ellis said nothing. He just gave that dark, predatory smile again.

"Yeah," Jay said slowly. "We should get some sleep. We've been up all day, and Han's running low, and it's super late!"

"Really, amazingly late," Han chimed in.

"So we're just gonna..."

"Go," Han finished.

"Go," Jay agreed.

They hurried for the door in record time, and barely remembered to say goodbye to Randall on the doorstep before Han put his arm through Jay's and dragged him away toward the tube.

Neither of them said a word.

THEY STAYED silent until they were well and truly back home, and even then Han locked all the doors and closed all the blinds and curtains before he was ready to try to put thoughts into words.

"Do you think Ellis has been, like... I dunno... Eating people?" It rushed out of Jay before Han got a chance.

Han shrugged out of his jacket and hung it, then kicked his shoes off. "You thought that too, eh?"

"Oh come on! Randall can't get him to eat for weeks, suddenly we put Richard in front of him and he was ready to sink his teeth in!" Jay flapped his hands helplessly, then busied himself with taking his coat off. "And he totally egged you on to do it, too." He hung it beside Han's jacket, and crouched down to unlace his shoes. "He wouldn't have, would he?"

"Don't ask me," he sighed. "I don't know. If you'd asked me yesterday I would've said no. Of course Ellis wouldn't have done that. But you saw the look in his eye. He was properly going to go for Gary."

"Can we at least call him Richard?"

Han pulled his tie off and folded it. Jay was absolutely right. He was being damn rude about Gar- about *Richard*, but in his defence the bloke had tried to stab him through the heart with a stake only that morning. "You're right," he conceded. "Richard. I don't know, baby. Maybe it's an after-effect of the, er..." There was no nice way of saying it. "The torture. That shit's got to have an effect. People come away with PTSD from less, and he's an art dealer, not a soldier." Han ran a hand through his hair, which had long since lost any styling product he'd put in it. "Maybe in his head he just doesn't want to hurt anyone the way he got hurt. Maybe he saw Richard and just..." He shook his head. "I don't know."

"Me either." Jay unwrapped his scarf, then moved straight on to unbuttoning his shirt. "Maybe we should just sleep on it.

Focus on the problem. I mean... I saw his weave. His threads. You're both made up of magic, and it's like a tapestry, and you're wound really tightly—"

"Tell me something new," Han chuckled.

"Ah ha," Jay said dryly. "Your tapestry is tight and neat. No gaps, no holes, no wiggling. But Ellis' is literally unravelling, just like he said. There's give in his threads and gaps between them. Some are broken, others are fraying. I got the feeling if I could just find and pull on the right one, he'd fall apart in a flash." His wry smile had faded fast. "What if that's painful? What if it hurts, each and every moment?"

Han bit his lip. "What you're saying," he murmured, "is that it might not just be one day of torture."

"What if every day since then has been torture?"

"Fuck." Han strode toward the bedroom so that he could get undressed. "Can you fix it?"

He heard Jay follow. He could pinpoint exactly where Jay was without even looking his way.

"I don't know," Jay admitted. "I've only just learned to see it, and Bryce had decades to try and figure out what made vampires immortal and she couldn't do it. What if I can't figure out how to stop one falling apart in a couple of weeks?"

Han shed his shirt and tossed it into the laundry basket. "Only two weeks?"

Jay's shirt followed his. "Maybe more, but I can't tell. I've got no reference point. Urgh, this is all horrible! How can I fix this? She had like at least fifty years of experience, and I'm this total newb!"

He could hear the panic rising in the race of Jay's heart and the tremble of his vocal chords. He could see it in the strain around Jay's eyes, the way his irises contracted to allow more light in through his pupils. Jay was keeping it together, but the cost was great, and it wasn't going to get any less.

Han shucked his trousers and stepped out of them, then lifted a leg so he could pull one sock off, balancing perfectly on the other foot. "Okay," he said with care as he tossed the sock and switched legs. "You can't solve a problem if you don't sleep, right?"

"But—"

He threw the other sock into the basket. "But you can't sleep if you're worried sick about how your best friend is doing, right?"

Jay nodded grimly. "Right."

"Well, you're going to have to try," he said bluntly. "For Ellis' sake. I'll do everything I can to help you, but your brain's the one we need in full working order here, so you have to take care of it."

Jay's shoulders slumped, and Han crossed over to him to place his hands on them. Jay's skin was like a furnace to his touch, and Jay gasped sharply.

"Oh my god, you're so cold!"

"Weather," he grumbled.

"No, you're hungry," Jay argued. "You said so earlier."

"And we agreed to shelve it until we got home," Han agreed.

They stood in silence, gazing at each other. They both knew what he needed, but it seemed an imposition to ask right now. How could they do this when Ellis might be suffering? Even if all Han did was feed, it would still arouse them both, and then one thing would probably lead to another.

Even if they didn't set out to have sex, the odds were that they'd get there if Han fed right now. That was one of the most horrible things about vampires. Their very existence was a withdrawal of consent. To their knowledge, Han was the first vampire ever created with actual permission of the human about to be turned. Until Ellis met Randall, he'd fed by necking strangers in bars and leaving them like they'd just had the most amazing heavy petting in the world, because it was impossible to say "Hey, actually I'm a vampire, is it okay if I feed off you?" Every law in town forbade humans finding out that vampires existed, and asking that question could get a vampire executed at the Council's order.

Han sighed and let go of Jay's shoulders. "I'm just going to run to the bathroom," he murmured. "Back in a tick."

Jay nodded, and Han turned away, heading into the bathroom and shutting the door.

He'd accepted tea earlier because it was hot. It warmed his body, both from the inside, and as he held the cup in his hands. But he had to get rid of it now, or he'd have no choice in the matter once the sun came up, and neither of them would want to get woken up by Han vomiting cold tea everywhere.

He placed his hands either side of the sink and leaned over it.

There was a trick to this. His body seemed to know what didn't belong inside it, and he didn't have to fuck around doing all those things students did to try and make themselves throw up if they'd got too drunk. All he had to do was sort of... *be ready*, and his body did the rest.

Well, he was ready now.

His gut convulsed, and the job was done. Neat. Efficient. Gross as shit. Han rinsed his mouth out and then brushed his teeth, because toothpaste was a better flavour to have lingering around. Then he washed his hands to get any residual mint off them so when he put his fingers in his eyes to slide his contact lenses out, he wouldn't get mint-eye.

He wiped his face with a cloth when he was done, then looked into the mirror out of habit.

There was nothing there.

Would he get used to that, one day?

No. He wouldn't have to, because it wasn't damn well good enough, and he would have to figure out a way to fix it. And if Jay could learn to interfere with the magic which constituted his body now, he might just have the right tools for the job at his disposal.

He patted his face dry and left the room, only to find Jay naked and sprawled on the bed with a welcoming smile on his face.

Apparently in Han's absence, a decision had been made.

FOURTEEN

JAY SLID his hands up behind his head and laced his fingers together, then wiggled his hips to make his cock bounce around. It was, he was certain, the most erotic thing Han had seen in the last five minutes. Guaranteed.

Han blinked, then laughed softly and shed his boxer shorts. "Only if you're sure," he said.

"We'll see how it goes," was his counter-offer. "Maybe if you wear me out I'll sleep better."

That was the hope, anyway, because he knew damn well Han was right. Jay couldn't do a damn thing to help Ellis if he ran himself ragged and spent the next two weeks wandering around in a sleep-deprived stupor. He needed rest, and the best way to guarantee rest was a good fuck.

Tomorrow, he could go back to Frederick's and take the rest of the books with him. Tonight his husband needed to eat, and Jay was more than happy to be the main course, because if there was one thing he never wanted to see again it was Han feeding from another guy. Great though it was for Edison to volunteer himself the way he had, the image played on Jay's mind and he really wished it didn't.

Han came closer and padded onto the bed on his hands and knees, and his golden eyes were filled with warmth, creased by his soft smile. "I can always wait," Han insisted as he eased across Jay's body and pressed lips to his jaw.

Jay raised his hands and traced them along Han's sides, gasping as Han's cold body slid over his own and settled against him. He shivered like the window had suddenly been opened. "I think you should do it," he whispered, "before I freeze to death."

Han chuckled and trailed kisses down his jaw, each touch of his soft, icy lips lower than the last.

Jay swallowed and tipped his head back. His hands found Han's hips and he squeezed them, holding tight.

Teeth ran along his skin, and he gasped, his cock thrumming with anticipation.

And then those teeth pierced his flesh.

His hands froze where they were. He had no choice about that. The wave of pleasure which rode the stab of pain down through his whole body made his cock stand tall and his nipples harden. His breathing quickened, and he heard his own soft gasps for air that took place entirely without his control.

His body was, in every way, Han's now. There was nothing he could do, and that usually wasn't a problem. It was *awesome*, in fact. But all he could think of was the look in Ellis' eyes.

Eat him.

Han pulled free and gently ran his tongue over Jay's skin, then his breath flowed across it to heal the injury, and Han was warm again.

And Jay was free.

He gasped, and his eyelids fluttered. "Oh god," he breathed.

Han raised his head and frowned slightly. "That wasn't an *Oh god, Han, that was so good* kind of oh god."

"No," he agreed. "I think he did it."

Han searched his gaze, then nodded gently. "Yeah," he agreed quietly. "You think it's what happened with Charles?"

"Maybe," he murmured, moving his hands to stroke Han's arse. "I was thinking Jonas. The guy who turned him."

Han sucked his teeth, then shrugged. "Not a whole lot we can do about it right now."

"Yeah," Jay agreed. Then he smiled weakly. "Sorry. Where were we?"

Han laughed. "I was around here." Then he dipped his head back to Jay's neck and gnawed playfully at him.

It tickled, and Jay laughed, and soon he was able to put Ellis aside and focus on the one man who mattered more. He squeezed Han's bum, then slapped it lightly, and Han's cock stirred against his own.

"Han," he whispered.

"Yeah?"

"We're out of lube."

Han snorted at him. "No we're not."

He rolled his eyes and laughed. "God, I can't even with you! Can't a guy crack a joke and get away with it any more?"

"No." Han laughed and slid hands over his chest, thumbs circling his nipples. "Unless you want to start seeing someone else."

Tingles of joy sparked from Han's fingers and through Jay's body, and he arched, which only served to grind their cocks together. "Never!"

"Well, you're stuck with me, then."

"Rather be stuck with you *in* me."

"Wow, that escalated quickly."

Jay laughed as Han eased off him to go fetch the lube, and

rolled onto his front, doing his very best *come fuck me* eyes while he propped his arse in the air.

Han turned back to face him, tube in hand, and gasped.

"Like what you see?"

Han looked to his eyes, then back to his bum, and cleared his throat. "Baby, I liked what I saw from the first moment I laid eyes on you."

Warmth flowed through him, and he couldn't help but smile. "You're the most gorgeous man I ever met," he breathed. "Get on and fuck me."

"Such romance!" Han smirked as he got back onto the bed and grabbed Jay's arse.

"I know. I'm all flowers and long walks in the park."

He closed his eyes as Han stroked his skin and leaned over to kiss the small of his back. He gasped as Han's nimble hands took his cock and balls and began to stroke both with tender care. And when Han eased lubricated fingers inside him and found his prostate, he lost control of the ability to use words.

Han entered him slowly. He knew exactly when to wait and when to push, and Jay didn't need to ask how. He didn't need to do anything other than lay here and enjoy the way his husband took him over and spoiled him rotten.

"How's that, baby?" Han breathed as his hips came flush with Jay's backside.

Jay's eyes fluttered, and he groaned. He'd *tried* to say it was great, but words had fled him. It didn't matter. Han would understand.

Hands rubbed his back gently, and then returned to his cock, stroking him off as Han began to fuck him.

God, he was amazing. Smart, beautiful, every bit as thoughtful in bed as he was out of it. Meeting him was the second best thing to have ever happened to Jay.

Marrying him was the first.

He gave himself over to Han's hands, his cock, the way his husband curled around him and whispered dirty things over his shoulder, and the closer he came to orgasm, the more he wondered what it would be like to be fed from right then. Right at the moment, the point of no return.

Would it be amazing?

His body seemed to think so. Just imagining it pushed him so close he began to cry out, to gasp, to buck in Han's hold and beg him to go harder.

Faster.

"Oh, fuck! Yes!" he managed, just before he came.

And then it was on him. The ravening, mind-shattering bliss of orgasm, the storm that swept aside everything else and replaced it with shuddering pleasure and peace, and a sense of unity like nothing else on Earth.

He cried out, wordless, then collapsed in a heap, panting hard, seeing stars.

Holy fuck, he really did have the best husband in the world, and he grinned feebly to himself.

"Suck it, bitches," he mumbled.

Han just laughed.

HE WOKE SUDDENLY, jolted by Han's sudden strangled yell.

"Sweetie?" He gasped. "What is it?" He sat up fast just as Han leaped out of bed and clutched at his gut. "Oh my god! Han? What's wrong?"

It couldn't be the tea. Han had gone to the bathroom and come back tasting of toothpaste, and he wouldn't have forgotten to sort the tea out, would he? No, that wasn't like him at all.

Bollocks. He wished he could still see the magic. Though even if he could, what could he do?

"I don't know," Han gasped. "Oh, god, it hurts! It—"

Han broke apart in the space between one second and the next, turning into wisps of darkness that fell across every surface from the bed and floor to the dresser and walls.

Crouched huddled in the darkness was Richard.

Jay gasped and clutched at his sheets, dragging them up over himself. "Han?" he yelled. "Han! Are you okay?"

Richard eyed the blackness all around his feet and scrambled up onto a chair. "Oh, god," he gasped. "It's a monster. I've never seen anything like it!" Then he stared at Jay. "Oh, *god!*" he added with such disgust that Jay immediately knew what he meant.

Jay grit his teeth and focused on the shadows as they pulled together and rose from the floor. Han was back in one piece, stark bollock naked because that's how they slept together, and looking slightly ill.

"Sweetie?"

Han waved his hand. "I think I'm okay."

"Jesus Christ," Richard spat. "Were you in *bed* together?"

Han blinked and turned toward Richard, who visibly flinched. "What the fuck are you doing here?"

Jay grabbed his phone and checked it, then sighed. "Sunrise," he concluded.

Richard curled up on the chair, clearly not even willing to put a foot on the floor, and eyed them both. "Fuck," he spat.

Han looked to Jay. "You think I had to spit him out because it's sunrise?"

"Makes sense," Jay sighed. "Like food."

"I'm not food!"

"Be quiet, sweetie," Jay muttered. "You're not going

anywhere all day, so you may as well be a good guest, or I'll open a fucking curtain."

Richard looked to Han, then sneered. "You wouldn't dare."

"I can turn into a shadow and hide in a wardrobe in the blink of an eye," Han countered. "Then we get your ashes vacuumed up and thrown in the bin. Are you going to behave yourself or what?"

"We could just see whether you can hold him again," Jay muttered, "once sunrise has passed."

"No!" Richard clutched at his chair, and a look of pure terror twisted his features. "Please, no!"

"Then shut the fuck up. And don't eyeball me when I get out of bed, arsehole," he added.

"Oh Christ, you're not going to go at it with an audience, are you?"

Han rolled his eyes. "No, we did that earlier."

Richard seemed even more appalled, and Jay slipped out of bed to head for the bathroom.

What a stellar fucking start to the day.

JAY'S CANTONESE wasn't yet good enough for a fluent conversation about astrophysics, but it was decent enough to chat with Han's family whenever there was a get-together, and it was good enough to make sure Richard couldn't eavesdrop on them while they showered.

"What are we going to do?" He kept his voice low anyway.

Han sighed and shook his head. "I don't know. I'm not looking forward to spending an entire day with him in here."

Jay nodded in agreement. "Want me to stay?"

"He likes to turn invisible and stab people," Han said dryly. "I think you should go."

He sighed at that and rinsed shampoo from his hair. "Fine, but once I'm a..." he hesitated, not knowing the word.

"*Mou-si,*" Han supplied.

Jay repeated it a couple of times to make sure he had the tonality right, and then he continued. "But once I'm a wizard, I'm going to..." He waved his hands then switched back to English. "Kick his arse."

Han chuckled, and remained speaking Cantonese. "But until then, I'll handle him. Who knows? Maybe stuck in here we can come to some arrangement."

"What like?"

"I don't know," Han mused. "But you know what Mum would say."

Jay groaned. "Oh no."

Han laughed and tilted his head, doing a startlingly good impression of his mum. "When the winds of change blow, some build walls..."

"And others build windmills," Jay concluded. "Okay, but if he kicks off, lock him up. I do not want to come home and find you..." He waved a hand again, but this time he knew the word.

He just didn't want to say it.

Han gave a solemn nod. "I promise."

FIFTEEN

HAN HELPED Jay get the suitcases to the door, but he had to hang back as Jay left. The hallway beyond the door had plenty of windows to let in light, and even though the sun was barely up he didn't want to give Richard the opportunity to slip out and escape.

Bloody hell. He was keeping a prisoner in his own home.

He waited until Jay locked the door, then he turned to face the other vampire.

"So what now?" Richard snapped. "We stay here all day? Together?"

"You're welcome to go outside." Han shrugged. "How old are you? Do you think you'll make it to the tube before you turn to dust?"

Richard eyed him, then stalked to a sofa and sat down.

"Didn't think so," Han muttered.

It was a gamble that paid off. Ellis had been told that sunlight was immediately fatal, and had only discovered otherwise by mistake. After that, Han had undertaken extensive exposure testing and knew that, if he had to, he *could* make it to the tube with plenty of time to spare. It wouldn't be comfortable, but he wouldn't die from it.

But if the general belief was that a few seconds of sunlight was death, Richard might not have been willing to risk it, and it turned out he wasn't, which meant they got to keep secrets a few hours longer.

Han just had to hope there was a solution that could be reached before sunset, or this would go south really fast.

"Am I under arrest?" Richard cut in.

Han turned away and wandered toward another sofa. He sat slowly, deliberating his answer as he tugged on the crease of his trousers to straighten it.

"If you take me to the Council, I'll bury you all with me," Richard snarled. "Even if your boyfriend—"

"Husband," Han cut in.

"Even if your husband is some kind of witch, they still won't want the other two to know about us. You've broken laws. They'll punish us all." Then he creased his nose. "Wait, husband? How?"

"Christ, you're out of date, aren't you?" Han rolled his eyes. "Look, the way I see it, we have a problem. And by we I mean you and I. Both of us. Your problem is that my job is on your territory, and then in your zeal to cause shit, you tracked me across other people's territories to snoop on me. Councillor O'Neill was more than happy to kill you for being on his turf without permission, and I've saved your life. Regardless of whether anyone else on the way might have let you pass, *he* wasn't going to."

Richard glanced away, then crossed his arms tightly. "What's your point?"

"I also have a problem." Han crossed his legs and leaned back against the sofa. "My husband's human, as are two of our colleagues, and they know what I am. They know what you are. Ironically they know about this because they're the only ones who can solve a very specific problem, which might actually benefit you in the long term." He laced his fingers together in his lap. "So here's what I propose. I tell you everything. All the gaps in your knowledge, I fill them in. I tell you what the benefits might be. You already know half, so you may as well know the other half."

At that, Richard's eyes narrowed, and he sneered at Han. "And then you kill me? What's the point?"

"And then I ask whether you want to join us," Han replied. "I ask you which side of all this you want to be on, once you have the full facts at your disposal. And then, maybe, if you don't want to be on our side, I take you back to Ellis and he can deal with you."

He kept his features relaxed. Neutral. But the fact was he knew damn well that taking Richard back to Ellis was a death sentence. Just because Han wouldn't be the one to do it, the look in Ellis' eyes had made it more than clear that he would quite happily murder a vampire in his house.

Taking Richard back there was as good as dropping the guillotine himself.

"Okay." Richard shifted in his seat to sprawl slightly. "I have to admit to some curiosity. What do you think you could possibly tell me that would make any of this all right? Go on. Astound me."

"Okay." Han met his eyes across the room. "There's going to be a revolution, with or without the Council's vote. Sooner or later — and I think it'll be sooner — these travel restrictions are going to get lifted. Everyone will have the right to travel around London. People might choose to maintain a territory of their own, but there won't be any more of this killing each other over it. You get to move freely. Interact with each other. Make friends, maybe even allies. The way this city runs is going to change forever, and you can either stick around for it, or you can be gone before it happens, but it *is* going to happen."

Richard shifted slowly from sprawl to upright, until by the end of Han's speech he was leaning forward, elbows on his knees, looking him straight in the eye.

"That's madness," he said slowly. "You're making it up. None of that is possible."

"It's possible," Han stated firmly. "And it's already underway."

Richard was quiet. Still as a statue, and just as silent, until two full minutes had passed.

Only then did he take a breath to speak.

"How?"

HAN LAID IT ALL OUT. He explained that if the Council didn't vote for it, that a revolution would occur to force it anyway. He didn't mention Barb, but he did point out that Ellis had a network of contacts far beyond his outwardly obvious means, and that he would leverage them to ensure that the Council modernised. He might have over-egged it a bit, making Ellis sound like some all-powerful mastermind, but what the hell. He had one shot at this, and if he couldn't make Richard buy the shit he was shovelling, he'd have to put the guy back in the box, and the box seemed genuinely frightening so he'd rather not if he could avoid it.

Richard got up and paced away from him, circling the room like it was his cage.

Which, to be fair, it was.

Han idly kept tabs on him without making it too obvious that he was watching. With a vampire who might become invisible at any moment it was probably best to rely on his hearing anyway, so he got his phone out and started checking his emails. If he couldn't get to the office today, he might as well get some work done anyway.

He was halfway through tapping out an email when Richard said something, and he paused his stylus.

"This would lead to chaos." Richard seemed to be mulling that over, rather than condemning it.

"How so?"

"If we can go anywhere, then we *will*. And if we aren't responsible for our own territory any more, how will the Constabulary solve any crime?"

Han shrugged. "The same way they do now?"

"Don't be facetious. They solve crime *now* by knowing whose territory the crime occurred in. Usually it's reported by the person whose territory it is, and they just—" he gestured with both hands, half a shrug "—hand all the information over, and that's that."

He stared at Richard. "Right, that's not actually solving crime. There's no deduction there. That's just turning up and going after whoever you tell them did it."

Richard shrugged. "It works."

"It doesn't bloody work," Han argued.

And then he had an epiphany.

"Oh my god," he breathed. "None of you know a damn thing about modern policing, do you? No, don't answer that."

It made too much sense. He doubted anyone had bothered turning a detective in the last hundred years, let alone the past ten. Aaron was probably the closest thing they had to any actual investigative skill or technique, and he wasn't trained at all. He was just really picky about the truth for his own reasons.

But otherwise, none of these people had been turned for

their problem-solving skills, and he very much doubted any of them had even known a real-life police officer, let alone anyone from CID.

They had an entire Constabulary to police vampires, and no knowledge of how to do it.

"So that has to change," he concluded out loud. "You're right, in a way. If we abolish territories, we have to implement a proper Constabulary, complete with training and standards and accountability."

Richard snorted and rose from his chair. "This is all speculative," he muttered. "The Council has clung to these laws for centuries."

"How do you know that?" Han turned to watch him this time. "What proof have you got?"

Richard stopped. He frowned. And then he glanced toward Han. "What?"

"Evidence. Proof." Han stood and spread his hands. "You're younger than seventy, right? You must be."

The other vampire gave the faintest of nods. "Of course. Only Devitt was pre-war, and he's gone."

"So the only evidence we have of what any of these laws even are, let alone how long they were in play for, comes from a guy we know to be a psycho, a liar, and capable of making people do everything he told them to." He dropped his hands and stuffed them into his trouser pockets. "And before the Blitz, he would have been one of the younger vampires in London. Not necessarily the youngest, but hardly in line for the Council, if that was even how the Council worked at all." He narrowed his eyes. "The entire way this city's been run could have been totally made up, by Charles Devitt, once he realised most of the others were dead."

Richard began to pace again. At the very least he seemed to be engaged now, rather than refuting everything Han said. "He can't have been the only one left," he insisted. "Why would he bother creating any others at all? He would have the entire city to himself to do whatever he wanted."

"Yeah. So he can't have been alone. And maybe he wasn't even the oldest. But if there were few enough vampires left, Devitt could have ordered them to form a system of government and a set of rules that basically put him in charge. He could even have told them all to forget everything before a certain date, or told them they were younger than him, or anything else. And then once the new system was in place and the population started to recover, he could have bumped them off one by one until the Council *was* all younger than him."

"Maybe." Richard clicked his tongue. "But ultimately it's irrelevant."

"No, because if it's true, it proves that this system hasn't been in place since the dawn of time. It's just a recent fabrication, and we're still dancing to someone else's tune. And that someone else has been dead for months."

They stood a while. Han's mind was racing through how on Earth to go about setting up a functioning police service from a bunch of vampires who were, for the most part, little more than enforcers, while Richard seemed to stare up at the ceiling like he'd stalled.

"Okay," Richard said. "Fuck it. I'm in."

Han raised his eyebrows at that and tore himself away from his own thoughts. "What? Really?"

"Are you kidding me? I'm not saying this is going to be a long-term friendship, but if we've all been living under rules that aren't there to benefit us, I want to know why, and I want things to be better. So I'm in. And until we get to the bottom of this, I promise not to tell a damn soul about your collection of humans." He approached Han and pursed his lips, then stuck his hand out. "Deal?"

Han eyed it. There was no way to tell if Richard was lying. Vampires lacked all the tells of a human body. No sweat, no heartbeat, no autonomic functions.

All he could do was take a chance, so he reached out and shook Richard's hand firmly.

"Deal," he said.

SIXTEEN

Jay really didn't fancy leaving Han with Richard all day, but he didn't see how he had much choice. Ellis wasn't going to get better by himself, and Han did have a point: Richard couldn't hurt him.

Well, not unless Richard managed to bite him.

He had to call an UberXL to get all the suitcases in, and even then he sat up front in the passenger seat, gnawing on his thumb all the way to Chelsea.

Vampires just didn't bite each other did they? Putting Ellis aside for the moment, was it the kind of thing they'd even think about in anger, or was it like the unspoken agreement between middle-glass blokes that you just don't kick each other in the balls, even in a pub fight?

The Uber driver pulled up outside Frederick's house, and Jay thanked him, then between them they got all his suitcases out onto the pavement, and Jay thumbed his phone to leave a tip while he shuffled the cases to the doorsteps.

He just had to trust that Han could handle himself. His

power was pretty freaking awesome, and if all else failed he could just melt into shadows and be completely untouchable.

Jay was busy wondering whether Han was able to slip under doors or pour himself down drains as Michael opened the door, and he shoved those thoughts away for now.

"Morning," he said brightly. "Hope I'm not too early?"

"There's no such thing when there's a deadline," Michael chuckled as he hopped down the steps and began to heft one of the heavy cases back up them. "Urgh, why does paper weigh so much?"

"No idea. Water's just as bad. Things you don't think weigh much but secretly do." Jay grunted as he began heaving a case up the steps. "We need to find a levitation spell."

"Or install a ramp," Michael muttered. "I guess London got mostly built before the invention of the wheel."

Jay laughed softly as they got the other cases inside. Each one had to be something like thirty kilos of dead weight, and by the time they were done and the door was shut, his arms had turned to jelly.

"Have you had breakfast?" Michael asked as he wheeled a case through to the living room.

"Actually I haven't." He followed and smiled to Frederick. "Morning."

"Good morning." Frederick eyed the luggage as it added to the clutter in the room. "Breakfast seems an excellent idea. Do you eat eggs?"

Jay nodded and smiled. "Yeah. No allergies or anything."

Michael chuckled and rubbed his hands together as he peeled off to head for the kitchen. "Eggs it is, then. And tea, I assume?"

"Oh god, yeah." Jay fetched another case, and this time Frederick came out to help him.

Together they methodically opened case by case, emptying

the books out. As Jay had already sorted through them at home, they were pre-arranged into magical and non-magical, English and non-English, and so Frederick began the task of sorting the non-English books into specific language piles.

Michael soon brought out simple omelettes and a pot of tea, but after a short break to eat, they were down to business.

As much as Jay loved organising, he would rather have been learning more spells right now, but there was little he could do other than start sifting through the English books to find any more of Bryce's notes.

It was going to be a long day.

HE FELL down the research rabbit hole. It was easy to do. Both Frederick and Michael were beavering away, working feverishly fast to catalogue the entire non-English collection, which left Jay with plenty of time on his hands, and millions of words to fill it with.

This must've been what life was like before Wikipedia, he figured. You opened one book, and then before you knew it you'd skim-read half a dozen of the things.

What seemed to be becoming apparent, the more that he read, was that every sorcerer out there who had ever put pen to paper had different ways of doing things. Sometimes those methods seemed similar enough to be roughly the same, and other times they were miles apart. He found two spells for examining the structure of wards, but one of them seemed way more bullish and antagonistic in tone than the other.

Was it a matter of personal style? Were there several roads to the same goal?

He took a breath and looked up, then hesitated. Frederick's

pen was darting across his ledger as he made notes, and Michael was tucking notecards inside books.

Maybe this wasn't the time for philosophy.

Frederick's pen halted, and he looked up, meeting Jay's eyes. "Hmm?"

Jay puffed his cheeks out, then let the breath go. He hadn't got where he was today by not asking questions.

"Is it me," he began, "or does there seem to be some duplication of effort among these spells?"

Frederick set his pen down and rolled his shoulders, and a variety of cracks and pops quietly accompanied the motion. "In what sense?"

"Well, like. I'm sure I've found a couple of spells that do exactly the same thing. They just, like..." He waved his hand. "Do it with different word choices and sigils and... that."

"Ah." Frederick reached for the next book on his pile and flipped it open. "Yes. As I understand it there are a variety of means with which to get the universe to do as you wish, and some are more forceful than others."

Jay pressed his lips together and frowned. "Are you saying it's possible to bully the world into going the way you want it to?"

"Essentially. Or you can ask nicely. Or find some middle ground." Frederick began to flick through the pages, eyes passing back and forth rapidly as he skim-read.

"Why would anyone force it if asking nets the same result?"

At that, Frederick burst out laughing, and he set the book down. "Why indeed, Jay."

He stood up and stretched slowly, eliciting a few pops of his own from his spine. "I basically just asked why some people are arseholes, didn't I?" he realised.

"Essentially," Frederick chuckled, clearly still amused. "Perhaps asking nicely takes longer. I can't attest to whether or not being brutal is more or less effective. I do know that sorcerers tend to classify themselves according to their methods. A witch will work with the natural order, for instance, and request aid. A warlock will bend the universe to his will and not care what he breaks along the way." His grey eyes clouded and he stood, turning his back as he stepped away from his desk.

Jay watched him. Despite not knowing the man for long, he was reasonably sure Frederick was one of those stiff upper lip types who could maintain a blank face during the apocalypse. This was about as much emotion as Jay had seen him convey at all, other than amusement.

What could shake a man like that?

Jay blinked slowly as the pieces all slotted together in his head. "Your father's a warlock?" he guessed.

Frederick pulled his phone out to look at it, then glanced over his shoulder to Jay. "Michael, why don't you prepare lunch for us?"

Michael set his stack of cards down and hopped to his feet with a soft smile. "I'll get right on it."

"Thank you. I appreciate it."

Once Michael left them alone, Frederick paced across the room, picking his way around books and suitcases, until he reached the tall windows at the front of the house. From there, the park across the street could be seen, and Jay watched as Frederick looked out at it.

"You are correct, of course," Frederick eventually murmured. He didn't look back to Jay. "And he has broken... plenty of things. I won't go into the details, so please don't ask me to."

Jay adjusted his centre of balance, shifting weight from one hip to the other, and nodded softly. "I'm sorry. Whatever he's done, I wish he hadn't."

"As do I." Frederick rubbed his jaw, then shook his head. "Still, that's in the past. But it should inform your future." He turned and faced Jay directly and slid his hands into the pockets of his cream trousers. "You are just starting out on this journey," he said. "And you must choose which path you will take."

He stared at Frederick.

Why did it feel like those few words suddenly added a whole new weight to his shoulders?

Jay sat slowly, elbows on his knees and laced his fingers together. "How do I choose when I don't even know how many paths there are?"

Frederick shrugged at that. "Every single step is part of a path. I'll be brutally honest here: the path I personally choose is not for everyone. I am quite willing to break eggs to get a good omelette. I am not a good person, simply one capable of doing good things. Every choice I make is weighted, evaluated, but very rarely do conventional ethics factor into it." He seemed utterly unruffled by what sounded to Jay a hell of a lot like an admission of psychopathy, but before Jay could worry about it, Frederick continued. "But your path? Your choices? Only you can make them. I can't tell you what to do in that regard. And in the end, we only really have one choice throughout our lives."

Jay blinked at him and waited, but Frederick said nothing, so he asked, "What choice?"

Frederick's lips twitched. "Whether our goal is worth the price."

Jay swallowed, but the lump in his throat seemed to remain. He squeezed his hands together, then raised them and bit his thumb softly as Frederick's words rattled around inside his head.

"I shall check on Michael's progress," Frederick said idly, as though he hadn't just tossed a grenade into Jay's lap, and he sauntered off through to the kitchen, leaving Jay well and truly alone.

What *was* Jay's goal? He didn't doubt he'd have plenty of different ones over time, but his goal right now?

Save Ellis' life.

Was he willing to threaten the universe to do it? Cajole it? If there was no other way, was he willing to bend reality to his will and force it to do as he wished?

Could he stand by and let Ellis die if the only way to save him was to become a warlock?

He didn't know. He really didn't. Sure, it seemed obvious to answer yes. Yes, of course he'd break things to save his best friend's life! Who wouldn't?

But nothing could shake the feeling that, for all Frederick basically claimed to be out for himself, whatever the duke had done was infinitely worse than being a bit selfish or demanding the universe give him free stuff.

Broken. That was Frederick's word. The duke had broken something, and left Frederick scarred somehow.

Was that what Jay wanted to become? The kind of man who left scars on the world around him? He could save a life, but what would the cost be?

Would it be different if that life was Han's?

He straightened in his seat and knew the answer immediately. He would tear the universe apart to save Han's life, if he had to. If there was no other way. Of course he'd prefer to do things gently and politely. It was always better to win success with a smile and a kind word than at the end of a loaded gun, but if the loaded gun was his only option?

Yeah.

He'd take it.

That was who he was, then. Maybe it wouldn't have been if

he wasn't able to use magic, or if he wasn't surrounded by vampires and werewolves. Maybe in a normal world with a normal life he wouldn't ever get pushed into a corner and forced to make life or death choices. But his life wasn't normal, and it never would be.

All he could do was hope for the best, but he was damn well willing to prepare for the worst.

SEVENTEEN

Since they'd reached some kind of uneasy truce, Han had decided he may as well spend the rest of the day asleep. He could lock the bedroom door and set an alarm to wake him before sunrise, and while he wasn't wholly comfortable trying to sleep with a stranger in his home, he managed to doze off in the end, and was pleasantly surprised to find himself able to wake up again when the alarm went off.

He fumbled the sheets off himself and tipped himself out of bed, then made it into the bathroom and had a quick shower. He was in no rush to spend an awkward evening waiting for sunset with Richard, so he took his time, brushed his teeth, did what he could to style his hair without access to his own reflection, and put his contact lenses in.

Once he was dressed, he checked his phone for messages, and found a few from Jay.

Things are going well. Found a handy spell. Will be here until late.

Hey sweetie. How's it going with that idiot?

Oh, Barb says Aaron couldn't find anyone suitable to help. Looks like we're on our own here.

Are you asleep?

Han chuckled and tapped out a quick response, then sent it. *Yeah, just woke up. I'll come over once I can.*

Great! was Jay's prompt answer.

He pocketed his phone, unlocked the door, and stepped out into the living room, half expecting to find that Richard had vanished, but he was there on one of the sofas, slowly sitting up and running a hand through his hair like he'd just woken up himself.

Han thumbed over his shoulder. "Bathroom's free if you want it."

Richard eyed him, still sullen, but at least no longer outright hostile. "No. Thank you," he added. "It can wait."

"All right." Han crossed to the curtains and reached for them, then glanced back to Richard. "How old are you, again?"

Richard leaped to his feet and backed away, alarm plain on his face. "Are you insane? What are you doing?"

"For fuck's sake, trust me. You can't be over seventy. I reckon not even close. So out with it." Apart from anything else, he lacked any scientific data from anyone older than himself, so if Richard started to burn it'd be useful to know his age.

Wait, he told himself. That was cold.

Or just thorough.

"Thirty seven," Richard spat. "What does that have to do with anything?"

"As a vampire, right? You're not counting living years?"

"Of course!"

Han nodded speculatively. "Okay. Trust me on this."

And then he yanked the curtain open.

Richard screeched and scrambled backwards, hands up to protect his face.

Nothing happened.

Han crossed his arms and waited for Richard to realise he wasn't dead, and once Richard hesitantly peeked out from behind his arms, he sighed. "It's a lie. It's all part of the lies they use to control you. Look." He pressed his own hand flat against the glass. "Now I'm not going to claim you'll be totally safe outside. I'm led to believe it affects us differently based on factors like our age and how recently we fed. But I promise you, even if you come stand over here, you're not going to turn to ash in a split second. Look." He turned his palm toward Richard to show it to him.

Richard eyed the window, and then Han's hand. He slowly lowered his arms.

"It doesn't make sense," he whispered.

"It makes total sense." Han stepped away from the glass and back toward the sofas, though he didn't sit. "It's all about population control. You stay indoors, you only go out at night, you don't even talk to each other. What kind of existence is that? Fucking hell, we only inflict solitary confinement on the worst of prisoners, and even then you have to ask whether it just takes criminals and turns them into monsters." He shook his head. "This situation is a monster factory. Tell me you haven't wanted to seek out someone you could just talk to about your existence? Someone who could listen and understand, know what this life is like? Even if you couldn't see them again for ten years, just to know you aren't alone in this could save you going mad, couldn't it?"

Richard's gaze darted to the glass, then back to Han. "We see the Council once a year," he said, sounding like he wasn't all that convinced that was a good thing.

"Yeah. And do you get to have a nice sit down chat with them?" Han shrugged. "You basically get hauled up in front of your jailers so that they can check you haven't died yet. And then they throw you back in your box."

God, the more he thought about it, the worse it seemed. Even if a vampire could mingle among humans every night of his life, sooner or later those humans would notice that he didn't age, and then that vampire couldn't just move to another part of town where he had no contacts.

He was stuck there, slowly losing the ability to even go out on his own turf in case any of his former mortal friends spotted him one night and began to ask the obvious questions — maybe not directly, maybe only among themselves.

Maybe they met other humans who had also found themselves friends with people who never grew old.

Charles might have been the only vampire with the ability to do whatever he wanted and get away with it, but maybe all the solitary living got to him, too. Who wouldn't go a bit bonkers if they got to be a hundred or more years old and were stuck on one little parcel of land that was designed to break them?

Richard circled the room slowly, approaching the window with extreme caution. Han just sat on the back of the sofa, watching him, saying nothing.

"This is insane," Richard muttered. But with extreme caution, he eased his fingers out into the weak evening sunlight, then snatched them back and examined them. "How did you find out?"

Han shrugged. He wasn't about to tell the truth, but at he could come out with something close enough. "I'm a scientist by nature. If someone tells me something is true, I want evidence."

Richard blinked at him. "You exposed yourself to the sun to see if it would kill you?"

"Very carefully." Han pushed away from the sofa and returned to the window, leaning his shoulder against it as he regarded Richard. "I don't doubt we wouldn't want to do this in the middle of August, but right now?" He crinkled his nose. "With this weather? I'd say you're probably safe for at least ten minutes, maybe even half an hour. More than enough time to run for cover wherever you find yourself."

Richard narrowed his eyes and looked out of the window, down at the Thames below. He paused, then lifted his gaze to Blackfriars station across the water. "We're on the south bank," he surmised.

"Yep."

"So running water..?"

Han shook his head. "Even I'm not willing to test that one. There's no way to do it gradually. We've got to use the tube to get there." He pointed at the station, fingertip against the glass. "Quarter of an hour to do a two minute walk."

Richard nodded grimly, but stepped back into the shade of the next curtain nonetheless, as though he still didn't entirely trust his newfound knowledge. "Why are you trusting me with all this?"

He laughed briefly. "Sooner or later we're all going to be able to talk to each other. You're going to find out. You're going to be able to make contacts, talk to people, and have a future. It's not remotely in your interest to maintain the current system. You're too young to have a shot at Councillor, and you're just about old enough to have lost all your human friends already. Right now, you're alone. But you don't have to be. Christ, we don't even have to like each other, Richard. I'm not asking you to declare undying friendship. We just met, and I locked you up straight away. In my defence, you did try to stake me, so I think we're about even, but it's not exactly going to be all Friendship is Magic around here. But that doesn't mean I want you to live in a cage for the rest of time." He shrugged. "It's more efficient to talk about it now instead of waiting five years."

Richard glanced to the window, then walked away from it, arms crossed so tightly he was almost hugging himself. "Every vampire in London thinks they can't go outside right now," he said softly. "I think you're right there. It *is* prison. And we think it isn't, because we can come and go. But all we're really doing is pacing around inside our own cells."

Han nodded faintly and stepped away from the window himself. There was no need to start slowly cooking himself. That wouldn't help matters. "Look. You know where I live. Worse, you know where my husband lives. You know where our friends live. You know everything you need to know to go straight to the Council and get all our heads chopped off. And all that will do is reinforce the walls of your prison. What's in it for me? You know what's on the table. Six lives are in your hands. And what's on the table for you is freedom. I'm not saying there won't be laws or rules, but I can't even begin to imagine what they'd look like, and I don't think you wouldn't get a say in them. It just doesn't make any logical sense to me that you would sacrifice six lives just to lock yourself back in your cell."

He wasn't negotiating from a position of strength here. What he offered was a vague promise of future freedom, and what Richard held was information he might think could benefit him right away. If he took it to the Council and exchanged it for a place on the Constabulary or as a Vassal he'd have the freedom Han was trying to offer him, and it would be power, because very few other vampires had it.

"Yeah," Richard said. "Yeah, okay. Fine. Like I said, I'm not going to promise anything long term, but for now?" He ran a hand through his hair, then nodded curtly. "For now I'm willing to see where this goes."

"Good. Thank you." Han crossed to the door and grabbed a jacket. "Do you have a phone?"

"There's no point. We can't use them."

Han rolled his eyes. "Okay. Then there are definitely things you need to learn, because these things are lifelines." He brought his phone out of his pocket for a moment, then stuffed it away again. "Go buy yourself a phone." He dug into another pocket and handed Richard his business card. "Get a stylus, too. You can't use the phone without it. Then text me. Send me a text message," he clarified, "to that number. I'll happily show you how to use it, and then I can keep you in the loop."

Richard looked uncertain, but sighed. "Fine. I'll see if I can pick one up."

"Great." Han unlocked the front door and pulled it open, then headed outside. "Let's go."

"Where to?" Richard stepped out after him, and pulled the door closed.

"Right now, to the tube. Then I'm heading to Chelsea. If you want to go your own way, be my guest. It might be safer for you, since you don't have travel rights." Han tapped the button for the lifts.

Richard nodded thoughtfully. "Okay. Yes, you're right. It's probably better to just go home, get a phone, and... do a text message."

"Okay."

Han got into the lift, and as Richard stepped in beside him he prayed he wasn't making an enormous cockup.

EIGHTEEN

"I WONDER if this might be of particular interest?"

Jay looked up as Frederick spoke, and found him rising from his chair with a book in his hands. The glow of this one was a pale yellow, almost invisible, and as he came nearer he turned it and offered it to Jay.

"What is it?" Jay looked to the spell written on the page, with all its instructions and sigils detailed opposite, but he just about recognised it to be written in Greek. The rest was beyond him.

"It purports to give the caster access to any language not their own." Frederick perched on the arm of Jay's chair. "Greek is quite tricky, pronunciation-wise, unless you have childhood experience of other languages that use similar sounds. Any Spanish experience would be particularly helpful."

Jay made a so-so motion with his hand. "We did a little bit of Spanish at school. Mostly French, though, and I've picked up Cantonese reasonably well."

Frederick nodded to himself. "Well, the best we can do is try it and see how you go. If your pronunciation is too far off it may not work, but it should certainly give you the ability to work through these books yourself, which would be insanely useful. Shall we give it a try?"

Jay set his own book aside, and grabbed his notepad. "Let's do it."

They didn't have much time, and the ability to read all the books that Frederick had to translate for him would save them so much that he didn't have to think twice.

IT DID TAKE some effort to get words right, but Frederick seemed pleased with his progress, and once Jay attempted to cast the spell he felt that distinctive hesitation all around, as though the universe was waiting on his every word, and when he was done, there was that faint wisp of pink that disappeared into nothingness as everything came back into place.

He put his notes down and checked the book in his hands.

It made sense.

"Oh my god!" He couldn't believe what he was seeing. He *knew* it was Greek. The letters in front of him didn't look English, they still looked Greek, but he understood them as surely as if he was reading English. "It worked! Oh my god this is amazing!"

Frederick chuckled. "Don't get too excited."

"Why not?"

The Viscount tipped his head toward all the non-English books. "Because now this means you can work your arse off."

Jay groaned.

"Bollocks."

HAN ARRIVED around an hour after sunset, so Jay interrogated him about Richard and then put him to work on the English books, since nothing here seemed to be written in any form of Chinese.

It was like being at university all over again, pulling an all-nighter 'round a friend's house. Except none of his uni friends lived in houses as posh as this one. They were either in halls of residence, or crowded rentals with five or six people per house. But apart from that, it was totally like uni.

It was almost midnight when he began to yawn uncontrollably, but just as he was ready to call it a night, something caught his eye.

He leaned forward sharply and re-read the spell. It wasn't what he was looking for. He'd been about to skip right past it. Very little in this book had anything to do with magical creatures, let alone vampires, but he'd got sucked in by the randomness of it. It had veered from rumination on the battle of Carthage and what time of year was best to harvest certain berries, and into theories on the nature of memory and knowledge, but one more page and there was a spell of such magnitude that he wasn't sure he could be sure he'd read it right.

Jay stopped. He ran his fingers across the paper as he studied it more slowly.

"What is it?" Han asked.

"I think it's like some major exam cram spell," he breathed. "I think it makes you remember *everything*."

"Holy shit. Really?" Han hopped over and sat beside him, then huffed. "Why did I even look?"

"Because it's late," Frederick chuckled. "Honestly, though, if you've found some sort of eidetic memory spell, that does seem invaluable. I feel as though my work here is accomplished. If you are able to read everything here and remember it, you don't require our assistance any more. Although I do still happily offer it."

"Yeah, I can't see how your help wouldn't still be useful. It's still a huge amount to get through, and the faster I find the *right* books to read—" he broke off into another yawn "—the sooner I can fix this."

Han eyed him. "But right now, you need sleep."

"No, I—"

"Sleep," Han insisted.

Jay looked him in the eye, then sighed. "Fine. Okay. Good point."

"Yeah." Han squeezed his hand. "That and I can't get home once the tube shuts down, so we need to get cracking."

"I bet you could do it," Jay mused as they sat on the tube together.

Only the Jubilee line went to Southwark, but it was a nice, modern line with quiet rolling stock, so it didn't seem to cause Han too much discomfort as they sped toward Westminster. It was the stretch from South Kensington to Green Park on the Piccadilly which had been more painful, even to Jay's ears.

"Do what?" Han eyed him suspiciously.

"Think about it. The tube's already underground." Jay glanced around their empty carriage before he leaned in closer and lowered his voice anyway. "The tunnels don't have lights in them. I bet you could stealth shadow your way through the tunnels once the whole thing's shut down and get around London any way you wanted. A locked station's not going to stop you, I reckon. You won't show on any security cameras. The only thing you need to do is make sure nobody actually sees you with their own eyes and you're set."

Han rubbed his jaw while he mulled it over. "But why would I want to?"

"It's just an option. Say you get stuck out after it shuts down. The night tube doesn't go everywhere, and even when it's on it's only Friday and Saturday nights. If you get stuck on the wrong side of the river on a Monday night you're buggered. So it's an idea." Jay rested his hand casually on Han's thigh.

Han nodded at that, then smiled a little. "I suppose you're right. Anyway, I've had a thought."

Jay looked to him. "What?"

"You can see what makes a vampire," Han murmured. "Maybe in all of Bryce's notes she's managed to identify different parts of that in her search for the one piece that creates immortality, right?"

"Right," he agreed. He'd seen many of Bryce's notes already, and she had at least identified what she'd had before she threw it away each time. "I think there's some of that, yeah."

"Okay. I'm going to ramble off for a second here. Do you know how permissions work?"

Jay laughed. "Sure. You ask me if I want to suck your dick, and I say yes!" He winked and squeezed Han's thigh.

Han nearly choked with laughter. "Yes! But more specifically with computers."

"Oh, well. Maybe? Try me."

Han leaned back in his seat and stretched his arm out around Jay's shoulders. "Okay. Permissions come in layers. They pile up on top of each other in what's called masks, and when a system looks at those from the top, whatever permissions are still visible through the mask are the ones that get granted."

Jay bobbed his head. "Sounds like magic."

Han snorted at that. "You can grant a permission, revoke it, inherit it from the mask below, or deny it altogether. Generally if you deny a permission it ripples through the whole stack so you can't grant it again after. Depends on the implementation... Anyway. My point is if something about the magic that makes up what a vampire is specifically revokes the permission to interact with electronics, mirrors, and the like..."

Jay sat up straight. "Then maybe there's a way to add a new permissions mask to explicitly grant that permission again."

Han's grin was so wide it threatened to split his face. "Bingo."

"But what if it outright denies those permissions?"

Han's smile faltered at that. "Well, then the idea's a no-go and I'll have to have another one. But that's never stopped me before." He rose to his feet and snagged the overhead grab handle as he offered Jay his other hand.

Jay took it and stood, and a second later he too heard the difference in train noise which meant the train up ahead was exiting the tunnel. "Okay, I'll look into it once I've got to the bottom of this thing with Ellis," he said.

Han waited until the train stopped before he let go of the handle, then led Jay off the train, hand still in his. "Yeah, no problem. Prioritise Ellis, that's the more urgent problem. Once that's done we can try and figure out whether it's possible to fix the tech issue, but there are workarounds for that for the time being."

"Great. And I'm pretty sure I should be able to cast whatever the fix is onto an item that you can just carry with you or wear. I shouldn't have to cast it every day or anything." He waved his free hand through the air. "I've seen a few comments about imbuing items with particular spells, and then those items are permanently working that spell, or have it stored in them, so it should be possible to do that. If we can solve it in the first place." He stifled another yawn as they parted their hands for the barriers. "So you really think Richard will be on board with everything?"

"No way of knowing. It's in his best interests to be on board, but since when do people do what's in their best interests?" Han took his hand again once they were outside, and they turned north to head home.

"It's so true it hurts." Jay glanced around out of habit. It was hard not to check your surroundings when you were holding another man's hand, even in a dead quiet part of town when you were with a man who could hear a pin drop at half a mile. He saw nothing to trigger his Spidey-sense, so he returned his attention to his husband. "Should I bring the books home, do you think?"

Han bit his lip briefly. "Depends. Do you value speed or access more highly? Bring them home, you have them to hand round the clock. Leave them at Frederick's, you have three people instead of one working on the problem *and* you get forced to leave and get some sleep. Which goes against your urge to work twenty-five-hour days, I know," he added dryly.

"How do I know whether working alone would be any faster?" Jay huffed. "There's no way to test it. Not with a limited time-frame."

"You don't," Han said simply. "I think you're just going to have to trust them. It's going well so far, right? They've even taken time off work to burn through cataloguing those books for you, and Frederick's been able to help you find the spells you need to do this more efficiently. The teamwork's functioning really well, and I'd be inclined to stick with it, even if they're half-way across town."

Jay huffed at him, then shook his head. "You're right," he confessed. "I should never have fallen for a guy who was smarter than me."

"Oh shut up. You're a genius and you know it. Even better,

I think we've finally found the one thing in the world that your particular brand of genius is perfectly suited for."

He eyed Jay and let go of his hand as they headed into the lobby of their building. That way it didn't look odd to any security footage that might get reviewed later on. He didn't even look at Han until they were in the lifts.

"You think I was born to be a wizard?"

Han grinned. "Maybe not. But I think you're going to be the best one there can be."

Jay poked the button and leaned back against the wall of the lift while it rose toward their floor.

There were so many books, filled with so much knowledge, and Jay now had a starting point. He could read them, and he could memorise their contents. His organisational skills and his ability to think on his feet were already second to none, and the ability to rifle through a mental map of every spell he'd ever learned and whip it out with precision under duress could be the difference between a mediocre sorcerer and a top notch one. If there wasn't some kind of innate limit to power or skill, which he'd found no evidence of yet, then a sorcerer's power all came down to his arsenal of spells. His knowledge. And his ability to cast the right one at the right time.

Jay had no doubt he could come to grips with all of that in time, so maybe Han had a point.

Maybe Jay had finally found his true calling.

NINETEEN

IT TOOK ALMOST a week for Jay to read everything he needed to, and Han had little to do but sit and wait. Well, sit and wait at work, anyway, because he couldn't justify continually taking days off on the hope that things got fixed soon. He had a business to run, and it was hard enough without Jay being there to field phone calls, but it would be impossible if he didn't ever actually turn up.

He wasn't used to doing nothing, and he certainly wasn't used to being utterly unable to do anything. With Jay working his backside off over at Frederick's house all day long, and Han trapped in the office until sunset, they barely got to see anything of each other, and everything was limited to swapping text messages throughout the day.

Jay seemed sure he was making progress, though. He'd already figured out how to make himself one of those imbued spell pendant things that Frederick and Michael wore to protect him from other sorcerers, and he'd picked up a few supplies to make working easier, including a foldable laminated card which was like a portable dry-erase board, and

140

a collection of pens that would wipe off it. That way he could draw whatever sigils and such were needed wherever he was, then wipe them off once his spell was done.

And still Han sat in his office, waiting to see if Richard would ever text him.

That was uncomfortable all on its own. Had he made a mistake trusting the other vampire? It was, he was sure, his only option at the time, but looking back on it now was there another way he could have handled the situation?

Short of eating Richard, of course, because that was downright gross and Han still hadn't quite forgiven Ellis for even suggesting it. He couldn't just pop over to see Ellis and ask what the hell he'd been thinking, either, because Ellis clearly wasn't in his right mind.

Han had no way of knowing whether he ever would be, either.

He sighed as he packed his things away into his desk and locked the drawers, then rose from his chair and headed for the door. The sun had gone down, it was time to go to Frederick's. At least that way he could escort Jay home when they called it quits for the night. It was better than just going home and watching television alone.

He waved to the handful of people still working as he left, and told them in no uncertain terms to go home themselves, but he knew some people just preferred to linger in the office until their partners left work, or their neighbours went out, or even just until the tube was less hectic.

He wasn't expecting to find Aaron waiting for him at the tube station, and he blinked at the sight of the lanky Constable. "Aaron?"

"Han," Aaron greeted. He thumbed toward the barriers. "Going in?"

"Yeah." He dug out his Oyster card and waited for Aaron to

do the same, then joined the throng of people heading through to the escalators. "What's up?" he asked once they were side by side again.

"Unofficial business," Aaron said, though he didn't seem at all relaxed about it. "You been speaking to a bloke called Richard, right?"

Han nodded. "Let me guess. I shouldn't have."

"Hole in one," Aaron said. He got on the escalator first, so that when it went down, he and Han were around the same height. He faced his back toward the direction of travel so he could look Han in the eye. "Which means we'll have a problem soon."

"More than one, I'm willing to bet," Han muttered.

Aaron was a Constable. He wouldn't have heard about any of this unless the Council had heard it, and the Council wouldn't unless Richard talked. And *that* meant that the rat bastard had sold him out.

God fucking damn it, he'd trusted Richard, and the rat bastard had stabbed him in the back first chance he'd got.

"Multiple problems," Aaron agreed. "Nobody's capable of reaching you before me, though. I'm the fastest thing in this city, and nobody else can get to you until at least ten minutes after sunset, maybe even fifteen. They're probably all checking your home address first, too, since they're old and think everyone stays at home until sunset."

Han swore under his breath. "He fucking gave them my home address?"

Aaron shrugged. "Proper sold you down the river, he has." He turned on his heel to step off the escalator at the bottom, then let Han lead the way. "I assume you're not heading home?"

"No. To Frederick's. Jay's there."

"They've got that address, too. And I wouldn't be surprised

if they're going to try to pick up Ellis while they're out. The Council would love a good reason to get shot of him. They never really wanted to give him the job, and if they bump him off it'll be Barb on her own where they can easily outnumber her."

Han nodded grimly and headed for the westbound platform. At least from Blackfriars it was a straight run through to South Kensington, but it was easily a twenty minute journey.

Twenty minutes to give Constables enough time to close in on Jay.

"Bollocks," he spat.

———

THEY EMERGED AT SOUTH KENSINGTON, and Han's nerves were already almost shot. As they exited the barriers and passed through the short shopping arcade which led to the station's exits, he found himself checking almost every nook and cranny that they passed, straining to listen out for footsteps that didn't seem to belong to anyone.

It was enough to drive a bloke up the wall.

"Right," Aaron said as they left the north exit. "I better make myself scarce. If they catch me near you I could be in the shit."

"What?" Han stared at him in mounting horror. "You're going to leave me to it?"

"No, I'm going to be right with you. Just not where anyone can see." He grinned and flipped a casual salute as he merged in with the flow of human traffic leaving the station.

Han stared at him, but true to his word he was gone within moments, stepping out of existence at such high speed there was no way even Han's eyes stood a chance of picking him out, so he skirted the throng of people waiting at the bus stop which sat right outside the station exit, and made his way along Thurloe Street away from the mass of people.

It took surprisingly little time to be free of the commuters, most of whom didn't come to South Ken to then head directly east into the expensive real estate. He was soon in quiet streets with narrow pavements and private homes, and he chose to skirt the edge of Thurloe Square Garden rather than risk attracting attention by jumping the low fence just to cut a corner.

Kensington and Chelsea were both littered with these private gardens, accessible only to the tenants surrounding them. Frederick's was the same, with its little crescent-shaped park across the road which Han very much doubted any of the residents even used, especially as Frederick's house also had a private back garden. Who wanted to go share a park with their neighbours when they could share their gardens with themselves?

That was London, though. Some of the most expensive real estate on the planet, and yet amazingly there were spots of land which remained free from the housing developers.

He crossed Brompton road, which was light on traffic and even lighter on pedestrians, and straight onto Egerton Gardens, which almost immediately became Egerton Crescent.

So far, no vampires.

As he walked alone — or, at least, seemingly alone — along the pavement, he couldn't help but grit his teeth as his imagination ran wild.

What if he was too late? Should he have run the whole way? He was walking as briskly as he could, but what if a sprint made all the difference?

No. The odds were that it made no difference at all. Anyone coming here had a half hour head start on Han, and they would prefer to arrest rather than kill outright. From what he understood of the way Ellis had been arrested by Hughes himself and how all that had ultimately played out, the Constables would take Jay, Frederick, and Michael to a holding cell, then haul them up in front of the Council one by one for questioning. Only after all that would they pass the inevitable death sentence, and that gave Han time to bust them out. Hughes had to know where all potential holding cells were. All Han had to do was check each one.

He had a plan, and he was satisfied with it. It would have to do.

He hopped up the steps to Frederick's, but there were still no signs of either vampires or a struggle, so he reached out and rapped on the door knocker.

A few moments later, Michael opened the door, and the sight of the curly-haired redhead filled Han with relief.

"Good evening," Michael said with a smile. "Come in."

"Thanks. I probably—" He broke off as a gust of wind snapped at his tie, then gestured at Aaron, who seemed to have appeared behind Michael. "I probably have a friend with me," he explained with a gesture to Aaron as he stepped inside.

Michael jolted back in surprise as he turned and found Aaron inches from him. "Fuck me," he blurted, his accent all-American for a moment. "Uh. I mean, er... What's going on?"

"Funny story," said Aaron. "We're up shit creek and all out of paddles."

Han shut the front door. "This is Aaron. He's a vampire. Part of the vampire police, in fact." He beckoned them to follow through to the living room, where he found Jay and Frederick up to their eyes in books. "Hey, gorgeous."

Jay bounced to his feet and flung his arms around Han,

kissing him quickly, then he glanced over Han's shoulder. "Aaron?"

"Jay. Sorry to bust in on you like this. We've got a problem."

"Let me guess," Frederick murmured without looking up. "That tiresome invisible vampire has decided to rain on our parade?"

"That's pretty much the size of it, yeah," Aaron said. "The Council's got its knickers in a right twist. Asquith's yelling for everyone to be arrested. And I mean everyone, not just you lot. I think he's screaming for the arrest of just about every vampire under thirty to get locked up."

"And they might have gone to get Ellis," Han added.

Jay stared at him, his eyes slowly growing wide, and then he gasped. "If they do that..."

Han nodded grimly. He didn't need Jay to elaborate.

"Christ, yeah," Aaron muttered. "Randall'l make mincemeat out of 'em."

"Yeah," Han echoed.

That or Ellis would straight up eat them.

Either way, they had to get over there, because there was going to be a problem, and neither Ellis nor Randall would handle it at all politely.

TWENTY

THE UNSPOKEN TRUTH was that if they didn't make it to Ellis' in time, Ellis might damn well eat whoever turned up to arrest him, and Jay didn't think even Aaron would let him get away with that one.

Assuming anyone did turn up, of course. Aaron seemed convinced that the Constabulary was in motion, yet nobody had arrived at Frederick's.

Maybe they'd gone for the higher priority targets first.

They hurried for the front door, and Han and Jay were about to set off along the pavement, but Frederick gestured toward a large black Porsche 4x4.

"Let's not spend half an hour jogging through town, eh?" he said. "Hop in."

Michael pulled out a set of keys and the Porsche unlocked, so Jay glanced to Han and didn't even ask why Han only had a Range Rover when he could've had a Porsche. That would be petty, and Jay absolutely was never petty.

Han just rolled his eyes like he'd read Jay's thoughts, and they hopped into the back while Michael eased into the drivers' seat. Aaron got in after Han, and Frederick rode shotgun.

"Address?" Frederick asked as Michael started the car and pulled away from the kerb.

Jay buckled himself in quickly as he gave Ellis' address, and Frederick tapped it into the satnav even as Michael began to head east.

THEY REACHED ELLIS' in little under ten minutes, and Jay sat in the back scrawling a spell onto his portable whiteboard, finishing moments before they pulled up outside.

He unbuckled and leaped out of the car, then dropped the laminated card to the pavement and stepped on it, reciting a spell as quickly as he could. By the time the other three were out and the car was locked, he was done.

He could see the magic which made both Han and Aaron, so he grabbed the whiteboard off the ground and folded it quickly, stuffing it away. He didn't have time to wipe it right now, but at least the other side was clean if he needed it.

"I don't see anyone else," he said after a quick look around. "They can't be taking this long to get here, right?"

"No," Aaron agreed. "Something's up."

"We haven't missed them," Han murmured. "I can hear two heartbeats inside." He nodded toward the house. "Randall and Tiberius, I'm guessing."

"All right. Then perhaps we'd best get off the street," Frederick said.

Jay nodded and hopped up the steps to knock on the door. "It's Jay," he said quietly out of habit, though he wasn't sure Ellis was in any fit state to care

The door unlocked a few moments later, and Randall was there, eyeing the lot of them in surprise. "What's going on?"

"We're coming in. It's urgent." Jay stepped out of the way so he could keep his eye on the street as everyone else filed past him, and only then did he back his way into the house, shut the door, then bolt it. "We've got a problem."

"What is it?" Randall followed everyone else through to the living room, and Tiberius bounced over to greet Jay, so he crouched down to fuss the German Shepherd.

"It's Richard," Han sighed.

"Gary?" Ellis sprawled across his desk and didn't look up. "Let me guess. You didn't kill him and now he's causing trouble?"

Jay looked up and let out a soft squeak.

Ellis' weave had gotten even more loose. Jay could almost see right through it now.

"That's about the size of it, yeah," Aaron said as he strode to the window and glanced outside. "He ran to the council and blabbed about Han talking to humans, and the Council found they didn't have a Han in the records, and Richard said you threatened him and told him to keep his mouth shut, so now basically the Council is gunning for the lot of you. Oh, and get this, apparently he also mentioned some sort of revolution that was on the horizon."

"Fancy that," Elis said, still without lifting his head off the table.

Jay sighed softly. "Well as we're here, I may as well try something. Hold on."

He hurried out to the kitchen to grab a cloth and wipe his portable whiteboard down, then he dried it with a tea towel and put it back in his pocket. He heard chatter from the living room, including from Frederick, so he figured that introductions were flying around.

"I assume," Ellis muttered into the table's surface as Jay re-entered the room, "that the Council has fed Aaron false intelligence to see what action he'd take."

"Nah," Aaron said. "I wasn't the only Constable in the room."

"But you are the only one who would zip out of there so fast they wouldn't see you go, after which they could hold the rest back," Ellis continued.

"Sounds a bit unlikely. Asquith's an idiot."

"Right, well, I reckon if they aren't here yet, that means I've got some time." Jay pulled a sharpie out of his pocket and made his way to Ellis' desk. "Sit up straight, sweetie."

Ellis groaned. "Don't want to."

"Randall?"

Randall bit his lip, but at least he approached Ellis' chair and rested a hand on his shoulder. "C'mon, El," he murmured. "Just for a minute?"

Ellis muttered something that Jay didn't catch, but he did slowly push himself off the desk and back into his chair, shoulders slumped like the motion had taken all his energy out of him.

Judging by the weakness of his weave, it may well have done.

Jay used his sleeve to wipe the desk surface free of the ash sprinkled across it and tried not to think too hard about how much of Ellis it represented. Then he spread the whiteboard across it and began to scribble furiously.

Ellis needed to be contained within a field which would give Jay direct access to his weave, but this room was carpeted, and the desk had bloody great gashes across it that would prevent Jay from creating an accurate circle. The whiteboard was too small for Ellis to lay down on, but at least Jay could get to work if he got Ellis into the whiteboard while everyone else worried about whether or not the Constabulary was coming for them.

"I suppose we get to find out how many vampires you can store inside you if this all goes pear-shaped," Frederick murmured to Han.

"And what happens if I run out of space," Han muttered. "God, that's not a nice thought. What if I just start spitting them out again?"

"Dear boy, I suspect that's the nicest possible outcome. You might end up condensing them all. Or losing them in the void."

"We really should send an exploratory mission in there to figure out how far it goes," Ellis said. "Get the tape measure out and everything."

"Oi." Han huffed at him. "I'm not having explorers in me. Bad enough storing Richard for one night."

Jay ignored it as they continued to chatter on about whatever theoretical realm Han might have turned into as part of his power, concentrating on getting his sigils right. This was Ellis' life he was about to try amateur surgery with, and if he cocked it up, he might end up killing the patient.

Which would, he supposed in a moment of black humour, save the Council the bother.

He bit the end of his marker as he considered the spell he'd drawn, then nodded to himself and put it on the floor next to Ellis' chair. "Right," he declared, capping the pen. "Ellis, I'm going to try and stop you from unweaving. Okay?"

Ellis shrugged. "Areet."

Jay beckoned Randall forward. "Just wheel the chair," he said. "We need him right in the middle."

"Okay." Randall pushed the chair forward, and used his foot to hold the whiteboard down as the wheels skittered across it.

Jay moved around them slowly, checking that Ellis was well

within the circle, then he nodded to Randall and crouched down to redraw marks that the wheels had scratched.

"Right. Ellis, I need you to stay totally still, sweetie. Can you do that for me?"

Ellis laughed bitterly. "It's all I'm doing lately, Jay."

Jay nodded, put his pen away, and stood. He raised his hands into the correct gestures for the spell, then began to recite it. "Universum, ut liceat mihi. Dirige manus..."

He felt the tell-tale pause as the world seemed to stop turning, just to listen to him. He could understand how some sorcerers felt like they had the right to do whatever the hell they wanted, however they pleased. The sensation of being at the centre of the universe, even if only for the duration of a spell, was like nothing else in Jay's life. Not even an orgasm felt so powerfully all about him and him alone. There was always Han there, sharing it with him, but this?

This was all him.

He reached the end and watched as the runes flared pink, only to then tinge Ellis' otherwise red weave with that pinkish glow.

"Did it work?" Randall breathed.

Jay nodded. "It's just the start, though. The spell that lets me do what I'm about to do."

"Then I suggest that the rest of us keep an eye out," Frederick drawled, "and leave you to it."

Jay nodded gratefully as the others took up positions by doors and windows, and he reached into the circle to begin grasping at threads.

Everything he'd read said this was going to take time, and Jay didn't know how much he had.

HE COULDN'T TELL whether Ellis had dozed off, and he lost track of time himself while he worked. He was able to discern threads of power and of energy, those which were Ellis' physical presence and those which made up some sort of aura which he suspected might have something to do with Han's idea of permissions masks.

What confused Jay the most was that everything he knew about vampires was that they had one supernatural ability. Above and beyond their enhanced senses and their peculiar relationship with pain, they each had a specific superpower, for want of a better word, which seemed to be a result of the interaction between the magic and the original body and mind. Ellis' power was that he could touch objects and receive visions from them, and the more emotional impact those objects had held, the clearer the vision.

But either Jay was misunderstanding Bryce's notes, or Ellis had multiple strands of power within his weave.

That didn't make any sense, but it undoubtedly contributed to Bryce mistaking Ellis for an Elder. Just by looking at his weave, Jay could see that there was simply *more* to Ellis than to Aaron or Han, despite the fact that Ellis was literally falling apart.

Sooner or later he would have to do *something*, though, and he had memorised the spells Bryce used to manipulate threads, so all he could do was get stuck in.

"Okay. Ellis?" He said it softly.

"Areet?"

"I'm going to try and repair the damage Bryce did to you. I'm sorry, but I think it might hurt."

Ellis shifted in the chair, but he didn't move out of it. "Do you have to?"

"You're going to unravel until you fall apart if I don't, sweetie." He reached out and gently lay a hand on Ellis' forearm. "But it's your choice. If you want me to do nothing, I won't pretend to understand, but I'll stand by you."

Ellis' head tilted toward Randall, and Randall reached in to squeeze his shoulder.

"I'm right here," Randall whispered.

Ellis nodded, then turned to face Jay again. "You can't make it worse," he said. "I'm already in hell. Do whatever you can."

Jay puffed out his cheeks. "No pressure," he chuckled as he withdrew his hand. "Okay. I'm basically going to try just... sticking everything back together again and hoping that your body can heal the rest once it's not, you know, drifting apart any more."

"It's fine," Ellis said. "May as well just crack on with it."

Jay nodded and murmured words under his breath. There were no sigil components to these spells. They were simple things, designed to work with the circle Ellis was already a part of, and so they were quick and easy to cast.

Then he reached in and grasped at threads to try and straighten them out so he could make sure he stuck the right ones together, and that's when Ellis began to scream.

TWENTY-ONE

HAN WINCED as Ellis started screeching like Jay was setting fire to him, but so far as he could see, Jay was just making weird plucking motions with his hands across Ellis' shirt. For one absurd moment he thought Jay might have decided to nurple the poor bastard, but that probably wasn't what was going on here.

"Hold him down," Jay said tersely as Ellis began to flop around.

Randall grimaced. He didn't look at all pleased, and Han totally sympathised with that, but he did as he was asked and gripped Ellis' shoulders.

"Do you need a hand?" Han asked Randall. Not that he wanted to be pinning his best friend to a chair while he was clearly in agony, but if it would help in the long run he'd do it.

"No other vampires in the circle, please," Jay said in the space between two screams.

"I'll do it." Frederick shrugged his jacket off and hung it on the back of the only other chair in the room, then moved over to stand beside Randall so that they could each take one of Ellis' arms as well as a shoulder and keep him in his seat.

Han backed away, taking up the position that Frederick had vacated, but he didn't like that this still left them with a lot less manpower covering the potential ways into the house, and Ellis' screeching made it next to impossible to hear anything outside.

It just got better when Tiberius began barking, too.

"He's not happy about the screaming," Randall yelled over the noise. "I don't think he'll get violent, though."

"You don't *think* he will?" Michael eyed the dog like it might have rabies.

"He's a guide dog. They're selected for nonaggression and obedience. Tiberius, it's okay. Quiet."

Tiberius gave another couple of barks, then tailed off into a disgruntled growl and tried to nose at Ellis' hand.

Aaron was at Han's side in the blink of an eye. "This is a clusterfuck," he said, too quietly for the humans to hear him. "I'm gonna wait outside. I can get good coverage up on the roof."

"How the hell do you get up onto a roof anyway?"

Aaron grinned. "Really fast. It's like a wall of death, just without the motorbike."

He was gone again a second later, and Han hurried out into the hallway just in time to see Aaron open the front door.

Someone was out there. Someone who made Aaron pause, so Han kept on hurrying so he could see what was going on.

There was a white guy out there just a little bit over Han's height, with sympathetically tragic sideburns and an equally unfortunate mullet. At least he'd slicked the mullet back so that it mostly just looked like he had longer hair, but the thinness of it past the neckline gave it away. He was wearing jeans and a hoodie, so the only thing that gave away any implication of age was those sideburns.

His eyes were pale amber, though. A dead giveaway.

"Constable Hughes," the vampire said.

"Constable Fitzwater," Aaron replied.

Fitzwater glanced past Aaron to Han, and looked about to disregard him, but then his head tilted. "Oh. Coloured contact lenses? They're pretty effective. Never seen anyone use them for long. You get bored of them in the end." He gestured in a half-wave. "You must be Han."

"Constable," Han greeted as he stopped behind Aaron. "What can we do for you?"

"Are you skinning a cat in there?" Fitzwater winced. "Come out here and shut the door so we can talk, will you? That's like nails on chalk board, it is."

Han glanced to Aaron, but Aaron just stepped down onto the pavement, so Han came outside and drew the door shut.

At least it cut out most of the noise.

"Funny story," Fitzwater said as he looked at Han some more. "You don't seem to be sanctioned."

"Really?" Han clasped his hands together behind his back. "Strange. Are you sure the paperwork didn't just get lost? What you need is a proper computerised system for this kind of thing."

Fitzwater chuckled at that and crossed his arms. "Nice. I doubt anyone would know how to use it, though. Anyway, as it happens, the Council's willing to make you an offer."

Han blinked and looked toward Aaron again, and Aaron frowned, shaking his head slightly.

That meant whatever this offer was, Aaron hadn't been told it, which didn't bode well for Aaron's status as a Constable right now.

"Is it a good one?" Han said to Fitzwater.

"Amazingly good, yes. If you give up the name of the person who turned you, they'll let you live. All official, tie a bow around it, you get a free sanction and not sentenced to death. I've literally never heard them offer this to anyone ever, so you should take it."

"Uh huh." Han ran his tongue along the back of his teeth. "And they execute whoever it was, right?"

"Probably," Fitzwater agreed.

Han shrugged. "And what if they're already dead?"

Fitzwater blinked and looked directly at Aaron, then back to Han. "You're not actually going to play that one, are you?"

Han followed Fitzwater's gaze just in time to see Aaron's eyes widen, and Han burst out laughing. "Oh shit. You think it's Aaron?"

Aaron stared at him, then joined him laughing until he was bent almost double, clutching at his own thighs to stay upright. "Me?" he wheezed. "Turn anyone? Are you off your head?"

"Well, I mean, there was that thing with Marc—"

Aaron was gone, and in the next second he was up against Fitzwater, one hand over his mouth, his ice-blue eyes narrowed and his mouth twisted in a snarl which showed fangs.

"You wanna think really fucking carefully about what you say next, Darren," he hissed.

Fitzwater's eyes widened as he stared at Aaron, then he bobbed his head briefly.

Aaron dropped his hand and backed away a couple of steps.

"Sorry," Darren muttered. "But that was never cleared up, was it?"

"Devitt did it," Aaron snapped. "He was a fucking shit and

you know it, and he turned Marcus, and if you so much as breathe Marcus' name ever again I will fucking end you."

Darren grimaced and glanced up at the house, then nodded before he looked back to Han. "Then I guess Devitt turned you?"

"That's right," Han said. "Like I said. What happens if he's dead?" He thumbed over his shoulder toward the house. "Councillor O'Neill lives here now. Devitt didn't have permission, but he's also gone, so if it's numbers you're worried about that's a straight one for one and nothing's changed."

"Then there's a territory problem."

"Yeah, and if Richard wants to try staking me again, he's welcome to give it a go." Han blinked, then took a step forward. "The little shit."

Aaron was quick on the uptake. "You're not seriously telling me he's run to the Council just to fix his territory dispute for him, has he?"

Han answered before Darren got the chance. "Of course he has. He can't kill me, and he knows I can kill him if I choose to. Argh, what a total wanker! We could've negotiated something, easily!" He threw his hands up and began to pace the pavement. "And he's got the entire Constabulary running around London looking for me just because he's a spineless little git."

Darren shifted his weight a little and looked between them. "What about all this talk of humans knowing things? Your husband?" he said to Han.

"Bullshit," Aaron said.

"I can hear heartbeats under all that screaming, Aaron. Don't push it."

Now it was Aaron's turn to cross his arms, and he did it with a scowl.

"All right. Yeah." Han shrugged. "He tell you the other stuff?"

"About this revolution or whatever?"

"No. The bit about my husband being a sorcerer."

Darren blinked slowly.

"Yeah, that figures. You want to think this over really carefully, because Richard's sold us all down the river here. You, me, Aaron, Ellis, the whole lot. He's trying to get the Council to kill a bunch of people just because he's got a territory dispute he can't resolve on his own. What is this, nursery school?" Han grit his teeth. "Right, this isn't bloody good enough. You go back to the Council and tell them I'm not having their deal, and I'm not having them threaten my friends just because Richard ran wailing to mum and dad. You can bloody well pull everyone off my flat, too, because I'm staying right here with Councillor O'Neill until this gets fixed."

He could see that Darren was growing incensed — or at least, mildly irate, but maybe that was as incensed as a vampire from an era of awful sideburns ever got. "I'm not your messenger."

"I think you might be, actually, because the other piece of this puzzle you're missing is that I'm Councillor O'Neill's Vassal."

Darren gawped at him, open-mouthed, then stared at Aaron. "Is this true?"

Aaron shrugged. "Yeah. He's busy screaming right now or I'd ask him to confirm it for you."

"Yeah, what *is* all that screaming about?" To Darren's credit he looked pretty sympathetic about whatever could make a vampire scream so much.

"Sorcery," Han said simply.

"If your husband's in there torturing a Councillor—"

"Yes, yes. Death on me, death on my house, death on my

cow, I get it. Believe me we aren't doing this for giggles. Look, it was nice meeting you, but if I'm not being arrested, I really need to get back inside. It's cold out here, and I don't like reaching ambient temperature in the middle of winter. I'm sure you're not a big fan of it either. Are we done?"

Darren scratched one of his sideburns as he narrowed his eyes at Han, then nodded. "Fine. I'll tell them. But you might want to stick near O'Neill if they don't like the message."

"I already said I'm staying right here." Han turned and hopped back up the steps. "Honestly, Darren, nothing against you personally. I know you're just doing your job. But I can't help feel you're of a generation that heard that excuse a whole bunch of times from Nuremberg."

Darren took a step forward. "Hey, there's no need for that. I'm not a fucking Nazi! That was uncalled for!"

"Just following orders?" Han raised an eyebrow. "Come off it. You must be smart, you made it to Constable. You know following orders is always a choice." He paused, then shrugged. "Unless Devitt gave them, but he's gone."

"It's not that easy."

Han grinned at him. "Sure it is. Join a revolution." He turned and knocked on the door. "Let me know what they say. I'd appreciate a head's up if they're going to send an army, but I'll understand if you don't want to be the person that gives it to me. It's not easy when on the one hand you've got a bunch of shady blokes who have no leadership credentials other than age, and on the other hand you've got a fella you don't know who's asking you to trust him. But that's life, innit?"

The door opened and Michael peeked out, then stepped back as he held it for Han.

"Look," Darren said. "I'll see what I can do, okay? I just... I can't make any promises."

"No," Han agreed without looking back. "But I can."

Darren was too smart to ask what that promise might be, which was good, because Han wasn't sure how many lies he could get away with in one meeting.

He strode back into the house, back into the reverberating screams, and left Darren behind.

It wasn't a problem solved, but it was a problem delayed, and that was the second-best thing right now.

TWENTY-TWO

Jay had to admit that he was impressed with both Randall and Frederick's ability to keep Ellis in his chair despite all the screaming. Even Tiberius settled down after a while, only offering the occasional grumble of disapproval.

It all meant that Jay was able to work.

God how he wished there were some way to anaesthetise Ellis, though. Everything Bryce had done to him, and here was Jay putting him through it all over again, though hopefully he'd be done more quickly than she was.

He reached through the mesh to get to trickier threads, and briefly wondered whether that meant his hands were actually inside Ellis' body, but he didn't dare so much as glance away from his work to see anyone else's reaction, because who knew what a single slip-up would achieve? This close to Ellis' heart, it could be the single error that turned him into ash.

Jay doubted Randall would remain nice and calm if that happened.

Each thread required a gentle touch to prevent it dissolving further, but he still had to stretch it to meet up with its counterpart. It was like tugging weak old elastic that could just snap at any moment, but when he did manage to get two ends to touch, if he held them in place long enough, Ellis' regenerating seemed to be the glue that made them stick back together.

It was slow, methodical work. He had to correctly identify both parts of a broken thread, because Christ alone knew what would happen if he just jammed random ones together. Then he had to hold them for what felt like forever, because they didn't repair with any haste at all.

His arms began to grow tired. His eyes were dry and sore, and he had to blink with increasing frequency to see straight.

He'd have to stop and hope that what he'd done so far was enough for now.

Jay withdrew carefully and drew his shoe across the whiteboard to break the circle, and the pink glow which coursed through Ellis' threads extinguished in a heartbeat.

Ellis sagged in his chair, and Frederick released him. Randall crouched down and grabbed his hand.

"El?"

Jay saw a little flicker of adjustment in Ellis' weave, but before he could identify it, Ellis lunged at Randall.

And latched on to his neck.

Jay shook his head and dispelled the magic which translated vampires into tapestries so that he had a better idea of whether Ellis was remotely in control of himself.

Ellis looked like self-control was something that happened to other people. His red eyes were wide, his face seemed pulled into a snarl, and their number one way of stopping Ellis from killing anyone was utterly incapacitated by the fangs in his neck.

"Well," Frederick said idly, "that's one way of dealing with trauma. Is this... going to be a problem?"

"I don't know." Jay pushed his hands through his hair as he tried so hard not to panic. "He's started regenerating at last, and he'd already lost a lot of blood and was refusing to eat. He might stop once he has enough for..." he tailed off. "For his immediate needs," he decided. "But if he doesn't, we'll have to stop him."

Han stepped back into the room, followed by Aaron, and Aaron swore softly.

"How do you reckon we do that?" Han said.

"I suppose with brute force and ignorance," Jay admitted. He glanced to Han and Aaron. "You can hear Randall's pulse?"

"Yeah. I can tell when it's getting dangerous," Aaron said. "It takes a while."

"Don't I know it," Han muttered.

Jay chewed on his thumb and fretted on the spot. Watching a vampire feed off someone else was an utterly horrible experience. True, it had been worse watching Ellis drain Han dry, for a multitude of reasons not limited to the sheer intimacy of the act. At least Ellis and Randall were an item and had been for around a year now. They both knew what the other was. Hell, Randall's werewolf blood was what helped Ellis survive in the sun way better than Han could, and it had healed his arm after a crazy vampire hunter had cut it off like it was barely a flesh wound.

Maybe Randall's blood was the best thing for Ellis right now.

"You're gonna wanna start trying to stop this pretty soon," Aaron muttered.

Jay nodded in acknowledgement. "Ellis? Ellis!"

Naturally he didn't respond. That would've been far too useful.

Jay stepped in closer and grabbed Ellis by the shoulder. At

least if Ellis switched targets, Randall had the strength to pull him off. "Ellis!"

Ellis just continued swallowing. Mouthful after mouthful.

It was obscene.

Han's power was weird. Maybe it had more strength than Han himself. They'd have to test it. Aaron's was super speed, which wouldn't help in any way Jay could see. And then he had Frederick, who certainly had the muscles of a rugby player, but whether he could pry Ellis off Randall?

"I presume if this isn't halted, we'll be losing Randall to blood loss and eventual cardiac arrest?" Frederick murmured.

"Most likely, yeah," Jay breathed. He shook Ellis shoulder. "Ellis, you have to stop! You're going to kill Randall!"

Assuming Ellis was even still in there after two rounds of torture separated by a month of yet more torture.

"All right." Frederick sighed as though this was a great inconvenience and pursed his lips.

Ellis blinked, then withdrew his fangs from Randall's neck. He even remembered to take a breath and exhale over the wound.

Then he passed out in his chair.

Randall swayed on his knees and gripped Ellis' arm to stay upright, blinking sluggishly. "Bloody hell," he whispered. "That was a close one."

Jay blinked and looked to Frederick, waiting for some kind of explanation, because it certainly *seemed* like he'd decided to intervene somehow, and then Ellis had just... stopped.

Frederick gave him the side-eye, then sighed.

"Yes, yes," he said calmly. "I might be slightly psychic."

The room erupted into chaos.

"WHAT THE FUCK IS 'SLIGHTLY PSYCHIC' supposed to mean?" Aaron demanded.

"What, like, telepathic?" was Han's question.

"What did you do to him?" Randall surged to his feet.

"Wait, have you been reading our minds this *entire time?*" Han asked.

Michael was, Jay noted, remarkably quiet.

He knew.

Jay sucked in a breath. "Oi!" he bellowed. "Everyone, cut it out!"

Randall had his hands balled into fists, and his skin seemed to be rippling slightly, which was probably not a good sign.

"What the fuck is the problem here?" Jay yelled, just in case anyone felt like talking over him. "We've got a room full of vampires, a sorcerer, and a bloody werewolf, for crying out loud, and he—" he gestured toward Frederick "—just saved Randall's life. Cut it out!"

The room quieted, most likely in shock at hearing Jay yell at them like they were toddlers.

"Thank you," Frederick drawled. "I'll make this as painlessly brief as I can. Yes, I'm telepathic. Yes, it runs in the family. No, my father is not telepathic, it comes down via my mother's side. Yes, I could make you all forget you ever met me should you decide to murder me horribly in my sleep. Yes, I have been lending my facility with languages to Michael so that we could process your books in double time," he said as he looked Jay in the eye. "Yes, I do rather prefer not to have to out myself, because despite the fact that there are people in this room who can turn into a black hole or literally reshape the entire universe to their will, telepathy is inherently repulsive and dealing with the consequences of people having that knowledge is a waste of my time."

A whole lot of things seemed to slowly slot into place. The fact that Frederick had even invited Jay up to his office to speak was just the start of it. He couldn't see the magic of the book Jay had been carrying, but he'd been able to see Jay's thoughts.

He could have made Jay forget ever meeting him, but instead he'd chosen to help, and the simple fact was that Jay wouldn't be able to stitch Ellis back together right now without that help.

"Okay," Jay said.

He heard Randall take a sharp breath, and looked to him.

"Randall," he murmured.

Randall bristled, but he frowned and crouched again, taking Ellis' hand. "What did you do?"

"Forced him to withdraw, then told him to go to sleep," Frederick replied.

"Couldn't you have told him to sleep through whatever Jay was doing?"

"Yes."

"But you didn't."

Frederick shrugged. "Look. I don't want to interfere with magic while it's in use. We have no idea what the side-effects of that would be. I wear an anti-magic talisman, and who knows whether even the weakest of esoteric contact while Jay was working could have backfired horribly. Who knows whether what he was doing could have interacted with Ellis' mind while I was doing the same thing. To be entirely honest, I'm afraid it was better to allow Ellis to suffer for a short while, and then mitigate his suffering at a later stage, once it became safe to do so. Which I'm quite willing to do, I shall add. I can help his mind heal from the ridiculous amount of horror the poor chap has endured these past few weeks."

Jay nodded slowly, then stifled a yawn. "Okay. We've had a bit of a shock. Apparently telepaths are a thing that exist."

"Exceedingly rare," Frederick murmured.

"Still a non-zero quantity," said Han.

Frederick inclined his head in agreement.

"And we're still all on the same side," Jay continued. "So why don't we all go home and get some rest, and we can come back tomorrow to continue?"

"Well," said Han, looking slightly shifty. "About that."

Jay blinked at him.

Why did he feel like this didn't bode well in the slightest?

TWENTY-THREE

ALL EYES WERE ON HIM.

Han cleared his throat. Was it hot in here all of a sudden?

"Constable Fitzwater just came to the door," he began with a gesture over his shoulder. "Richard threw us under the bus, but the Council had an interesting offer to make."

"If by 'interesting' you mean 'downright suspicious'," Aaron added.

"Probably the same thing in this case, yeah. They're willing to let me off for being unsanctioned, so long as I tell them who turned me."

Jay gasped, and his eyes grew wide.

"You didn't," Randall said, uncertainty making his vocal chords tremble slightly.

"To some degree." Before Randall could rip his face off, Han added, "I told him it was Charles."

Jay blinked, then his lips curved into a sly grin. "You're a genius."

"Got the Mensa card and everything," Han agreed. "But the problem's a bit bigger. I'm not sure he bought it."

"Agreed," Aaron said. "But I don't think it really matters."

"Because?" Randall had his hand curled around Ellis' fingers while Ellis slept through the entire thing.

"Richard's using the Council to settle his territory dispute," Han explained. "He's got so much dirt on all of us that the Council's gunning for pretty much everyone in this room. Me for being unsanctioned, you lot for being human and knowing what we are." He looked to Randall. "I'm very close to a hundred percent sure that they don't know about you. I told them flat out that my husband is a terrifyingly powerful sorcerer who could turn them all into frogs or something cool—"

"But—" Jay cut in.

"They don't need to know," Han said, just as quickly. "I also told him I'm Ellis' Vassal, otherwise I've been all over town without permission and that's probably also a hanging offence. I'll get tarred and feathered in the town square. Anyway, Fitzwater's on his way back to the Council to tell them what I've told him, and I basically said that he was welcome to join the revolution if he fancied it."

"Barb must be pissed," Randal muttered.

"If they haven't already got her under lock and key," Jay scowled.

"They haven't. She was doing a pretty good job of telling them all to go fuck themselves, though." Aaron grinned at them. "Pretty sure she's loving the chaos. It gives her more leeway to pull her revolution together while the Council's looking the other way."

"Right. So basically they're going to go chew this over, then either come arrest the lot of us, or wave their hands and let Richard sort out his own disputes like a grown man."

Frederick cleared his throat. "How callous would you say this Council is?"

"Completely," Randall declared.

"Plenty," Aaron said at the same time.

Frederick nodded. "Then they'll either want to eradicate everyone in this house, or somehow force you to give up the names of your collaborators in this revolution of yours and *then* eradicate you. I imagine it's best to prepare yourselves for an assault." He glanced to Aaron, and added, "I wouldn't doubt that they will have lumped you in with the rest of us by now."

"Agreed," Aaron muttered. "A revolution threatens the power structure. They'll want to squash it before it can gain any momentum."

"Which means they'll want to come back here tonight," Jay concluded, "before any of us have got away to places they don't know about."

"Charming," Michael murmured, though he didn't seem at all worried.

Jay bit his lip a little, and glanced to Ellis. "Maybe if you wake him up," he said to Frederick, "Ellis can help? He's a Councillor."

"It may be best if he remains out of this," Frederick countered. "He requires time to heal, and I'm doing what I can to suppress his pain while he does so."

Han blinked, but didn't bother asking the dumb question. Of *course* Frederick could do that, otherwise why had he said it? "Okay. Then we need to know what's coming at us. Aaron?"

Aaron rubbed his jaw and began to pace the outskirts of the room. "Darren Fitzwater isn't too scary. He can mimic any sound he's ever heard. Great for proving a suspect said something. Not great in a fight. Councillor Asquith can control small animals, which doesn't sound so bad until you realise how many fucking rats there are in this city. Councillor Stanley can do the whole traditional turn-into-fog thing, and Councillor Hillier can control water."

Han blinked, then let out a few choice words. He stuck to Cantonese, though, to save Tiberius from such language. "What you mean is that Hillier can walk back and forth across the Thames whenever he pleases, and can take an entire army with him at any time?"

Aaron blinked slowly. "Yeah. I suppose he..." He tailed off. "Fuck."

Now all eyes turned to Aaron, which at least took the pressure off Han for a while.

"Charles used to get down to Battersea way past the tube's closing time," Aaron muttered. "I never figured out how he did it. I guessed he was having Victor drive him around, but it's a long way from any tunnels."

"And Battersea's literally just across the water from here," Jay breathed. "You think Hillier was being used, or was it voluntary?"

"If it was voluntary, Hillier could have motive for wanting to pursue some good old-fashioned revenge against Ellis," Han said.

"I dunno," Aaron countered. "Unless he was okay with having Ellis on the Council just to keep an eye on him."

"Either way, he clearly can't be trusted," Frederick drawled, "if he's on his way here to trounce the lot of us. I would say that his motives don't matter a jot if he's busy trying to drown us all."

"So what've we got?" Jay crossed to Han's side and threaded his arm around Han's waist, leaning against him slightly. "A werewolf, two conscious vampires, a rubbish sorcerer, and a psychic who's busy keeping our third vampire from screaming all night long. I don't suppose you've got something up your sleeve?" He looked toward Michael, and the hope in his voice was only half-hearted.

"Totally regular guy," Michael said apologetically as he

spread his hands. "Reasonable at chemistry, and we're not in a lab. What about the dog? Is he secretly a trained killer attack dog?"

"No," said just about everyone at once.

"Shame," Michael muttered.

"I'm, er." Randall ran his hand over his short hair, and looked sheepish. "I'm not exactly the most amazing fighter around."

"Oh shut up," Jay laughed. "You turn ten feet tall and have claws the size of a man's head. You're fine."

"Maybe I can call in some of my pack?"

Han couldn't blame Randall for sounding uncertain about that one. It was basically the closest they could get to declaring an all-out war between vampires and werewolves, and who knew what the repercussions of that could be. It might be hundreds of years of unnecessary conflict.

That and Randall had already lost people close to him in fights just like this.

"No," Han said gently. "We can handle this. Aaron's faster than any of them, I can stuff people away in some weird-arse pocket realm, and Randall's got the big guns. I don't think we should need anything more than that. The squishy people can stay indoors, and we can go out and take care of it." He looked to Frederick. "Can you make sure there aren't any witnesses?"

"Easily done," Frederick said.

"Right. Then all we do now is sit tight and wait for them to come."

Jay looked to him and opened his mouth, then instead he looked to Aaron. "When did you last eat, Aaron?"

"Me? I'm fine." Aaron flashed a grin. "You?"

"Likewise," Han said.

"Better get ourselves settled in, then," Aaron said cheerfully.

Frederick ran a finger across his lower lip, then looked to Han. "A word, if I may?" He turned toward the kitchen, but paused, glancing back.

Jay released Han's waist and squeezed his fingers, and Han leaned up to kiss his cheek, then followed Frederick, curious about what on earth the Viscount could want with him.

Frederick grabbed the kettle and held it under the tap to fill it, and then murmured, "I hope you don't mind, but I've taken the liberty of having this conversation wholly in your mind. I don't believe you would wish the Constable to overhear it."

Han blinked and looked around, then back at Frederick. "Is this... Are you speaking telepathically?" Then he paused. "Am I?"

"It's a little more complex than that. But that's the essence of it, yes." Frederick set the kettle back on its base and turned it on, then crossed his arms and leaned against the worktop to regard Han across the room. "I think there is something that you should know regarding your friend O'Neill."

Han wavered. Had Frederick found something while he was in Ellis' mind trying to dull the pain? And if so, did Han want to know anything that had been uncovered against Ellis' will? "Is it essential?" he asked, which he felt was the best of both worlds.

"Possibly. Maybe not." Frederick glanced toward the door behind Han, then murmured, "your deduction about O'Neill's predatory habits is not incorrect, although I would argue that on both occasions he acted in self-defence, and a revulsion against cannibalism seems quite outdated when applied to creatures who already feed on blood to survive."

Han narrowed his eyes. He hadn't mentioned what he'd worked out to anyone except Jay, and nor had Jay, which meant Frederick had got it out of one of their minds at some point. "Just how much have you been digging into?"

"It's always safe to assume that I pick up everything," Frederick drawled. "It can't be helped." He gestured toward his own head. "It's ongoing. However, I don't go around sharing other people's secrets... Unless they could be of use. Devitt knew what O'Neill had done, and he also learned the side-effect of it, which is why he promptly ran off to eat a couple of Councillors himself. He undoubtedly would have got to the remaining three if O'Neill hadn't destroyed him, and with Stanley's power to turn to fog, Devitt would likely have become quite invincible in the short term, much as you yourself are."

Han's jaw dropped, and then he clamped his mouth shut.

There was a lot to unpack in all of that.

"Devitt knew... No, I mean... With Jonas?" Han bit his lip. "Shit, are you saying that eating another vampire gives you their power?"

"Exactly that. Ellis has Jonas' ability to speak and understand any language. He also has Devitt's power to control people, though he has yet to master it fully. He does not yet know whether he has also gained the abilities of those Devitt consumed — one was immune to silver, which would be awfully handy perhaps once every century, and the other could see auras, which I'm sure O'Neill wouldn't be able to use even if he did inherit it." Frederick licked his lips briefly. "Ellis knew exactly what he was saying when he told you to eat Richard, Han. He wants you to steal Richard's invisibility, because he believes it will mesh well with your existing ability and allow you to do what you do with relative impunity."

Han didn't know what to be appalled at first: the fact that Frederick had been turning over all these stones all this time, or the revelation that Ellis could be so cold and calculating as to suggest killing someone for something so petty as stealing their power.

"I feel it necessary to advise that I am in agreement with O'Neill," Frederick murmured. "Make of that what you will. I am not going to pretend to be a good person and tell you that it's the morally right thing to do. But it is an incredible tactical advantage that will be with you for the rest of your existence, and you shouldn't dismiss it out of hand."

For a moment, Han had a crystal clear vision of what exactly he could achieve if he *could* become invisible. While he could undoubtedly merge in with any dark shadows and disappear right now, the ability to slither his way around barriers without a single person spotting him was incredibly alluring.

But the cost?

Yes, Richard was a total dick. He hadn't even thought to invite Han to the negotiating table. He was an ableist arsehole who thought Ellis would be easy to knock over because he was blind. He ran to his superiors to solve his problems for him. And absolutely none of that meant he deserved to get fucking *eaten alive.*

And Han wasn't sure he was at all willing to even think about intentionally putting his fangs in another vampire to drain dry. It was murder, pure and simple, and while Richard had been happy to try and get people to do his killing for him, Han wasn't that guy.

He ran a software firm that made games and apps, for crying out loud.

"No," he said firmly, as much to himself as to Frederick.

Frederick shrugged. "Not my circus," he said languidly, "not my monkeys. If you wish, I can make you forget this conversation."

Han balked at him. "What the fuck? No! Why would you do that?"

"Because you have information that O'Neill would never

divulge, not even in confidence. You may wish not to hold onto it." Frederick tipped his head, then tutted. "I think it's about to become moot," he added. "They're here. Everything you say from here on out is verbal, and will be heard by any and all vampires in range to do so."

Han opened his mouth, then shut it again, silently seething. But there was too much going on for him to put into words, so it'd have to wait.

There were indeed footsteps outside the house, coming closer, and not a single one of them was accompanied by a heartbeat.

It sounded like a hell of a lot of vampires, and maybe their own numbers weren't looking so great after all.

But he was damned if that meant he was going to start eating people to level the playing field.

TWENTY-FOUR

HAN HURRIED BACK through to the office just in time to catch Aaron and Randall's rush toward the front door, and Jay's accelerated heartbeat as he watched them go then turned to Han.

"They're here," Jay breathed.

Han nodded. There were footsteps outside, though they were settling down now, and he could see glimpses of figures out on the street.

Bloody hell, it was like a Western out there, and Ellis' house was some saloon bar that was probably going to get its windows shot out in a few minutes.

Michael and Jay hurried to Ellis' chair and pulled it away from the window, then Jay reached down and snatched up his whiteboard, folding it and stuffing it into his pocket.

Han stopped by his husband and gripped his shoulder, and Jay leaned in to kiss him desperately.

"Be careful," Jay whispered.

Han nodded. "Stay in here. Don't go outside."

Jay gave him a swift nod, and Han stole another kiss before he let go and hurried after Aaron.

Randall opened the front door and headed out onto the lowest doorstep, and Aaron went out to stand by his side, so Han followed them up, and shut the door behind himself.

There was, he decided, a right shower of bastards waiting for them, and they were outnumbered two to one. Three of them were probably either the Councillors or their Vassals, and the other three were most likely Constables. Han figured if he were a Councillor he wouldn't turn up to a stupid thing like this himself, but whether he'd risk anyone else in his place was another matter.

Still, maybe the Councillors would rather lose a Vassal than risk their own arses.

Richard wasn't there, but that didn't surprise Han in the slightest. Why would the bloke who'd gone to so much trouble to make other people fight his battles for him then turn up to them himself?

"Councillors," Aaron said as he crossed his arms and spread his feet slightly. "We're honoured you came yourself. Where's Councillor Applegate?"

One of the vampires took a wheezing, rattling breath, and snorted with it. "Treacherous hag refused to come. She'll be off the Council once we're done with you lot."

"That's Asquith," Aaron said absently without turning to Han. Then he pointed. "Stanley. Hillier. Constables Glover and Ratcliffe, and Vassal Weatherford. What's the matter, no other Vassals available on short notice?"

"We're not anticipating a need for them," Asquith wheezed, "because you're going to come quietly."

"Why on Earth would we do that?" Randall murmured.

Han heard a distant rustle and snap, and he turned toward

the door. Beyond the heartbeats and walls, more footsteps. They couldn't be in the back garden, surely?

He narrowed his eyes.

"Because your humans are about to be rounded up," Asquith chortled. "And they won't be made comfortable, if you get my meaning."

Randall let out a growl which most definitely wasn't human, and his skin began to ripple in anger. He turned and took a step up toward the door, but Han put a hand on his chest and tried not to shit himself at the look in Randall's eyes.

"They're safe," Han murmured.

"Like hell they are," Asquith insisted.

He heard the tinkle of breaking glass from inside the house, and he shook his head at Randall. "Trust me," he said. "They're way safer than you know."

"Ellis—"

"Trust me," Han insisted.

If Frederick was capable of erasing Han's memories of their conversation, he could damn well make some vampires forget why they'd just broken into a house, but he didn't want to reveal that card out in the open. He just had to get Randall to refocus and hope he was right.

Randall bit his lip, then snarled again and turned back to the vampires.

"Sounds like that was a universal declaration of 'fuck you'," Aaron said cheerfully.

In the blink of an eye he was gone, and a second later Stanley broke apart into a thick, dense fog that rolled toward them even as Aaron reappeared with stakes in his hands. He gave one to Han, and hung onto the other himself as the fog closed in.

Han grit his teeth and stood his ground. If he could avoid

showing off his party trick he would, and perhaps with Aaron and Randall able to act freely thanks to Stanley's fog cover he might be able to get away with just standing guard on the door. He heard the most horrible wet tearing and dry snapping sounds from Randall, and suddenly the breathing came from way over Han's head, and the heartbeat was twice as loud.

He was kind of glad he couldn't see whatever the fuck had just happened.

Then there was chaos. He heard screams and grunts, footsteps and swear words, and so far none of it seemed to be coming his way. The stake was plucked out of his hand by a gust of wind he never even saw, and Han had a momentary glimpse through the fog of dark shapes that disappeared as the gaps in the fog closed up again.

Han turned his ear toward the house, but there were no sounds of a fight in there. The right number of heartbeats, and nothing else, so he turned back toward the fight.

He heard the rustling of leaves and the pitter-patter of hundreds of tiny feet. That had to be Asquith's super rodent powers, or whatever the hell that was all about, and just as he realised that, a swarm of rats and squirrels emerged from the fog at his feet and began to climb his trousers.

"Oh, fuck, no!" he declared, and transformed himself without a second thought, consuming every last damn rodent around himself and spreading out across the pavement.

It was much easier to see, now. Glover and Weatherford were already staked and laying on the floor, spread out across Han's body like they'd been abandoned there. Randall was absolutely huge, and tearing chunks out of Ratcliffe while Aaron was speeding around Hillier and landing jabs here and there as Hillier dragged water out of the drains to lash out at him with.

Han didn't see how this couldn't go their way. Aaron and

Hillier were restricted to what amounted to a slap fight, since neither of them were carrying lethal weapons. Randall would easily turn Ratcliffe into ash sooner or later, and Asquith didn't look like he was going to try hand to hand with anyone.

Han swallowed up the two who were staked, pulling the wood out of them as they passed his event horizon or whatever the hell he wanted to call it. He lashed out a tendril of darkness and jammed one of the stakes into Asquith's heart, then swallowed him up and pulled the stake free all in one go.

"You may as well stop," he said, hearing his own voice echo around inside the fog. "You can't win this. You were buggered from the moment you came here."

He'd said it to sound intimidating, but at the same time he realised it was true. The Council had been hopelessly outmatched even without Han's presence.

They weren't used to not getting their own way.

He swallowed up Ratcliffe before Randall could destroy him, then for good measure he dropped Hillier and his fistful of water through to the other side.

That only left Stanley.

Could Han swallow *fog?*

"You're done here, Stanley," he rumbled, spreading himself out to find the edges of the fog. "Maybe we can't touch you, but you can't touch us. How do you want this to end?"

He wasn't sure if he was going to get an answer, but moments later the fog began to recede, rolling down the road.

Randall turned into that horrendous set of noises just before the fog was completely gone, and by the time it was done he was there butt-naked in the street, nothing left of his clothes but tatters spread all across the pavement.

"Oi," Aaron said. "Bloody hell. Let us in—" He stopped as he looked at the door. "Shit, he's not awake, is he."

The door opened anyway, and Michael stepped back from

it, so Randall scooted inside as quick as he could, and Aaron followed.

Han poured himself in through the door as fast as he could, and continued into the office so that he could swallow up the three vampires who were standing in the middle of the room like ornaments — Darren and two Han didn't recognise.

Only then did he re-form.

Jay was blinking at the spot the vampires had stood on, then he rushed to sweep his arms around Han's neck and kiss him. "You're okay!"

Han nodded and wrapped his arms around Jay. "Yep. But we need to find more secure accommodation for our guests, or I'm going to vomit them right back up again at sunrise."

Jay's nose crinkled, and he backed off, dusting down Han's shirt. "Oh, no, sweetie. I could have done without that mental image."

"I could have done without learning it the hard way," Han countered. "Will you be okay while Aaron and I go take the rubbish out?"

Jay glanced to Frederick, then nodded to Han. "I'd be surprised if we weren't," he murmured.

Han nodded, then looked to Aaron. "Right. Where do we need to go?"

Aaron moved toward the door again. "I've got just the place."

They left the house together, and there was no sign of the fog outside.

Wherever Stanley had gone, Han hoped he'd just be sensible about this whole thing.

But he doubted it.

TWENTY-FIVE

JAY WRAPPED his arms around himself after Han and Aaron left, and he looked through to the broken window in the kitchen's back door, then he glanced to Frederick.

Frederick held a hand up a moment, then nodded. "It's safe to talk," he murmured.

"How did you stop them?" Jay breathed. "That was you, wasn't it?"

Frederick simply nodded. "The same way I've put O'Neill to sleep. The mind is a ridiculously vulnerable thing if one is equipped with the correct tools."

Jay shook his head numbly. "Unbelievable. I suppose your whole family is like this?"

"Not remotely. My twin brother's gifts are radically different from my own, and my youngest brother..." He tailed off. "Is something of an enigma. I cannot read my own family's thoughts," he explained before Jay could ask. "Whatever Nicky has tucked away up his sleeve, he hasn't revealed it to me."

"You could've averted all of this." Jay pointed toward the

front door. "Could have made them turn tail and leave us alone?"

Frederick sighed and wandered over to perch on Ellis' desk. He hooked one leg up and hung it over the corner, and laced his fingers together to rest his hands on his thigh. "It would not have solved the underlying problem."

Jay went over to check on Ellis. He certainly seemed flush with life, warmed through in a way he hadn't been in weeks, and he wasn't shedding hair or anything else any more, so all in all things seemed to be going well there.

"Surely you could make them forget the underlying problem, too," Jay concluded as he straightened up.

"Dear boy, there are a lot of things I can do." Frederick sighed softly. "It isn't quite so easy. Things work out best in the long run with a light touch, not a heavy hand. Let's say, for instance, that I made the Council tonight — and their hangers-on — forget all about us. How would that play out?"

Jay folded his arms across his chest and genuinely tried to think it through, and then he huffed slightly. "Richard would report us all over again. So you include Richard in your sweep-up."

"And when Richard next encounters Han in his territory?"

"You make Richard think his territory excludes that patch!"

Frederick grinned like he was enjoying this. "And when he reports to the Council next year and they ask him why his territory has changed?"

"You, uh..." Jay clicked his tongue. "You make them—"

"And how long do you intend for me to put myself at your disposal constantly fixing your problems?" Frederick arched a brow. "I do have a life of my own, Jay. I've put it on hold for you. I'm gladly helping out, even though I intensely dislike placing myself in potentially dangerous situations. Should I ever call on your knowledge in the future, in no way would I expect you to dedicate several years of your gifts to fixing my messes, because you too have your own life. By all means we can help each other out, but I wouldn't expect you to jump to extinguish each and every fire around me when simply solving the root cause would prevent those fires from even breaking out. Do you see?"

Jay narrowed his eyes and looked down to nudge the edge of a rug with the toe of his shoe. Then he let out a long-suffering sigh and raised his head. "You're right. I'm sorry, I'm being so fucking extra right now. Of course it's better to fix the actual issue than to just keep sticking plasters on it and hoping it'll stop bleeding all on its own."

"It's quite all right. There's no need to apologise. Were I in your shoes I would absolutely try and make me wave a magic wand." Frederick chuckled a little. "It's just that minds are incredibly complex and robust, and you cannot control everything. Sooner or later, whatever the difficulty was will arise once more, and history will repeat itself." He glanced past Jay and toward the door.

Jay turned just in time to see Randall walk into the room, this time thankfully with some clothes on, and the werewolf looked suitably apologetic.

"Sorry. Clothes are hard," Randall murmured as he returned to Ellis' side. "What's happening here? Is he still healing?"

"I can't tell without doing the spell again," Jay said. He looked to Frederick.

"I'm only muting the pain," Frederick murmured. "I don't know whether that means he's still healing, I'm afraid."

"So what do we do?" Randall gnawed on his lip as he rested his hand on Ellis' shoulder.

"We remain here and protect O'Neill," Frederick murmured. "You," he said to Jay, "need to cram some more useful spells into your head, I think. Being able to stitch O'Neill back together is all well and good, but you're completely defenceless against any vampire that chooses to punch you in the face, let alone bite you."

Randall blinked. "Bryce had wards," he said. "Aaron and Barb couldn't enter Bryce's warehouse until we broke them. But she had like some personal anti-vampire shield, too. Nothing Aaron or Barb did could touch her. They literally bounced right off her without even laying a finger on her." He gestured with a flick of his hand, like he was miming bouncing a vampire off himself.

Frederick looked to Michael. "Take the car," he said. "Make sure Jay gets there in one piece."

"Yessir." Michael strode for the door and flashed Jay a grin. "Shall we go read some books?"

Jay eyed Frederick, then looked to Michael. "What if they come for us there?"

"Then we'd better find this spell really damn quick," Michael said.

"So what's the deal with you two?" Jay said almost the moment Michael pulled away from the kerb.

Michael glanced to him, then laughed. "You mean are we lovers?"

"Wow. That was a bit more blunt than I would've put it... But yes." Jay smiled faintly. "Are you? 'Cause sometimes you kinda act like you might be, but other times... I don't know. You're both hard to figure out. I hope you don't mind me asking."

Michael shrugged as he wove west through little house-lined streets that seemed a world away from the major thoroughfares Jay knew to be just another few hundred feet in either direction. "Yes. We're lovers."

"Oh. But..." Jay felt suddenly awkward. This really was none of his business, but on the other hand nobody wanted to be the friend who didn't speak out when they saw something odd. It wasn't like there were any red flags, but there also wasn't a whole lot of affection that Jay could see. "I mean, he's..." He hesitated, then picked the safest phrase he could. "Kind of bossy?"

Michael laughed at that. "I think you mean hella bossy," he said, his American accent peeking through a little more strongly. "Yeah. He likes to be in charge, and I like that. But I think the puzzle piece you're missing is that he's aromantic."

Jay blinked, then it all fell into place. "Oh! Oh, I'm sorry! I didn't even think about that! Are you aro too?"

Michael shook his head. "Nah. More like demiromantic. But it's okay. Frederick's good at faking it when I need him to, and he knows when I need it. It works out well for us both." He glanced to Jay again. "But thanks for asking. For looking out for my safety even though you don't really know me. That's really kind of you."

Jay shrugged, still feeling like a total prick despite Michael's thanks. "No, thank you," he argued. "For answering my questions when it's none of my business."

Michael shrugged at that and looked forward to watch the road. "Hey, if more people asked questions when they saw something they didn't understand, the world would be a better place."

Jay nodded to that. "Can't disagree with you there."

THEY MADE their way into Frederick's house and Michael locked the door, "Just in case a door's enough to stop a vampire."

"It'd stop most," Jay admitted as they hurried through to the stacks of books in the living room. "Okay. Bryce's books..."

They both sat side by side on the floor, cross-legged, and began to sift quickly through Bryce's spellbooks. They worked in silence, and Jay ignored pages about the composition and structure of vampires because he'd already memorised those, and the wards weren't in there.

The only sound was the flick of pages being turned, and Jay wished they could've had Aaron's help, because he'd get through all this so fast they wouldn't even notice what he was doing.

He wondered whether time felt differently to Aaron. Did the vampire feel like he was doing things super fast, or did the rest of the world seem really slow to him, like someone had hit pause on the livestream?

"Jay," Michael said, with the kind of tone people used when it wasn't the first time they said it.

"Oh, sorry! Uh. What is it?" He rubbed his eyes and tried his best not to yawn out loud.

"Is this it?" Michael passed him a book and tapped at the left-hand page.

Jay focused blearily on the spell and quickly read it, then burst into a broad smile. "Yes! Perfect! Nice one, Michael! Hang on!"

He put the book to one side and pulled his whiteboard out, and clambered to his feet as he unfolded it. The thing still had spells scrawled on it, so he hurried through to the kitchen to wash them off, and dried it off with a tea towel before he brought it back through to the living room.

"Oh! Wait!" Michael was looking at the book again as Jay returned. "This could be even better!"

"Better than a vampire-repelling forcefield? How?"

Michael stood and handed the book to him. "Like this."

He took it and skim-read it. And then he read it again more slowly.

And then he gasped.

"Right?" Michael grinned. "I mean I'm reading it right, yes? It lets you make one of these—" he tapped his own chest, presumably where the amulet lay beneath his shirt "—specifically against vampires, and that'd save you having to cast it every time you want to go outside?"

"That's exactly what it says," Jay agreed. "Shit. Now I need something to cast it onto!" He bit his lip as he studied the instructions. "Shit, it needs to be something silver."

For the first time in almost a year, Jay wished he'd never melted down the knife Barnes had stabbed Ellis with. It'd be handy right about now.

Michael glanced to the windows. "I can't think of anywhere that sells silver that's open in the middle of the night." He licked his lips, then looked a little shifty. "But I've got an idea."

Jay eyed him with some suspicion. "This idea looks like a bad one."

"No, it's a great idea." Michael picked his way around all the piles of books on his way to the kitchen, and he tugged open a drawer. "Fork, knife, or spoon?"

Jay gaped at him, but all Michael did was look at him like he was waiting for an answer.

"You have solid silver cutlery," Jay stated.

"How about a teaspoon? It's nice and small, and there's no risk of you getting arrested for carrying it." Michael plucked one out of the drawer and turned it over to squint at the back. "Yep. Hallmarked with a lion. Not plated."

"You want me to make a vampire-repelling teaspoon." Jay sounded skeptical, and he did so intentionally.

"No," said Michael. He drew a fistful of teaspoons from the drawer and grinned. "I want you to make us one *each*."

Jay stared at him like he'd gone mad, but actually the bloke had a point. If vampires couldn't so much as lay a finger on any of them, then the threat became totally obsolete, and Jay would have solved all their problems in a single evening.

Well, he'd have to put his spoon down if he wanted to touch his husband, but other than that he had to agree with the logic of Michael's plan.

It was just a shame it had to be teaspoons and not something cooler.

TWENTY-SIX

Aaron led him to a church that had to be hundreds of years old. It was small and quite simple-looking, surrounded by London's ubiquitous cast-iron railings, and Aaron pulled heavy iron keys from his pocket to let them inside. They were only a stone's throw from Hyde Park, and it had taken them about ten minutes all told.

Every door and gate on their route was locked, and Aaron had to use a different key for each one. Han hurried down stone steps so worn with age and use that each step actually dipped in the middle, and then through a heavy iron-banded wooden door through to a row of cells.

There was no other word for them. Solid iron bars ran from floor to ceiling straight down the middle of the room, then separated the cells, too. Each cell contained a simple metal bed that looked like it'd been rescued from a WWII bomb shelter, and there were no windows as they were underground.

It was the perfect place to hold vampires captive.

One of the cells seemed reasonably recently repaired, or

even replaced altogether. There were new bars which looked more like steel to Han's eyes. They had that dull, unpolished sheen to them, and the smooth surface of machined metal.

He blinked and looked to Aaron. "This was where you kept Ellis," he realised.

"Yeah. Randall fucked that cell up good and proper getting him out."

"What even is this place? Why does a Church have cells in the basement?"

"Christians are weird is why," Aaron said. "They had monks who genuinely believed they should have like zero home comforts, so they slept in cells at night, because that's healthy." He shut the door behind himself and locked it, then went and locked all of the cell doors, testing each one after he was done to make sure. "All right. Chuck 'em in."

Han turned to shadow and flowed through the bars, spreading out to occupy all six cells. Then he spat out everything he had inside himself, restricting the Councillors to one cell each, and then spewing out rodents and other detritus like he was shaking out a vacuum cleaner's dirt bag.

He retreated through the bars and plucked the stakes out of the two Aaron had stuck with them on his way. The poor bastards were already behind bars, there wasn't any need to add insult to injury. He offered the stakes to Aaron as he re-formed, and the tendrils which held them became hands.

"Mate, that is some freaky fucking shit, I don't mind telling you." Aaron took the stakes and put one in each of his coat pockets, their sharp tips poking out of the tops.

"Where the—" Asquith began, but then his eyes widened. "How dare you!" He stormed to the front of his cell and gripped the bars. "How *dare* you! Let me out at once!"

"Us," said Hillier, bristling with irritation, half of which seemed aimed at Asquith.

"Look," Aaron snapped. "You came for us, not the other way around." He gestured to the rodents that had run as fast as they could for whatever corners they could find. "There's even a buffet. Now just fucking sit tight and we'll get this sorted out!"

"There is nothing to 'sort out', Constable!" Asquith roared, which only made the rattle of his lungs worse. "This is treason! You'd better hope we don't get out, because your head is on a damn platter if we do!"

"Maybe threatening to kill him isn't the best way to sue for peace," Hillier snapped.

"Don't you bloody start, Hillier!"

"You and your 'let's go en masse, it'll be a show of strength'!" Hillier snarled and moved toward the bed in his cell. "Christ, I was going to catch up on some telly tonight, too!"

Asquith looked stunned.

"Right," Han cut in before they could continue to bicker. "Like Aaron says, just sit tight, and we'll figure this out. You've been used by Richard because he couldn't just talk to me decently about our dispute—"

"And all your humans," Asquith interjected. "And—"

"Yes, yes, I'm sure we've broken all the ridiculous and stupid rules that Devitt made up."

"These are our ancient laws!"

"And you can prove that?" Han stepped toward Asquith, though not so close that he could be grabbed. He didn't fancy a tussle. "You can prove that these laws have been around since before the Second World War?"

"Of course!" Asquith barked.

"I mean, they were handed down to us," Hillier murmured. "By Devitt."

"Well they're oral tradition," Asquith argued.

"So you have no evidence," Han sighed. "Right. Sit here, get some rest, eat a rat. We'll be back."

He led Aaron out of the dungeon as the vampires in cells erupted in uproar, but the weighty door drowned the yelling out remarkably well.

THEY WAITED until they were well out of earshot. It was easy to tell. Once they couldn't hear Asquith ranting any more, he'd either shut up or they were too far away.

"How *do* we sort this out?" Aaron mused.

Han let out a slightly nervous laugh. "I have no idea, mate. I was hoping you'd have some suggestions. You've been around longer than the rest of us, and you know people." He glanced around as they walked. "Where's Barb, do you reckon?"

"Knowing her?" Aaron shrugged. "Probably going 'round making sure her revolution buddies are tucked up safely or something. At least that way she hasn't showed her hand yet. If she sprang up out of the blue to defend us they'd know she was on our side."

"They seemed to kind of think that already."

"Yeah. Probably just because she refused to turn up on their behalf. Asquith's one of those black-or-white kinda blokes."

Han nodded to himself as he tried to work out how exactly to fix this mess after promising everyone that was exactly what he was going to do.

Logically it was just a personnel problem. The most sensible way to resolve it would be to bring everyone to a negotiating table and hammer out a deal, but everyone they'd just left in a cell would be convinced that the laws were immutable and not to be ignored or rewritten.

Or... perhaps not. Hillier seemed slightly tired of Asquith's shit, so he might actually be willing to stop and think.

"Does the Council vote?" Han asked.

Aaron nodded. "Yeah. That's why they want an odd number, so there's always a tie-breaker."

"And there's still a tie-breaker with only three," Han mused. "They're not going to let Ellis or Barb vote on shit right now."

"If they even still consider either of them Councillors," Aaron agreed.

He nodded to himself. If they could convince Hillier, that just left Stanley as the unknown quantity, and Stanley seemed pretty keen on self-preservation, once it got down to it. He'd run the hell away rather than get captured, even though it'd be easy for him to escape any cell they tried to put him in.

Maybe then it was just Asquith who wouldn't negotiate, and Hillier and Stanley could outvote him.

"Okay," he breathed. "I think I've got a plan, but we're going to need Richard."

"That sack of shit?" Aaron snorted. "What do we need him for?"

"We've got two out of three Councillors. We've got most of the interested parties. If we can get hold of Richard too then we can sit our arses down and bang out a deal."

"What's in it for them?"

"Peace in our time, et cetera?"

Aaron laughed. "You're young. I like the optimism especially."

"Oh come on. We have to try." Han chuckled. "This is how business works. You get everyone to the table and you put down the proposal and then everyone decides what it's worth, and then there's either a deal or there isn't, and if we end up with no deal we can rethink the situation, but if we don't even try to negotiate then... I don't know what that makes us."

"It makes us dictators," Aaron muttered. He sighed and kicked a bit of stray rubbish into the gutter. "Fine," he said. "You're right. I just can't see it going well. And how do we even get Stanley to the table? He turned into fog and floated off. He could've gone anywhere."

"Right," he agreed. "But I bet he didn't go *anywhere*. I bet he went somewhere he knows. He'll be at home, or the Council chambers, or at his Vassal's house, or somewhere else he thinks is safe, right? He isn't going to just hang out as fog for the next hundred years. If his thing works at all like mine then he might not even be able to maintain that form during sunrise, so sooner or later he'll need arms and legs and all that good stuff, and *that* means he'll want to be somewhere secure for the day."

"Right, so we worry about Richard first," Aaron concluded. "We can go have a word with him, see if he's willing to talk, then we can try and find Stanley. I know a few places he might be, and I can check them all before sunrise if I go alone."

Han glanced to him. He knew Aaron was right, of course, but he still wasn't entirely happy about the Constable running all over the city without any backup.

He could all but hear his mum's advice in his ear, and he shook his head.

"What is it?" Aaron asked.

"Just imagining what Mum would say about all this."

"Yeah? What would she say?"

Han looked to Aaron with a sigh. "She'd say '*tōu jī bù chéng shí bǎ mǐ*'. It's a warning. When you try to steal a chicken, but you fail *and* end up losing the rice you used as bait."

Aaron eyed him, then looked ahead. "Well that's the risk

we take, innit? You wanna take a huge risk, sometimes these things don't pay off."

"Yeah. But I don't want to lose you in the process."

Aaron flashed a grin at him. "I won't get lost. No fucker's quick enough to catch me. It'll be fine. The worst that can happen is Stanley isn't anywhere I think he might be, then I run home before sun-up. Safe as houses."

Han rubbed his jaw, but nodded slightly, and decided not to mention all the times that houses burned down.

TWENTY-SEVEN

Jay double- and triple-counted the teaspoons. "Right. That's one for you, one for me, one for Frederick, and one for Randall." He sucked his lip as he moved them from one pile to the other one by one. "I'm not forgetting anyone?"

"Not unless you want to give them out to strangers on the street," Michael said as he picked up two of them. "We should get back."

Jay nodded and dropped the other two into his pocket. "They'll do short-term," he said. "I'd rather replace them with something more secure further down the line."

"You don't want to turn teaspoons into brooches?" Michael grinned. "We could just solder a pin onto the back. Might start a hot new trend."

"Michael, literally nobody is going to mistake lapel-spoons for a trend." He laughed as he headed toward the front door.

"Tell them it's an Alexander McQueen teaspoon and they will," Michael countered.

Jay considered it, and then he considered some of the awful

tat that other non-Ellis galleries sold for hundreds of thousands of pounds.

"Fair point," he admitted.

———

THEY GOT BACK TO ELLIS' house and parked up outside, and Randall let them in.

"Spoon for you," Jay said cheerfully as he offered it over.

Randall reached for it, then snatched his hand back when he was barely an inch away. "Fucking hell, Jay! Is that silver?"

Jay blinked, then turned and planted his forehead against the wall. "I'm such an idiot. Sorry! I didn't realise. The spell needs it to be silver for it to work."

Michael looked between them, then his eyebrows lifted and his mouth formed an O. "Ohhhh! So that's a thing? With werewolves?"

"I mean, I'm sure I'd love a spoon?" Randall squinted.

"It's a vampire-repelling spoon." Jay pulled away from the wall and wiggled the spoon in the air. "I could just drop it straight into a pocket for you?"

"Then how do I touch Ellis?"

"Er..." He puffed out his cheeks and headed through to the office, pausing to put the spoon down on a bookshelf. "Fine. Okay. I'll just leave it here. If you ever have the need for it, it's there. But I'll make something more useable for you. Maybe just pop it in a leather pouch or something so you don't have to touch it."

He had to admit he felt like a total bloody idiot. Of *course* Randall didn't want to touch anything silver. The house was totally devoid of the stuff. Even when it had been Charles' house, the only silver thing from basement to roof was a photo frame from back when Charles was still alive — in the beating heart sense, not in the undead sense.

No vampire or werewolf kept that stuff laying around. It was dangerous. The silver knife had been enough to slice Ellis' entire arm off, even though it was soft metal that would've bent if anyone tried to stick it into a human target. There was no way he'd want to put his hands on it accidentally while feeling around to find something else.

Jay nudged the teaspoon right to the back of the bookshelf just to be sure it was safe there, but he still felt like he'd taken a grenade into a bunker and dropped the pin at the door.

It was so late now that Tiberius didn't even twitch when there was another knock at the door, and Randall went to let Han and Aaron in.

Jay was having real trouble staying awake. He didn't want to admit it, but he could use some matchsticks right about now.

"Right," Han announced as he strode into the room and headed straight for Jay. "We've got a..." He tailed off as Jay back-pedalled fast, his hands up defensively. "Oh! You found it?"

"Yep!" Jay exhaled with relief and flourished his own teaspoon. "I didn't want you to bounce off me like I'm a trampoline."

"Not until later, anyway."

Han's grin was filthy, and Jay blushed so hard he could feel the heat in his own cheeks. He didn't drop his head, though. There wasn't a damn thing to deny there, and he was damned if he would even try to.

"Anyway, like I was saying, we've got a plan," Han continued. "We're going to go talk to Richard, see if we can drag him to the negotiation table. Then Aaron's going to run around like a blue-arsed fly and try to track Stanley down."

Jay nodded. "Okay. You really think any of them will talk?"

Aaron barked a short laugh.

Han shrugged. "I think we need to try."

"Fair enough." He stifled a yawn. "Why don't I come with you to Richard's? Then Aaron can get straight on with tracking down Stanley. It'll save an hour."

He wasn't a hundred percent sure he wanted to try and talk to Richard while his brain was this fried, but maybe some fresh air and a walk would give his brain a little extra boost. That and he got to tell Han how sure he was that this idea would fail without doing it in front of a whole bunch of spectators.

Han tilted his head, then smiled. "If you're sure?"

"Yep! Totally sure! That's me, sure!"

"Great. Then let's go!"

***

"YOU THINK I'VE GONE MAD," Han observed once they'd been walking at a brisk clip for twenty minutes.

Jay laughed warmly and, out of habit, veered closer to take his arm, but he had to pull away again when he realised what he'd been about to do.

God, sleep deprivation was a giant flaming turd.

"I think it's noble," Jay murmured, stuffing his hands in his pockets to make extra sure he wasn't about to accidentally shove Han out into the road with a touch. "I don't know if it'll work, but I agree it's the right thing to do."

Han nodded to himself, then glanced around before he lowered his voice. "Frederick agrees with Ellis," he whispered.

Jay blinked at that, and his tired brain took far longer than he would have wanted to connect the dots. "About Richard?"

About *eating* Richard, but he wasn't going to say that out loud.

Han's head bobbed. "He spoke to me, like... Telepathically, I suppose. Before the Council turned up. He said..." He glanced around again. "He said Ellis totally did it, but that there was a reason Ellis said I should do it."

It. Fucking hell, they sounded like teenage boys talking about sex, when they were actually talking about murder.

Jay crinkled his nose. "Go on."

"Apparently if we do this, we get the goods from whoever we do it to." Han frowned darkly. "Ellis has Jonas'... thing. And Charles', too. Frederick even thinks he has the things from the guys Charles did it to, too."

Jay worked to unravel that statement. Thing obviously meant power, but if that was true, then Han was saying that Ellis could speak any language *and* control people just by speaking. He didn't know whatever powers the two Councillors Charles had eaten may have had, but it all matched up with what Jay had found while trying to stitch Ellis' threads back together.

And why Bryce had mistaken him for an Elder at first glance.

"Shit," he breathed. "You mean I didn't need to go hunting for help with these bloody books after all?"

Han blinked at him, then got his thinking face on. "Not sure Ellis could do it," he mused. "If you can't pronounce what you're reading out loud, it might be gibberish to him."

Jay huffed at that.

And then it was Han's turn to look affronted. "You mean I bloody learned Mandarin to help him with his customers and I didn't have to?" He gritted his teeth. "Christ, I suppose it was a big secret. Still is. I mean, I don't even know if Randall knows."

"And Frederick told you because..." He tailed off.

This answer came more easily, and Jay felt a little queasy.

"Oh, god. Because you'd have Richard's thing and it'd be pretty fucking immense," he realised.

"Yeah. Exactly Ellis' reasoning, though I'm willing to give him the benefit of having been tortured a hell of a lot." Han clicked his tongue. "Frederick's logic was much more, uh... I mean, I know he's helped us out and everything, but it was... Harsh. No, I mean... Cold. It was cold."

Jay nodded a little at that. "I mean, it *would* be amazing. But you'd have to kill..." He took a breath and shook his head. "You can't. You're not considering it, are you?"

"No!" Han looked appalled. "Hey, who'd you marry?"

"You."

"Who's got your back, always?"

The black clouds of Jay's mood began to part. "You," he smiled.

"Right. So let's find this bag of dicks, solve all our problems, then get back to shagging like bunnies."

Jay laughed softly, and nodded.

"All right."

THE REST of the walk was along the Victoria Embankment, which was very pretty at night with all the street lamps and other lights which were reflected by the choppy waters of the Thames. It could be a lovely romantic way to spend a late-night stroll if only the circumstances were different.

Still, Jay smiled to himself as they walked briskly along. "I'm really proud of you, you know."

"For being so awesome?" Han grinned at him.

"Yeah, pretty much. Not everyone in your shoes would be

able to adapt to these situations. And not everyone would walk three miles across town in the dead of night to try and save everyone else's life when they've already been offered a way out for themselves."

"I don't think it was as much of a way out as it was sold." Han shrugged faintly, hands still in his pockets. "They offered me amnesty for being turned without permission, but not for you. I suspect they'd still have screamed 'orf with his head' the moment I gave Ellis up. That's not to deny still being awesome, mind you."

Jay laughed softly. "No, of course not." He let his laugh fade, then he added, "I love you."

"I love you, too, baby," Han murmured. "And I'm proud of *you*, you know. You're kicking arse learning all this magic stuff. You've pulled out all the stops, and you're doing great."

"Urgh, I know." Jay feigned flicking hair away from his face as his threw his head back. "I'm basically the best."

"I mean, second best," Han protested.

"Joint best?"

Han pursed his lips, then nodded. "Okay. I'll share my podium spot with you. Seems fair."

"That's right!" Jay grinned again, then he looked up ahead, to the mass of Blackfriars station in the distance. "Have you got an actual plan for finding Richard?"

"Well, not as such, no. Aaron gave me his address."

"So we're going to knock on his door like really early Jehova's Witnesses and hope he's in?"

"Bollocks to that," Han snorted. "I'm going to break in and check, just in case he decides to jump out a window or anything."

Jay sucked on his teeth thoughtfully. "It'll only take a few seconds to get inside, right?"

"In theory..." Han trailed off and narrowed his eyes. "No."

"Oh, come on! It's the only way we'll ever find out what's in there!"

"What if what's *not* in there is air?"

"Well that's why it'll only be a few seconds! I can hold my breath!"

Han bit his lip, so Jay stayed quiet while he worked through the problems.

"I did take in all those rats and squirrels," Han finally mused, "and I didn't pop them out again until maybe half an hour later, and they were fine."

"So there has to be some air," Jay said. "It'll be fun!"

Han eyed him, then pursed his lips. "What about the teaspoon?"

Jay felt his face fall in dismay. "Shit," he said. "I didn't think of that. We could shove it under the door?"

"Yeah, he won't be alerted by receiving a teaspoon at four in the morning!"

Jay threw his hands up. "Fine. I'll wait outside."

Han nodded in agreement, and they walked the rest of the way in amiable silence.

TWENTY-EIGHT

They separated at Blackfriars Bridge. Han reasoned that as they were three minutes from the flat, Jay may as well go there to wait, where he could score a power nap and be safe at the same time, and Han headed north toward Richard's address.

Territories this side of the city seemed to be smaller than to the west. Aaron had detailed Richard's little parcel in case Han didn't find him at home, and it was nowhere near the comparative sprawl of the boroughs that Ellis claimed for his own. Richard seemed to be stuck in the space between Farringdon Street and Arundel Street, bordered by Fleet Street and Strand to the north, and the menace of the Thames to the south.

If Han had been restricted to such a small area for decades, he suspected he might be willing to defend it by whatever means necessary, too. The poor bloke was probably insane with loneliness by now.

He turned to shadow long before he reached the terrace on Temple Avenue, choosing not only to not have footsteps suddenly stop outside Richard's flat, but also to experiment some more with how he travelled.

As much as the idea initially disgusted him, he'd spread himself all over London streets and hadn't picked up dirt and litter like he was made of silly putty, so he sank down a storm drain and travelled through the sewers a little while. It seemed like a great way to get around unnoticed, except it didn't take long to hear the banging and swearing of humans reverberate along the Victorian stone tunnels. It took him a while to figure out that they had to be maintenance workers after he pieced together some of their words, but it did put the kibosh on rushing around down here with impunity, so he bled out of another drain and went back to stretching himself along the most shadowed parts of the street and rolling forward that way instead. For the most part that meant he could sink into the gated wells the terraced homes had around their basement windows, then flow up the wall, across a doorstep, and down into the next basement well.

When he reached Richard's building, he slipped himself beneath the front door like it was nothing. The single millimetre gap was more than enough to pass under, and he made a mental note to experiment some time with more modern fitted doors to see if he could get around those.

He continued up the stairs. There was little point trying to hide here, he could hear that anyone who was in this building was either asleep or watching television quietly. Nobody was in the stairwell, so he continued up to Richard's and double-checked the number on the door frame, then seeped inside the flat.

Richard's television was on with the volume so low that any human would have a hard time hearing it, but was plenty for a vampire's ears. Han pooled by the front door and listened, sending tendrils closer to the living room to enhance his hearing in that direction, and was soon rewarded by the occasional scratch of pen on paper, unrelated to the noise from the television.

Han re-formed and spoke softly. "Richard? It's Han. I'm here to talk. I'm not armed. I know you can just turn invisible and jump out of a window if you want to, though that seems really pointless, but I really think you'll appreciate what I'm here to say." He paused. "May I come in?"

He heard footsteps, and Richard appeared in the doorway to the living room, looking absolutely livid.

"Looks like you're already in," he snapped. "What the hell are you doing in here?"

Han spread his hands gently and did his best to look inoffensive. It was one of the advantages of being relatively short. Most people underestimated him even before he was turned. "We need to talk." Then he nodded toward the living room. "Can we sit down?"

"No." Richard backed into the room, though, and grabbed a stake from somewhere out of sight.

Han blinked at him. "Seriously?"

Richard looked to the stake, then grit his teeth and tossed it aside again. "Fine. Come in. Sit down. What do you want?" He backed away again, and turned to go sit in an armchair.

Han tailed him at a distance to help him feel safe, and entertained himself by looking around the flat as he followed. It seemed fine, as flats went. Richard was probably fortunate enough to have bought it back when it was a fair price, but these days London property prices were anything but reasonable. Although Han's flat was four times the size of this one, it had cost way more than four times whatever Richard paid for it even if he only bought it twenty years ago.

Still, it was in the heart of the city, on the right side of the Thames, and more than plenty for one guy living on his own even if he was alive and needed to store things like food. The windows looked out onto the street, so Richard had a pretty decent safety mechanism. If it weren't for Han's power, Richard would be well aware of any approaching vampires and had plenty of time to prepare himself, or just turn invisible and wait for them to leave.

He crossed to the sofa and settled into it. Despite looking like it dated from around the Seventies or Eighties, it felt like new under his butt, and all that did was emphasise Han's sense of Richard's loneliness. Who managed to keep a sofa so like new for fifty years?

Someone who hardly ever had guests.

"What's so urgent that you felt the need to track me down and break into my house?" Richard snarled.

Han rested his hands on his thighs and focused his attention on Richard. "I trusted you, and you sold me down the river, all because you can't behave like an adult and negotiate. The problem is that the Council came to arrest me, so now they're all behind bars, and negotiation is your only remaining option."

Richard stared at him. He even began to rise from his armchair for a moment, before he sank right down into it again. "Behind bars? What the hell did you do?"

Han shrugged. "I've placed them under citizen's arrest. They're cooling their heels in cells while I've come to invite you to the table." He waved a finger toward the windows. "Your territory is tiny. There are very few bars and pubs in it. The longer you stay here the greater your risk of discovery. It's in your best interest for us to abolish the idea of territories altogether. So come with me, we'll sit down with the Council, and we'll hammer out an agreement."

This time, Richard did bounce out of his chair. "Are you mad?" Then he rocked his jaw and narrowed his eyes. "Is this some fucking joke?" He stormed away toward the windows and looked out as though he thought Han might have backup out there, then he stared back at him over his shoulder. "You're still on about this stupid revolution? When are you going to get it into your head that the Council won't ever allow it?"

"The Council who are currently behind bars, you mean?" Han just shrugged slightly. "How ever will they be persuaded to talk? I mean, ultimately we can leave them there for decades. Pop in and check on them every few years to see whether they're willing to negotiate yet. And in their absence, total chaos. Do you fancy total chaos? Because it's not really my cup of tea, personally. That's when you get people running around killing each other or creating new vampires with wild abandon. Hell, they might even decide it's a good idea to blow our existence wide open for public consumption."

"Oh, and you haven't already done that?"

"No, actually. My husband is a good keeper of secrets, and so is his teacher, otherwise you would have heard of sorcerers long before now, wouldn't you?" He tutted faintly, as though Richard wasn't quite keeping up.

There was no need to let Richard find out that Jay was so new he could cast maybe ten spells at most, and that Frederick couldn't even use magic. That wasn't a card anyone needed on the table.

Richard ground his teeth and turned his back to the window, then stepped sideways to stand with his back to a stretch of wall between that and another window. He crossed his arms with a scowl. "You're never going to get this stupid revolution off the ground," he muttered. "Do you think it hasn't been tried before?"

Han shrugged. He had no idea whether it had or hadn't. It didn't matter. "Do you really think that three Councillors who we've already managed to put behind bars are really a threat to us?" He crossed his legs and leaned an elbow on the arm of the sofa. "Look, here's the simple facts, whether we like them or not. The revolution is already underway. There's no turning back now. You can either come sit down at the table with the rest of us and we can hammer out how things are going to be moving forward, or you can stay here and miss out on being not only the first to know what the new laws like, but to actually have a hand in shaping them. Because that's what I'm offering you here, despite your attempts to have me killed." He allowed a faint smile. "A hand in how this city is run for the next hundred years. You know, until some kids come along and overthrow it. But that'll be a hundred years that you—" he pointed directly at Richard "—had a hand in."

Richard tapped his fingers against his bicep while he glanced toward the window, and Han took the opportunity to get a better look around the flat.

There was definitely some confusion in the decor going on, that was for sure. Stuff from the seventies and eighties mingled with much more modern things like a flat-screen television and a fake fireplace. Han idly wondered whether Richard just bought new stuff whenever the old one broke, or whether this was some kind of heterosexual bachelor aesthetic.

"Well I'm not going out now," Richard huffed. "It's far too late."

Han raised an eyebrow. "It's not even five yet."

"I don't like being out so close to sunrise."

Han resisted the urge to throw his hands up. That might not aid negotiations at all. "Tomorrow, then. First thing."

Richard nodded. "I'll be here."

He eyed Richard, but stood slowly anyway. "Is that like how you were totally not going to run to the Council and tell them everything?"

"Fuck you and get out of my house," was Richard's angry retort.

"All right." Han turned to shadow right there in the living room because he was an arsehole and he knew it'd put the shit up Richard.

It did. Richard pressed back against the wall in abject horror, eyes wide with it.

"If you're not here tomorrow," he rasped from every inch of his blackened surface, "you don't get a say in your fate. I might be inclined to repay you for everything you tried to do to me." He even waved some tendrils of darkness across the walls for extra spooky effect.

He seeped away down the hall and under the front door, and felt somewhat satisfied by the sound of Richard hurriedly turning lights on as though that could somehow make Han leave faster.

Joke was on Richard, though. Waiting until tomorrow just gave everyone the chance for a good day's sleep.

That just gave Jay's snark batteries time to recharge, and if Richard thought he was scared of Han, he hadn't met Jay in his ultimate bitchy form.

It might even be worth the wait.

TWENTY-NINE

W HAT WOKE Jay was the sensation of fingers lightly brushing over his stomach, and he stifled a yawn while he swatted at them.

"Evening," Han chuckled against his shoulder.

"Oh my god, what time is it?" He rubbed his eyes and wriggled so that he could roll over and face his husband without breaking free.

"I dunno. Sun's still up, though."

Jay settled down again as he nestled up against Han's body and leaned forward to kiss him slowly. "How did it go?"

"Great. Let's do it again!" Han leaned in for another kiss.

Jay laughed against his lips and slapped his arse lightly. "I meant with Richard. Was he in?"

"I'm right here, naked, we have plenty of time, and you want to talk about Richard?" Han's hand came down to Jay's bum in return and squeezed gently.

"Oh, well, when you put it like that..."

Han laughed and squeezed his arse again, so Jay shimmied down beneath the sheets and took Han's cock into his mouth.

Yeah. That put an end to the laughing.

He sucked softly, slowly as he encouraged Han's cock to grow, and then once it was hard enough he shimmied right back up again and pushed Han onto his back so that he could straddle him.

Han's hands went to Jay's thighs and stroked them. His golden eyes looked straight up at Hay, attentive. Fixated.

Fuck, he was so gorgeous, especially while his hair was still wild from sleep and he hadn't put his contacts in.

Jay didn't wait around. He sat up and arched his back so that he could guide Han inside himself while he was still wet enough to do it, and then once Han was in him he closed his eyes and licked his lips, taking a moment to savour the sensation of fullness, of being so thoroughly stuffed that he couldn't move.

"Fuck," Han whispered. "You got up on the horny side of bed today."

"Yeah, well." Jay grinned down at him and rested his hands on Han's chest. "We keep talking about it, but things got busy. Now they're less busy, so now we can *get* busy!"

"I'm not complaining." Han grinned and wrapped a hand around Jay's cock. "Go on, then. Fuck yourself on my cock. I like watching you do all the work."

Jay just groaned at that. Han's words wrapped around him like a blanket and made him feel warm and gooey on the inside, as well as made his own cock harden and his nipples tingle.

His husband *did* like watching him. Jay knew that. But to hear him say it, too? The honesty and truth in his words? It was a better aphrodisiac than any other he could imagine.

He began to rock slowly at first, letting himself adjust to having Han inside him, but once he felt ready he leaned forward, curving so there was still space for Han's hand.

Han raised his head from the pillow to meet him, and their lips clashed as Jay rode his cock hard. Every lift thrust his hand through Han's fingers, and every push rubbed Han's cock against his prostate, and soon he was lost to the push-pull inside of him. Han's lips fell away from his at some point, and Jay sat back again so that he could put on a better show as he rocked and fucked himself toward orgasm.

"Fuck," Han growled. "You're so fucking amazing. Look at you. You keep this up and I'm gonna cum inside you in no time!"

"Oh, shit!" Jay's breath hitched, and he gasped for air and sparks rippled through him. He couldn't last much longer, and just the thought of Han filling him with cum didn't help. "Bite me," he gasped.

Oh *shit*.

He hadn't meant to say *that* out loud.

Han sat up and coiled his free hand around Jay's waist, and began to rock with him.

And then he sank his fangs into Jay's shoulder.

That was it. Jay was gone. He couldn't move a muscle, and Han's cock was insistent inside him, his hand now moving to stroke Jay as he swelled and groaned and spilled inside Jay's arse.

All Jay could do was gasp quick, shallow breaths as the pleasure from the bite coiled around the need from his orgasm, and the two combined to shove him over the cliff and into freefall. He couldn't even cry out, so his orgasm took him harder, more roughly, stealing the energy that would've been used to make a noise and releasing it through his body in savage crests of waves instead.

He was only able to sag once Han's fangs withdrew from his skin, and he collapsed against his husband like a weak and hollow sack of bones.

"You're getting kinky in your old age," Han whispered against his skin.

Jay felt his lips twitch into the best approximation of a grin he could manage right now, and he lay his cheek against Han's shoulder.

That was everything he'd imagined it to be, and they were definitely doing it again one day.

"So how did it go with Richard?" Jay repeated once they were both showered and dressed. He stood in the kitchen cooking an omelette because he was feeling super basic right now.

"Who knows?" Han lounged in the dining room and answered him through the open door. "He's probably going to agree to negotiate, but only in his own self-interest."

"Isn't that the only reason anyone negotiates?" He chuckled as he flipped the omelette out onto a plate, then he turned the hob off and grabbed a fork. "Do you want me there?"

"Yes." Han watched him as he came through to the living room. "But I don't think it'd be wise. If we have Richard and the Council all in one place, they'll probably want it to be a very vampire-only space."

"Figures." Jay curled one leg under the other as he sat, so that his knee rested against Han's thigh. "In other news, though, I think I might be able to do this permissions mask thing you were asking for."

Han blinked at him. His eyes were still golden, and Jay guessed Han wasn't expecting to bump into anyone he knew today. Not who thought he was living and breathing, anyway. "That would be amazing."

"It would. But I suspect I have to kind of customise a few things. I've seen Bryce's notes allude to a few bits here and there about the nature of vampires not having reflections and such. Apparently the theory used to be that it was part of vampires' reaction to all things silver, since mirrors were backed with silver back before people figured out how to do it more cheaply, but then when electronics came along all of that got disproven." He used the edge of the fork to slice a piece off his omelette. "But I think actually she had some ideas about the source of the problem being a kind of curse, a fundamental part of the magic which makes up a vampire. She thought that vampirism came about from a sorcerer's attempt to become immortal."

Han put his hand on Jay's knee as he listened, and then he blinked. "So all of this rubbish, all these vampires, is just because one person didn't want to die?"

Jay ate his bit of omelette and shrugged. "I mean, that's people, isn't it? We'll cause all kinds of fuckery just to not die. It's pretty fundamental to the human condition. Anyway, I'm not saying it's a hundred percent confirmed. It might be somewhere in the rest of the books. But if it *is* true then it should be possible to do some tweaks to, like, modernise you."

There was a brief moment's pause, then Han barked a laugh. "You want to do a firmware upgrade on me?"

"Oh sweetie, I want to do all kinds of things on you!" He winked as he ate more omelette. "But I suppose the firmware update is a good start. So if you're going to go do all this negotiation tonight, I suppose you want me to have a back-up plan for when it all goes pear-shaped?"

"That might be good. What kind of back-up plan?"

"Literally no idea. I was thinking perhaps we totally overthrow the Council and install a new system of government, so maybe I should research systems of government and rank them in order of speed of implementation."

Han laughed again and squeezed his knee. "You want to overthrow the Council just because negotiations don't go well?"

Jay snorted. "Of course not. I'm a Millennial. I want to overthrow the Council because it's an outdated patriarchy full of bigots, and overthrowing patriarchies is what we do."

Han bit his lip as he tried not to laugh any more, but his eyes creased with humour. "That's it? You want to take some avocado toast with you or something?"

"Shut up, you're only a couple of years older than me. Technically you're a Millennial too. Overthrow the patriarchy, sweetie. It's good for you."

There was a deep sigh and a distinctive roll of the eyes, before Han said, "Fine. But only because it'll make you happy, baby."

Jay laughed and nudged Han with his elbow. "That's how I know you love me." Then he leaned back and made his face look far more serious, just in case Han assumed what came next was a joke. "I could just throw teaspoons like grenades."

"No."

He huffed. "I could throw Ellis like a grenade?"

"No."

"Fine." He finished off the omelette. "Then I suppose I have a few hours to come up with an actual plan."

"Yep." Han smirked. "You work best under pressure anyway."

"Oh, yes. I know! But just once it would be super nice to not have to!"

Han nodded along with him. "Totally agree." Then he leaned in and kissed Jay's cheek. "Love you, baby. Be careful, okay?"

"Me?" Jay booped the tip of Han's nose. "Sweetie, you're the one about to spend a night trapped in talks with a bunch of people who all want you dead."

"Right," Han agreed. "So we both be careful."

He nodded.

But he didn't feel reassured.

This was going to be one hell of a night.

THIRTY

To Han's surprise, Richard was actually at home and waiting when he arrived after sunset, and opened the door once Han knocked on it.

Han raised his chin. "You're coming?"

"If I don't, there's no telling what kind of deals you might strike with the Council," Richard spat.

Han smiled beatifically, as though butter wouldn't melt in his mouth. "That's right," he agreed. "Car's waiting." He turned lightly on the balls of his feet and strode away to the stairs without looking back.

"You want me in a car with you?"

"Oh I'm sorry. You're right." He didn't slow down, but he knew Richard could still hear him as he descended. "I'll drive, and then we can all sit around talking about what an arrogant shit you are for making us all wait for you to eventually turn up."

He heard the door slam and footsteps hurry down the stairs at his back, and just smirked to himself as he led the way out to the Range Rover.

HE DROPPED Jay off at Frederick's with a quick wave, since a kiss was out of the question with that bloody teaspoon around, and he took the opportunity to check his phone and see if Aaron had managed to track down Stanley.

Mission successful, was all Aaron's text said.

Han tucked the phone back into his breast pocket and pulled away from the kerb.

"Where are we going?"

"To the Council."

Richard pointed the other way. "They're in Aldwych."

"Not right now they're not."

He refused to explain further. Richard might have a moment if he knew he was being carted off to prison.

THERE WASN'T ANYWHERE to park directly outside the church, but he did at least see Aaron and Stanley waiting at the gate. Han stowed the car around the corner and walked the rest of the way with Richard walking a couple of steps ahead. He was probably itching to make sure he reached the Council first, and Han wasn't about to play posture games with the guy.

"Councillor Stanley!" Richard jabbed his hand out and stopped a couple of feet away from Stanley, who eyed the hand then shook it briefly.

"Yes," said Stanley. He sounded testy, and Han couldn't blame him. "Shall we get on?"

"No problem." Aaron whipped his keys out and led them inside, and Han brought up the rear.

It was as though their approaching footsteps had flipped a

switch, and the ruckus from the cells fired up just before Aaron put the key into the door to the jail.

"About damn time," Asquith yelled. "Who is it? Get us out of here!"

Stanley walked through first, and Richard balked in the doorway, so Aaron and Han pushed him inside and then hurried in behind him.

Aaron slammed the door and locked it.

"What is this?" Richard gasped. He turned toward Han and his hands balled into fists. "You lied! What is this!"

"I didn't lie," Han replied calmly. There was enough shouting going on down here without him contributing to it. "This is exactly what it looks like. A hostage situation. Nobody gets out of this room until some agreements are reached, and since Aaron's got the keys, it better be an agreement he likes."

"Stanley?" Hillier sounded uncertain. "Are you on their side?"

"He's the traitor!" Asquith bellowed. "All this time we thought it was Applegate, but it's you!"

"There is no traitor," Stanley sighed. He walked away to the furthest cell and broke apart into fog so that he could seep through the bars, then he re-formed on the bed, sitting cross-legged with his back to the wall.

Han admired the sheer chutzpah at the manoeuvre. It made the playing field almost look level, but made it equally clear that he was here of his own free will and could fuck off again any time he wanted.

"I don't need to be here," grumbled Constable Ratcliffe. "Not if you're gonna be negotiating shit all night long."

"Why are there rodents in here?" Richard demanded as a rat ran over one of his feet.

"I'm only a Vassal," Weatherford insisted. "I demand you release me!"

"You little shit!" Asquith turned on Weatherford. "I see your Vassal is as much of a coward as you, Stanley!"

Han opened his mouth, but he heard the rush of air as Aaron sucked in a full lungful, so he waited.

"Shut the fuck up the lot of you or I swear to god I will start fucking staking people!" Aaron bellowed.

The fella could make a lot of noise for such a slim frame. Han was impressed.

It took a couple more instances of Aaron screaming at everyone to get Asquith to shut up, and then Han stepped into the fray.

It was his turn now. He negotiated deals all the time for work, but by and large those were with people who wanted to trade. Negotiation with a munch of fractious childish man-babies was beyond his usual remit, and it was going to take every single ounce of his skill.

He wished Ellis was here. That man could sell snow to Norwegians.

"All right," he began. "Let's begin by going around the metaphorical table and outlining what each one of us wants out of these talks. Richard, why don't we begin with you?"

"Why—" began Asquith.

"Because it was Richard whose actions kick-started this whole chain of events," Han cut in, "and if you can't learn to wait your turn, we'll have to implement a talking stick as though we're all toddlers. Do you want me to treat you like you're five?"

"You filthy fucking—"

"Stick," Han said.

"As you wish." Aaron turned and picked up a stake from the sideboard.

Asquith's eyes widened, but he shut his mouth so tightly that his lips formed a straight line.

"Right. Let's try that again." Han gestured to Richard. "What is it you'd like to get out of these talks?"

Richard eyed Han like he was expecting this to be some kind of trap, but he cleared his throat and spoke anyway. "I want you to face trial for your crimes and get the punishment deemed fit within our laws."

"Is that it?" Han blinked. "You don't want some icing on that cake?"

Richard shrugged. "I just want peace and quiet."

Han shrugged at that, then moved on to the next in line. "Stanley?"

Stanley pursed his lips and was quiet a while, and Aaron had to waggle the stake toward Asquith to stop him from cutting in yet again.

"I would like an actual democracy," Stanley finally decided. "I'd like the Council to become an organisation any vampire in London can aspire to become a part of, whose job is to serve the entire community and not just the oldest vampires in town. I would like the Council to actually take responsibility for vampire wellbeing, instead of just laying down laws and executing the detractors."

That only made Asquith start yelling again, so when Han heard footsteps outside and Ellis' voice, he was almost relieved by the distraction.

Aaron unlocked the door and let Ellis into the room, then quickly locked it again while Ellis felt his way forward with a soft *tap tap* from his cane.

"Ellis," Han said. He was surprised as hell that Ellis was up and about, let alone that he'd turned up here of all places.

Ellis stopped just as his cane found Han's toes, and he gave a considerably saner smile than the last one Han had seen him give. "Areet, Han? I heard you were looking for Councillors."

"Oh now we've got the cripple, too?" Asquith sneered.

Ellis tipped his head slightly. "Shut up, Asquith," he said, his own voice soft. "Or I'll come over and share that cell with you."

Han glanced to Asquith and noted the Elder's mouth opened and then shut again.

None of them knew how Ellis had survived all the attempts on his life. They didn't know how he'd defeated the oldest and most powerful vampire in London and claimed his territory.

They were afraid of Ellis, and Ellis knew it.

Christ, what the hell had Ellis endured in the short amount of time since he'd been turned and was then forced to turn Han to save his life?

He looked to Ellis and reached out to touch his elbow briefly. "Are you sure you're ready to be here?" he murmured.

Ellis nodded. "Fresh as a daisy," he replied. "It's like waking up from hell and realising you do actually still have a life to go back to. I'm okay, Han. Let's just get on."

Han nodded to himself, then turned his attention on Weatherford. "All right, Weatherford. You next. What is it you want out of all of this?"

Weatherford blinked and glanced around, then stepped to the front of his cell. "Me?"

"Yes. You. You're here. Consider yourself the voice of anyone not old enough to get a Council seat. What would you want for the future?"

Weatherford licked his lips and glanced to Stanley, who nodded at him.

"All right." Weatherford crossed his arms. "I want a bigger territory. I want to be able to become a Councillor one day. And I'd really like to know who the fuck owns the territories around me."

Han nodded and continued down the line.

He wasn't looking forward to reaching Asquith, but otherwise, so far so good.

———

BETWEEN THEM, Han and Ellis seemed to be getting things moving forward, at least. The Constables were mostly confused as to why they were even being consulted, except Aaron, who took it in his stride. Asquith remained outraged that mere Constables were having their say, but was even more outraged that Richard and Han were present at all, since they had no rank whatsoever. Hillier seemed mostly to be coming down on Asquith's side, though not for any love for Asquith, that was certain.

Stanley was taking a far more neutral middle-ground, which at least facilitated continued talks. Richard just wanted everything to go back to the way it was last year, which mostly put him on Asquith's side. Weatherford seemed quite happy to agree with Stanley, and Han suspected that Weatherford was actually Stanley's Vassal.

Glover and Ratcliffe were dithering, and Han suspected they were both trying to avoid generating political discord in case it meant they lost their status as Constables whoever won, but their failure to fully support Asquith was just making Asquith all the more angry.

Han suspected that people's existence was enough to make Asquith angry, though. There wasn't much he could do about that.

And then there was Aaron, who stood firmly on the side of burn it all down and let it sort itself out. If Han harboured any suspicions that the bloke was an anarchist at heart, they were well and truly blown out of the water now.

The talks came and went in waves. There would be lulls in

which progress happened, and then there would be tides in which Asquith and Hillier just yelled at each other before Aaron offered to shove wood in their hearts. He even unlocked Asquith's cell and got the tip of a stake up against Asquith's ribs within the blink of an eye at one point, which seemed to calm Asquith down for a whole half an hour.

Ellis took his glasses off and pinched the bridge of his nose in clear exasperation, then looked toward Han. His eyes were blue again, which made Han blink in shock.

Had Jay's magic actually worked?

Han almost said something to him in Cantonese so that they could talk without everyone else here eavesdropping. He knew Ellis would understand it. But then what might happen? So far as Ellis knew, his possession of Jonas' power was a secret, and if anyone present cottoned on, this whole thing would go to shit.

Cantonese wasn't a language most white people bothered to learn.

"This could go on a while," Ellis murmured.

"Right?" Han agreed with a soft sigh. "Thanks for coming. Are you sure you're okay?"

"Okay enough. Better than I've been in ages." Ellis paused, then turned his head away, tipping an ear toward the door.

Han heard it a second later. Heavy boots clumping down the stairs, and then a thump on the door.

"Oi," Barb yelled from outside. "Aaron! It's me! Open up!"

Aaron dug his keys out and unlocked the door, and Barb stepped through it, pushing it wide open and spreading her arms.

"Hey everyone! Miss me?" She grinned.

Han glanced to her foot. The back of her heel was pressed against the door to keep it open.

Something was wrong, and he didn't know what.

He reached out and pressed his hand against Ellis'. "Take my arm," he hissed.

Ellis didn't argue. His hand traced up Han's arm swiftly until his fingers could settle in the crook of Han's elbow. "Barb?" He smiled anyway, turning his head toward her. "Glad you could make it!"

"Yeah, come in, you're causing a draft," Aaron added as he beckoned her away from the door.

"I would," she said, "but then how would everyone else get in here?"

And then the sound of many more vampires rushing down the stairs hit him, and Han hurriedly led Ellis away from the door. Rats and squirrels — those who hadn't already been eaten — scurried around in panic.

The vampires flooded into the room, and Barb kicked the door shut.

"What the hell is going on?!" Asquith screamed.

Barbara laughed and rubbed her hands together. "Get 'em, boys! Vive la revolution!"

So that ended the negotiations pretty quickly.

THIRTY-ONE

It wasn't too surprising that almost everyone started yelling again the moment Barb's revolutionaries surged toward the cells. Aaron blinked out of existence and in the next step two vampires were staked and falling to the floor, but there was a finite supply of stakes, and now Aaron was reduced to wrestling a third vampire and trying to steer him away from the cells, but that just left plenty of space for others to rush past.

They had keys.

"What the hell is going on?" Ellis hissed tersely.

"Barb's decided to come murder the Council, I think," Han replied.

"Well that throws a spanner in the works," was Ellis' reply.

Han snorted and braced himself as a vampire rushed toward him.

"Not them, you fucking idiots," Barb yelled. "Do they look like they're behind bars?"

The vampire veered away from Han at the last moment

with a brief, apologetic look on his face, but then he threw himself at the bars to Stanley's cell and reached through them, trying to get to Stanley, who was far too far away for that and just looked mildly bemused by the attempt.

Cells unlocked one by one.

"Fuck," Han breathed. "I'm going to have to—"

Ellis' fingers tightened on his elbow. "Do what, Han?" He said it quickly. "If you save them, Barb will keep coming for them, and they won't always be in one place for you to protect. The only answer here is diplomacy..." He tailed off. "Okay, the only *good* answer here is diplomacy, but when people are this pissed off diplomacy just leads to death anyway."

Han frowned at the haunted look in Ellis' gaze. This wasn't the time to ask what had happened or what memory had just been dredged up.

Rats swarmed past and began to attack a vampire who screamed and began trying to pull them off his legs.

Someone was hanging from the ceiling. Barb, he realised, standing with her feet on the ceiling and her blonde hair hanging down while she observed the fight and barked orders to direct people.

Han knew Ellis was right. He could save the Councillors right now. And their Constables, and poor Wainwright. But once they were all at home, Han couldn't protect them any more. It would delay the inevitable.

But since when did that mean he shouldn't try?

"Barb!" He looked up at her and spread his hands. "Stop this! Please! Just for a minute, so we can talk!"

She turned to face him and grinned, but upside down it looked almost demonic. "Wotcher! You know they're never gonna accept you, right? They're never going to accept anything that takes their power away."

"Stanley might," Han countered. "He's been the voice of reason so far!"

She looked toward Stanley, who just shrugged to her. "Hey. Stanley. How's it hanging?"

"Let Wainwright go," he countered. "He's done nothing."

"Hey! What about us?" Ratcliffe yelled, around one second before he got punched in the face.

"Wainwright!" Barb barked.

Wainwright looked up to her. "Yes, Councillor?"

"Are you a sexist, racist piece of shit?"

"I hope not," he replied. "I'd like to think if I was either of those things someone would call me on it."

Barb pursed her lips, then yelled, "Leave Wainwright and Stanley alone. Get Asquith!"

The flow of bodies adjusted at once. Even the guy Aaron was in a brawl with backed away, and Aaron blinked to Han's side, his hair tousled and his clothes in disarray. "Well this passes the time," he muttered. "Maybe you should step in, Han?"

"You know," Han said calmly, "I'm not all that sure I want to." If he had a pulse, he figured it'd be racing by now, despite his outward display of cool.

Could he really stand by and watch Asquith get murdered?

And what about Hillier, or the Constables? How far would this go once they'd destroyed Asquith?

He swore softly and turned to shadow, quickly absorbing Aaron and Ellis. The least he could do was protect them both. He spread across the room, blackening the floor, the walls, the ceiling, and he sucked in Stanley and Wainwright as he passed them. He swallowed Glover and Ratcliffe too, since the poor bastards had only been trying their best to preserve their own arses.

Then he dragged Barb inside himself and flowed away up the stairs, leaving the rest of the mess to sort itself out.

———

FREDERICK'S HOUSE WAS CLOSEST, and Jay was there, so Han favoured it over Ellis' place. He darted through sewers and storm drains where possible, surfacing now and then to make sure he was heading the right way, then he oozed out of the drain nearest Frederick's door and seeped in through the letterbox.

"Jesus Christ!" Jay yelped as Han entered the living room. "Careful, I've got the teaspoon."

"I'm counting on it," Han answered.

He spat everyone out. Well, at least he tried his best to deposit Ellis upright, but the rest he was quite happy to dump out onto the floor before he spread himself across the room to swallow up all the books just in case anyone felt like stealing some.

"Han?" Ellis said, sounding uncertain.

"Right here," Han answered. "So is Jay. Where's Frederick?"

"In bed like a normal person," Jay said. "It's nearly five o'clock."

"What have you done?" Barb stamped her foot on the shadow, likely on the off-chance that it would do some good. "Where are we?"

"Just somewhere we can talk without getting murdered." Han finally re-formed and did a quick head-count to make sure he'd spewed out the right number of vampires. "Look, I know you've had this whole thing planned for some time, but I'm not all that keen on watching it happen, okay?"

"But you're *letting* it happen," she countered.

Han shrugged faintly at that. "I suppose I am, yeah."

Jay gasped. "What the hell is going on?"

"Barb here decided to start World War Three," Han muttered. "Rocked up with an army, attacked the Councillors."

Jay blinked, and his posture shifted. "Would these be the Councillors who want us all dead?"

"Those ones, yeah," Barb said.

Jay nodded. "Fuck 'em."

Even Aaron looked startled at how casually Jay said it.

"Wow," Han said once he found the ability to speak. "That's... hard, Jay."

"Yeah," Jay agreed. "They want you dead, sweetie. They want me dead. They want Barb and Aaron and Ellis and Randall and Frederick and Michael dead. Asquith could choose to change a few laws here and there if he wanted to, but they use fear to keep everyone in their place, and it's never going to end unless he's stopped." He nodded toward Barb. "Barb's done us all a huge favour."

Barb smiled and rested her hands on her hips. "Thanks, Jay."

Jay shrugged. "I had to think long and hard about who I am when I was starting to learn magic, because if you go into it without knowing yourself, you can make some awful mistakes. I decided I was the kind of person who would do whatever I had to in order to protect the people I loved. I might not be in there jabbing Asquith with silver, but I'm not going to rush in to save his bigoted arse, either. Revolutions happen. It's how societies grow sometimes. I won't let you get hurt."

Han crossed his arms and didn't know whether to feel flattered or chilled that Jay had thought this all through. Not right now, on the spot, but coldly and calmly several days ago. Maybe Han should have been working these things out, too. He knew Ellis' world was more dangerous than his own. A blind man had already had to kill two other vampires just to survive more than a year. They were cutthroat, heartless bastards, it seemed, and maybe they just got worse as they got older.

Maybe all this infighting and destruction was how they saved themselves from immortality.

He snorted at the notion, and lowered his hands to his pockets.

"What is it?" Ellis murmured.

"I was just thinking," Han said. "Whether this immortality is as everlasting as we tell ourselves it is."

"Ah. Well, aye," Ellis chuckled. "It's one of those things, isn't it? Like freedom or perfection. It can't ever really be achieved, yet everyone wants it."

Han blinked, then laughed. "Jìnghuā shuǐyuè," he snorted.

Ellis looked about to speak, so Han cut in, just in case Ellis revealed that he'd understood what Han had just said.

"It's an idiom. Mirror Flower, Water Moon."

"I don't follow," Barb said.

"It's something that can be seen but not touched, like a flower in a mirror, or like the moon reflected in the surface of a lake," he explained.

"Like you," Aaron grinned and clapped his hand on Han's shoulder. "Except, you know, not when you're like this. When you're all shadowy and spooky."

"That was cool, by the way," Barb said.

"It was all right," Stanley sniffed.

"Oh yeah, just because you can turn into fog, you think you're so awesome," Aaron chuckled. "Anyway. Reckon they're done yet?"

Barb checked her watch. "Oh yeah, they should be."

Han sighed as he ran a hand through his hair. "So what happens now?"

"Chaos?" Aaron sounded hopeful.

Ellis snorted. "Ultimately we don't really want chaos. The city expects a Council, so I suggest one gets formed, and we can take it from there." He tipped his head toward Stanley. "Any objections?"

"No. I happen to agree," Stanley murmured. "Forming an interim Council until a new system of government can be worked out is just common sense. People will still turn up for their census dates and won't know a bloody thing until then."

"You want in?" Barb said to him.

Stanley shrugged. "I think it would add some legitimacy for people to see at least one familiar face when they turn up."

"Right. Ellis? You sticking around?"

Ellis pursed his lips, then sighed. "For now. The Council can't very well modernise if I promptly hand off to older vampires the first chance I get."

"Right, then it's you two," Barb said as she pointed to Aaron and Han.

Aaron blinked. "Wait, what? Me?"

"And me?" Han echoed. "I can't do that, I have a day job! A business to run!"

"So have I," Ellis argued.

"Right, but—"

"And you can help them get all their data off paper and onto computers," Ellis added.

"I'm not a data entry—"

"I think it'd be good," Jay chirped.

"You're all mad!" Han rubbed his forehead slowly. "What about Ratcliffe? He seems..." He didn't really know what Ratcliffe seemed. Politically cowardly? Unwilling to jump off the fence?

"No thanks," Ratcliffe muttered. "You get enough enemies as a Constable without sitting in a big chair as well."

"Yeah, count me right out," Glover agreed.

Han looked to Wainwright, who just shook his head. "No."

"Bollocks," Han muttered. "What if I refuse?"

Barb widened her eyes. "Well I'd be bummed, but you gotta do what you gotta do, mate."

Well, it was better than suggesting she'd drop her mob of revolutionaries on his head, that was for sure.

"Okay," he sighed. "But first thing we do is disband your pitchfork-wielding followers, because if you just let them trundle on without steerage someone else will step in to fill the void and point them at whoever they don't like. That's the joy of angry mobs. They're easily led."

Barb held her hands up. "Totally agreed," she said. "I've seen people co-opt riots to get their own axes ground. I'll take care of it."

"And what about Richard?" Jay said.

Everyone fell quiet.

"You know he will have disappeared right out of there," Stanley finally said. "He's a cunning little shit, he's not just going to stand there and let a mob kill him."

"Yeah," Aaron agreed. "Maybe I should go 'ave a word?"

"No," Han said. "Leave him to it. He might find things more to his liking once they settle down. He was only trying to protect his own arse because he didn't believe we could pull off a coup. Now he knows differently, fifty quid says he'll want to suck up, especially to Barb."

She laughed. "Yeah, good luck with that one."

"I suppose," Ellis said without much enthusiasm, "we really should go check on how it all went."

There was some silence again.

"I'll go," Aaron finally said. "I can be in and out without anyone noticing." He pointed at Barb, and said, "Don't even say it."

She just smirked at him and checked her watch.

Han went to the front door with Aaron and unlocked it for him, then offered his hand. "Good luck."

Aaron shook it, but smiled. "Don't need it, mate."

Then he was gone, and Han closed the door.

How the shit had he ended up a Councillor?

More importantly, how long would it damn well last?

THIRTY-TWO

AARON REPORTED BACK WITHIN MINUTES, and while Jay wasn't all that surprised to hear that both Asquith and Hillier had been killed, he did feel slightly underwhelmed by the news.

"Maybe we should all just, like... Go home," he murmured. "Sleep on this. See how we feel tomorrow. Uh, today. Later. After sleep."

"I'm going to need a little assistance," Ellis said. "I've no idea where we are. Randall walked me to the church, but I assume we didn't pass him on the way out?"

"I don't know," Han said. "I went underground as soon as I could. He might've been right across the street."

"Why don't I walk you there?" Aaron said. "If he's gone, there's still plenty of time to get you home before sunrise."

"I'll just text him," Ellis smiled. "But a lead home would be great. Thanks, Aaron."

"I could give you a ride?" Han offered.

"I'd rather chew my own face off. It's like being in a sensory deprivation tank."

240

"It is pretty awesome," Barb agreed.

"It's horrific," Stanley muttered.

Jay bit his lip and took Han's hand. "Well, we should clear out of here and let the homeowners sleep."

Han nodded, so Jay ushered everyone out of the house, and then pulled the door shut and checked it had locked.

There were some farewells on the doorstep, and Jay waited for everyone to leave before he set off at a slow dawdle along the crescent.

"You need to find some way to turn that teaspoon off," Han chuckled "How can I walk with your hand in mine if I can't touch you?"

Jay smiled faintly, but it was tinged with melancholy. "I know. Hopefully once all this is done I'll have a better way of doing it. There are ways to imbue a spell into an item and activate the spell later, so maybe I can figure out how to do that. Or hopefully there won't be the risk of vampires randomly attacking me anyway."

"I think that might just... always be a risk," Han said quietly. "They seem a pretty violent bunch. At least we're underway on the whole overthrowing the government and installing something better, though."

Jay nodded. "I think it's rare that a revolution isn't bloody. Doesn't mean we have to like it, but..." He sighed and shoved his hands in his pockets.

He really didn't want to think about the cost of what they wanted to achieve. Overthrowing patriarchies was all well and good, but the fact was nobody at the top wanted to step aside voluntarily. Who ever wanted to walk away from power once they had it?

And yet he had sat in Frederick's house and determined that he was the kind of person who was willing to pay those costs. So while he hadn't yet learned to deal with it, he could.

He would.

And he no longer needed to come up with a plan to overthrow the Council, because Barb had waded on in there and just got the job done. In his defence, she'd been planning for way longer. She'd made contacts across the city despite the restrictions the vampires lived under and she'd struck fast the moment she had the opportunity.

"How do you think Barb knew where everyone was?" he mused.

"Wouldn't be surprised if Aaron told her," Han replied. "She *is* on the Council. He might've hoped she would come negotiate and be another vote on our side."

Jay pursed his lips and let his mind wander back to when Aaron had first caught them discussing things they shouldn't at Barb's flat. Back when Barb had revealed the whole existence of her plans for revolution to Aaron.

Maybe Aaron had acted in good faith like Han suggested. Or maybe he'd seen an opportunity for Barb to act.

Either way, did it matter?

Barb had got the job done. Arguably a job that nobody but Ellis was willing to do themselves. They all wanted change, but didn't want the mess that change required, and at the end of the day Han was no killer. He was an adorable nerd who ran a software company.

And speaking of Ellis.

He'd seemed remarkably together tonight. Had Frederick done something to him? Ellis seemed like his old self again, the warm and affable man he'd been before Bryce put him through the wringer.

The man who had eaten two vampires.

Jay would have to ask Frederick whether he'd interfered with Ellis' mind in some way. It wasn't a question he was looking forward to, but he needed to know the answer, because if Frederick *hadn't* interfered it was possible that Ellis was burying a lot of things that might come back to bite them all in the arse one day.

He sighed faintly to himself and packed all that away for now. It would have to wait. Instead he glanced to Han. "You better not have got all the books mixed up. We spent forever organising them."

Han blinked, then laughed. "I don't think so?" he offered. "I seem to be able to put things out exactly how I want them."

"You better, or you're going to be the one sorting them out again." He bit his lip, then grinned. "I think we're going to need more bookshelves. They can't live on floors forever."

Han nodded in agreement. "I thought maybe we could get rid of one of the spare bedrooms and you could take it over as a laboratory or sanctum or whatever you want to call it. Library," he added. "Wizard's tower."

"You've already seen my wizard's tower tonight," he smirked.

Han feigned a gasp and pretended to be shocked, his eyes wide and eyebrows high. He covered his mouth with one hand. "Jay Newfield you are a disgrace!"

"Oh yeah." Jay grinned.

Han slowed to a halt, his head tilted, and then he frowned and turned away.

Jay stopped immediately. If Han had seen or heard something, his chances of nailing it down would be best if Jay was quiet as he could be.

"I know you're there," Han said. "Stop fucking around, Richard, you can't stake me."

"I don't need to," Richard snarled. "You've destroyed everything. Absolutely everything. Half the Council's dead, and you get to just walk away from it all like mud doesn't stick. And maybe it won't."

"It won't," Han agreed. "I'm on the Council now."

Richard snarled, and he sounded absolutely furious. "Then at least I can make you regret what you've done forever!"

Jay saw Han lunge forward, his arms outstretched, but he didn't seem to make contact with anything, and then Jay felt a strange little tingling sensation as the hairs on the back of his neck lifted.

Richard appeared, inches away from Jay, and was thrown back through the air until he landed flat on his back a few feet away.

Jay's heart thudded in his chest. Adrenaline crashed through him, urging him to run, and he had to fight the instinct just to hold his ground.

"What the hell?" Richard rasped.

The ward must have kicked in. Jay dug the silver teaspoon out of his pocket and blinked at it, then stared at Richard, who was stumbling to his feet in equal horror.

"Did you just try to *kill* me?" Jay gasped. His voice trembled.

He didn't think anyone had actually tried to murder him in cold blood before, and certainly not just to piss off Han.

How utterly cheap.

"You just tried to kill my *husband*," Han hissed. He stepped forward, his hands balled into fists, gold eyes flaring with absolute rage. "For what? For some petty revenge? To hurt me? You're willing to kill a living being just to troll someone? What the hell is wrong with you?"

"Let him go," Jay breathed. "Let him crawl back into whatever hole he crawled out of, sweetie. He's a sad, lonely little man, and he's never going to change."

Richard's eyes went to the spoon, clearly not even understanding why Jay was brandishing it at him. "You're carrying silver?" He blinked. "A spoon? Why not a knife or a stake?"

"Because it'll hurt more, cousin?" Jay sighed without any enthusiasm. "Just get lost, Richard. Leave us alone."

"You're on *my* territory!" Richard stopped backpedalling. Either he was getting over his fear, or his anger was the greater force right now. "You've ruined my whole life. Sooner or later, I *will* have revenge!"

Han flashed his teeth, then melted into a puddle of shadow, and the darkness raced over the pavement to Richard. Richard turned on his heel to run, but Han swallowed him whole within three seconds flat, and then the shadow was still.

Jay clutched at his own shirt in shock, and his hold on the spoon tightened. "Sweetie?"

"In a minute." Han's voice was a thousand copies of itself, coming from all around him as the shadow bled back toward Jay.

Then the darkness spat out Richard's clothes.

Jay blinked as the pile of material and pair of shoes got left behind, and Han re-formed by his side, his gaze distant.

"Sweetie?" Jay bit his lip a little. "You can't keep him in there forever. And why is he naked?"

"He's not naked," Han breathed. He glanced to the clothes. "He's dead."

Jay blinked at that. This wasn't the kind of thing Han would joke about, which was good, because it wasn't funny either.

"How?"

Han crossed his arms and turned his back on the clothes so that he could look Jay in the eye. "I pulled his head off."

"Inside..." Jay tailed off. "Does that mean you've got ash in there now?"

Han nodded a little. "I don't want to leave it by the clothes. It'll look suspicious."

"Bloody hell." Jay hurried to the clothes and emptied the pockets. He rescued a wallet and some keys, but that was all. "You killed him," he breathed, as though repeating it to himself might make it more real. "Are you okay?"

"I don't know. I think I might be?" Han sighed and scuffed his shoe along the pavement a little. "I'll sleep on it." He raised his hands and mimed pulling something apart. "It was just like breaking a glow-stick. I thought I'd just... I don't know. Pop his head off, and..." He tailed off.

Jay wanted to reach out to him, to take his hand, or even to hug him, but that damn spoon. He didn't dare ditch it on the street in case they got attacked by someone else.

"You thought it'd just inconvenience him," he murmured. "You didn't realise it'd kill him."

Han nodded. "We heal from everything. Fuck. How was I supposed to know this was some Highlander bullshit. I even feel like..." He stopped himself again.

Jay narrowed his eyes and leaned forward a little.

Han *did* look a bit more flush than he had earlier.

Like he'd just eaten.

"Oh, god," Jay gasped.

Han just shook his head and set off walking again.

THIRTY-THREE

TROUBLE WAS that Han knew damn well he'd fed. He could feel the strength and vitality flowing through him, every ounce of Richard's blood now forever mingled with his own. The power felt incredible, especially as Han usually only took a few millilitres from Jay at a time, and there was absolutely no way he could mistake it for anything but feeding.

He'd eaten someone.

God, he felt sick. Nauseous. Worse to know that he was carrying all this corpse ash around inside himself somewhere, but he could get rid of that in a tunnel.

Out of sight.

How did Ellis deal with this? Knowing that he had blood on his hands?

That didn't help Han in the slightest. He wasn't Ellis, and he sure as hell didn't know what Ellis had been through to get where he was now. Maybe they could talk about it sometime, once Han was ready to, but for now he just wanted to sweep it all under the rug and pretend that everything could be normal again.

They stopped at Blackfriars bridge, and Jay looked to him with a heartrending look of sadness and hope.

They were only parting for a few minutes, but it felt like something more. Han needed Jay's touch right now, but instead they were going their own separate ways, and it wasn't a pleasant feeling at all.

Jay blew a kiss to him. "I'll wait for you in the lobby," he promised.

Han nodded. "Be there quick as I can."

He turned away and crossed the road toward the station, and glanced around himself as he ducked behind an awning and turned to shadow once he was sure nobody could see him. He seeped around barriers and shutters, down escalators and onto the Circle Line, where he sped into a deserted tunnel and sprinkled Richard's ashes into the darkness.

This was Richard's burial. No matter what life he'd lived before he was turned, this was where he ended up, and come the morning the winds which passed through the tube network would have scattered his ashes far and wide. Han might not share his mum's superstitious nature, but he was still fully aware of her beliefs, and he couldn't help but agree that this was a tremendously disrespectful way to say goodbye to a once-living creature.

He didn't want to end up like this, spewed out so that his loved ones had nothing to grieve.

He swooped through Embankment station as fast as he possibly could and slipped between the gaps of the Jubilee Line's barriers to switch tunnels, and then he was in Southwark in almost the blink of an eye.

Han oozed out of the station and checked the coast was clear before he re-formed, and he hurried past the quiet buildings and closed fast-food places on his way home.

Jay was, as he'd said he would be, waiting outside their

building. Han didn't know why he thought Jay might not be there, but he was immensely grateful to see his husband on the street corner, and he broke into a light jog to close the distance.

Jay looked at him oddly, tilting his head. "Is everything okay, sweetie?"

"Sure," Han croaked. "Yeah."

Jay just nodded, and his expression didn't change. He led the way inside, and Han darted after him to make the security footage look as natural as possible.

They stood in opposite corners of the lift. Han had no idea of the radius on Jay's enchanted teaspoon, and he didn't really want to find out the hard way, so it wasn't until they were inside their flat and Jay pulled the damn thing out to put it down with his keys that Han was finally able to step in closer.

Jay moved away from the spoon and grabbed Han's hand, pulling him to safety like he was rescuing a drowning man.

Maybe he was.

Jay dragged him into a tight embrace, hands rubbing over Han's back, cheek resting against his hair, and Han felt like he was melting, conforming to the shape of Jay, letting Jay become everything his world needed.

"I'll always love you," Jay whispered. "Whatever happens, I'll always have your back."

"I know," Han breathed. He eased his arms around Jay's waist and hugged so tight that he felt like he could just cling on forever. "You know I've got you too, right? I won't ever let anyone hurt you."

"I know." Jay tilted to press a kiss against the side of Han's head. "And if anyone touches you I'll pull them apart so fast they won't know what happened."

Was that supposed to be reassuring? It was the kind of things heroes said in films all the time, but Han wasn't too keen on the visual that came with it. Jay was kind and adorable and astonishingly smart — all qualities Han had fallen in love with soon after they first met — and the image of him tugging on strands to make vampires fall to pieces didn't seem to gel with that.

Maybe it was Han's turn to evaluate what he was willing to do. How far he could or would go in defence of everything he loved. Jay had already worked those things out for himself, but if Han didn't do the same it could tear them apart.

He sucked in a breath and stepped back to gaze up at Jay. "I need your help."

Jay nodded softly. "What can I do?"

"How do I deal with this?" He ran both hands through his hair. "I didn't mean to kill him. Or..." He sighed. "Maybe I did? Maybe some part of me just wanted to kill him? Why else do you pull someone's head off, for crying out loud?"

"It's okay to not know," Jay said softly as he stepped in closer. His hands raised to Han's shoulders and held them tight. "We'll get there. We'll work through it. Do you think you did want to kill him?"

Han opened his mouth, then shut it again.

Maybe if he wanted to pull something off he could have gone for an arm, but that seemed like torture. But the *head*?

Like popping the cork out of a champagne bottle, he'd resisted the urge for so long, but once he finally did, the pressure was released.

"I must have," he breathed, "on some level. I think I knew it was the only way he'd ever stop." He blinked, then he looked up to meet Jay's eye. "I knew he was going to kill you, or at least try, and all it would take for him to succeed would be one single moment when you were unprotected. He made that situation. He decided that he would kill you. And I couldn't let that happen. Not ever."

Jay nodded again. "So you made a choice," he murmured. "And now we have consequences. But life *is* consequences, sweetie. Maybe you'll decide never to kill again. Maybe you won't. But I think you need some time to accept what happened, to look at it with a little bit of distance, gain some perspective by leaving it for a few days. And then when you're ready to examine it we can turn it over a few more times, come at it again, and see how it goes."

Han felt like a weight had lifted from him. Jay was absolutely right, but then he usually was. This wasn't a puzzle for Han to try and solve, and it wouldn't just be fixed with a wave of his hand or snap of his fingers. It would take time and effort, and all Han had to do for now was accept that fact, rather than leap to a magic solution right this very second.

It gave him space in which to breathe. To accept that it might take a while to understand and even accept what had happened, and to find a healthy way to deal with it.

He lifted his head and met Jay's beautiful hazel eyes, finding only love and comfort waiting for him there, and he smiled softly. "How do you do it?"

Jay laughed and slipped his hands around Han's to pull him closer, their fingers entwined. "Do what? Be absolutely amazing all day, every day?"

"Yeah." Han chuckled. "That."

"Oh, well, you know." Jay flicked his head aside as though he were flipping hair out of his face. He wasn't, of course. It was far too short and neat for any of that. "I'm basically just the most awesome person ever, and you've gotta deal with it, sister."

"Can I deal with it tomorrow?" Han leaned against Jay's chest and pressed a kiss to his jaw. "In some indescribably sexy way that we can think of the closer it is to fuck o'clock?"

"Sure. I think that's a good idea. And for now we can just

lay down, rest, get some sleep, and the world can just damn well wait for us to be ready for it." Jay turned to kiss the side of Han's head, and his lips were soft and warm, full of reassurance.

God, that sounded great. Some rest at last. No blind panic, no fear of getting executed by a bunch of vampires. Just a duvet, his husband, and several hours of peace and quiet.

Jay began to walk backward toward the bedroom, his hands pulling on Han's, raising their arms between them. Han allowed himself to be drawn through the flat, and spent the time appreciating all the fine details. The strands of Jay's hair which had broken free of the mousse's hold and drifted across his forehead. The way his pupils dilated or contracted with the smallest changes in the light they walked through. The soft and steady beat of his heart, the core of his being, the pump which kept him alive. Each breath was a gentle song, and every step was a drumbeat which backed that siren's call.

The more he allowed himself to be wrapped in every single facet of Jay's living, breathing existence, the more he became sure that he'd done what he could.

What he had to.

But that was a decision for another day. For now, this was more than enough for him.

It was everything.

THIRTY-FOUR

JAY COULD'VE SLEPT for weeks, but that was probably a bad idea, so he turfed himself out of bed before sunset and showered, then assured Han he'd be back soon. He grabbed the teaspoon though, just in case he got caught out after dark. It'd be daft to get sloppy immediately after the total disaster of the past few days.

He hopped on the tube to Temple and walked uphill through the back alleys until he reached Devereux Court, and then he hit the buzzer for the solicitor's office.

"Hello?" answered a female-sounding voice.

"Jay Newfield," he said. "Looking for Frederick d'Arcy, if he's available?"

"Come up. Second floor."

The door buzzed, and Jay slipped inside, ignoring the lift and taking the stairs two at a time. By the time he reached the receptionist's desk, she had the visitor's ledger open and was pushing it toward him with a smile. "He's available," she said. "Pop your name in the book. You know the way to his office?"

Jay picked up a pen and scribbled down his details quickly. "I do."

"Then you're all set." She took the book back and closed it, before offering him a visitor's pass.

"Thank you."

He pinned the card to the lapel of his coat and headed along the corridor, tapping on Frederick's open door once he reached it. He popped his head inside for good measure.

"Come in," Frederick said. "Close the door. Have a seat."

Jay did so, and unbuttoned his coat to keep from overheating all of a sudden. "I'm glad you were free," he said, glancing to the view from the window.

The white front of the Royal Courts of Justice really was very pretty, and it felt so strange to be eye-level with one of London's most famous buildings. Well, famous to Londoners, anyway. He didn't know whether it meant anything to tourists, but it was on the news every other day locally, and when he looked down, he could see yet another journalist and camera crew setting up outside the huge wooden doors.

He looked back to Frederick and offered a small smile, somewhat sheepishly.

"As am I. It would've been a waste of a journey otherwise." Frederick put his pen down and leaned back in his chair. "What can I do for you?"

Jay crossed his legs. "I mean, you already know, right?"

"Well, yes. But the art of conversation is never to be underestimated. Would you like me to skip ahead?"

Jay rubbed his jaw and considered it. "Yeah, okay. Why not?"

Frederick laughed at that and stood up, then wandered toward the windows to look down at the film crew. "Then yes, I did indeed provide some assistance to your friend O'Neill. He isn't aware of it. I leave that in your hands as to whether or not you mention it to him. I have mitigated a great deal of the suffering he endured, both from his torture at Bryce's hands and the subsequent unravelling, and the pain of your repair work. He will be in a much better place for the time being. Obviously I cannot protect him from future suffering, but at least I can prevent what he has already lived through from settling in to become a long-term problem."

Jay swivelled his chair to watch Frederick. He wasn't sure whether he'd really expected the Viscount to leap straight to the reason for Jay's visit even though he'd offered to do exactly that, but Jay was impressed that every single one of his points had been addressed so neatly.

Maybe there were advantages to this whole telepathy thing.

"I can't say that I'm not satisfied with the way things turned out," Frederick continued. "It perhaps could have been a little less messy, but at least it's done and dusted, which is for the best. You are, of course, welcome to get in touch any time you have need of me, and I would hope that you would be willing to aid me should I approach you with some magical problem in the future."

"I mean, I wouldn't promise to be able to fix things," Jay murmured. "But I'd be happy to look and see if there was anything I could do."

"I think that's more than fair," Frederick agreed. "I also have something for you."

Jay lifted his head. "What's—"

He broke off as words and sigils blossomed into existence in his thoughts, then settled to become knowledge. It was the strangest sensation, as though he'd just crammed for an exam without even reading a book. He closed his mouth and pictured the new spell so that he could work out what it was.

Then he looked to Frederick, gobsmacked.

Jay had just been handed the keys to keeping Frederick out of his head.

"Consider it a gesture of trust," Frederick murmured. "Which is not something I often offer. It is my understanding that this spell will protect you from my particular brand of telepathy."

Jay nodded in agreement. That had been his assessment of it, too. "Where'd you get it? Your acquaintance?"

"In a way. My brother dug up a spell to protect him but wasn't given the opportunity to use it. The version they had was not designed to be cast upon oneself, but I found something similar while trawling through your books, et voilà." Frederick turned and perched his bum on the windowsill. "I shan't be at all offended if ever you choose to use it."

He nodded slowly and propped an elbow on the arm of his chair. "That must be hard for you. So thank you." He pursed his lips, then added, "I understand you told Han that eating Richard would be a good idea."

"Mmm. While I'm sorry that it occurred the way that it did, it's for the best. Han should take full advantage and learn to use Richard's power as quickly as he can. He knows what it is, so it should not be too difficult to learn."

Jay grimaced at the way Frederick was so casual about killing Richard, but Jay wasn't a hypocrite. He had to admit that he too agreed that things would be easier without Richard around. "You must've known more about Richard than we did," he prompted.

"He would not have stopped, if that's what you want to know." Frederick nodded. "He was even less pleasant than myself. He had hopes of becoming a Vassal one day, and was willing to kill you both to get himself noticed. He didn't give a damn about anyone but himself before he was turned, and that didn't change once he became a vampire."

Jay stood and wandered to the window himself, stuffing hands in his trouser pockets while he looked down to the street. The film crew had set up, and the journalist was speaking into her microphone while looking at the camera, and Jay had to wonder what big story was in progress while they stood up here discussing magic and murder.

It was a whole other world. At first, when Ellis had been turned, Jay hadn't realised how big this all was. So there were a few vampires dotted around the city. So what? They kept themselves to themselves, they did their best to go undiscovered, and Ellis' existence was a spanner in the works but it still felt small. Personal.

But now it had taken over Jay's life. His husband was a vampire. He stood here with a telepath. A good friend was a werewolf. And Jay was like some lost survivor of a forgotten genocide which had happened all around him yet somehow missed him completely.

He was the only sorcerer in the country other than Frederick's father.

He glanced toward Frederick.

"No," was all Frederick said.

And maybe he had a point. He'd already stressed that the duke would kill Jay as soon as look at him. But what was to stop him killing Jay if he ever found that Jay existed?

"He wasn't the one to start the pogrom," Frederick murmured. "I doubt he has any interest in tracking you down. He simply won't want you stepping into his life. If you do nothing to interfere with his world, he won't interfere with yours. He's..." Frederick paused a while. "Selfish," he finally said.

"I suppose that we all are, in our own way," Jay sighed. "We all want to protect those we love."

Frederick smiled faintly. "To the death," he murmured.

Jay couldn't disagree.

THIRTY-FIVE

IT TOOK a couple of weeks for things to settle back down to some semblance of normal. Han was able to go back to work, and while his evenings were then dominated by Council meetings, they managed to chew through the majority of the admin tasks pretty fast, and could get back to one meeting a week after that was sorted out.

Han, Ellis, and Barb all had experience with running their own businesses which helped to streamline all that stuff. They knew how to create workflows, delegate tasks, manage projects, and craft lines of effective communication, and within that fortnight they had appointed new Vassals — largely chosen at random from vampires dotted across the city who had the most diverse skillsets around — and invited a few new faces to become Constables.

Han hadn't so much as tried to use Richard's invisibility. He felt sick just knowing he even had it, and the idea of trying to kick-start it felt like a step toward accepting what he'd done.

He wasn't ready for that.

One day he'd need to have a private chat with Ellis, though. They'd both done the unthinkable, only Ellis wasn't aware that Han knew, and Han wanted to know how the hell he was supposed to reconcile it all.

He felt like there was a storm on the horizon. He couldn't shake the visceral knowledge of what he'd done to protect Jay, and he couldn't keep from questioning the lie he'd told both to himself and to his husband.

Who the hell pulled someone's head off and *didn't* expect it to kill them?

It was bullshit. Maybe even at the time it was bullshit he'd believed, but looking back with the perfect vision of hindsight it was even more obvious that he hadn't acted out of some childish urge to pull wings off a fly as though Richard would learn from it.

No.

He'd set out to kill.

Han could try and justify it all he wanted. After all, Richard had tried to kill Jay, and then made it clear he was going to keep on trying until he succeeded. Han had tried negotiation with Richard and it had failed so spectacularly that everything which happened since was Han's fault. Richard running to the Council, the deaths, the revolution, all of it had been kicked off by Han trying to talk things over with a guy who had the mentality of a toddler.

Jay insisted it wasn't fair for Han to blame himself. Barb's revolution had been in the planning stages since before they'd even met her, he pointed out. Things would have come to a head there sooner or later, maybe even with more bloodshed, if Barb's hand hadn't been forced.

Jay was far too reasonable sometimes. Together they could defeat anything with logic and rationale.

Han just needed to remember that not every threat was rational.

"I think I've got it." Jay strode into the living room, iPad in his hand.

Han looked up from his book. "The herps?"

"Don't be gross, sweetie." Jay grinned and turned the screen to face Han. "I think I've worked out how to make spells from scratch."

Han slid a bookmark into his book and put it on the table before he looked at the screen. There was a circle on it which touched the edges of the display, and it was lined with sigils. Beneath it was a short piece of text in English.

Dear Universe,

It would be awfully nice if you could grant the listed permissions to the wearer of this pendant.

Thank you.

Han blinked. "Is that a spell?"

"Yes!" Jay hopped on the spot, which made the iPad's screen auto-rotate to try and keep up with him.

"What pendant?"

Jay plucked a necklace from his trouser pocket, and a military-style dog tag hung from it. Both the necklace and dog tag were black. "This one! It was on sale. It's stainless steel."

Han pursed his lips. He wasn't sure whether he liked the implications of a dog tag, but at least it wasn't gold. "Don't spells have to be in Latin?"

"Ah, well!" Jay waggled his finger, and the necklace swung from his fist with the movement. "Apparently if you're the first person ever to invent a spell, you get to do it however the hell you want. Latin might be easier, but I don't speak it, and I didn't want to run to Frederick for every little thing. If this doesn't work I can go back to the drawing board." He grinned. "And I thought that with a pendant you could take it off if ever you wanted to sneak into places. If I cast it on your wedding ring and you lost it, I'd have to withhold sex rights, maybe forever."

Han shuddered at the thought. "Okay. So, what do we do?"

"Hopefully very little!" Jay put the iPad down on the table and carefully piled the necklace in the centre of the circle, then he gave the screen a quick tap to keep it awake.

Han kept his mouth shut as Jay held his hands over the iPad and read the words of his spell out loud. He heard Jay's heart pick up speed, and saw the tiny muscles in his eyes and face begin to move toward a smile that broadcast excitement before Jay's features had even shifted into a broad grin.

Still, Han decided to play it cool. "Did it work?"

"Yes!" Jay squealed loudly and snatched up the necklace, swinging it back and forth as he gazed at it. "Oh, wow! That's brilliant! I'll have to load a bunch of spells onto the iPad. It'll make things so much quicker! Here, try it on!" He thrust the necklace toward Han and bit his lip.

Han took it and slipped it over his head.

He didn't feel any different, but at least it wasn't making him scream.

Jay took several steps back, like he expected something to happen, then he bounced on his toes again. "Oh my god! Okay, now try it!"

Han raised an eyebrow, then reached for the iPad and tapped it, fully expecting it to ignore his touch.

The image scrolled under his fingertips.

Han blinked slowly. It had to be a trick of the light. Maybe the screen just tried to scroll because he'd nudged it.

He hit the home button and pulled up a browser, then typed in a URL.

It worked.

No stylus. Just his fingers.

"Oh my god," he breathed.

"Get up! Get up," Jay squeaked as he bounced in close and grabbed Han's arm to drag him to his feet.

Han stood, feeling numb. This seemed too good to be true. Jay hadn't cracked it, had he?

Jay whipped out his phone and leaned in. "Say cheese!"

Han blinked.

The shutter clicked.

The phone had snapped them both.

"Ahhhh!" Jay flapped his hands with so much excitement that he almost threw his phone across the room.

Han backed away. He stepped around the sofa, then turned and ran for the bathroom.

To the mirror above the sink.

Where his reflection waited.

Shit, the gold of his eyes really *was* obvious, even without the glow.

Jay ran in after him, tears brimming in his eyes, cheeks flushed with his jubilation. "Obviously we'll need to test it," he breathed. "We can't just assume I managed to remember everything that might be a problem."

Han nodded slowly. It was hard to tear his attention off the mirror.

He still owned a face.

It was hard to put into words the toll it took not being able to confirm that he truly existed. To rely on touch for styling his hair or brushing his teeth or even knowing that he'd cleaned himself properly. To need Jay to tell him that his eyes weren't dark brown any more.

To remain convinced that he was a person.

But now his reflection was back, now he could use a touchscreen, he was back in the game.

He grinned slowly, and drew Jay into his arms.

"You," he whispered, "are a genius."

"I am!" Jay beamed, and his joyful tears were blinked free of his eyes.

"But if we do refine it, can we not make it dog tags?"

Jay laughed at that. "Okay. Fine. Cross my heart." He leaned in for a kiss, and gripped Han's shoulders. "Love you, sweetie."

"Love you," Han replied. "My husband."

Things were looking up.

TOOTH & CLAW

Blind Man's Wolf

Blood Moon Rising

Balance of Power

Monsters Within

Mirror Flower, Water Moon

Visit https://ravenswordpress.com to discover more about the characters and world of Tooth & Claw, and to sign up to the newsletter.

Join the Discord server at https://ravenswordpress.com/discord.

ACKNOWLEDGMENTS

Mirror Flower, Water Moon was absolutely necessary after Monsters Within. I left Ellis in a state where he was quite literally falling apart (much as my life was in 2018, frankly) and needed outside help from his friends that he wasn't in any condition to ask for. Also, I'd always known what Han's power would be, and felt it would be way more fun to find out alongside him, rather than from Ellis' perspective.

That and I love throwing out the occasional "other guys" perspective.

We'll be back with Ellis and Randall for the next instalment, though!

If you'd like to get sneak peeks of upcoming releases, why not join my Discord server? You can find it here:

https://ravenswordpress.com/discord

Love,

Amelia Faulkner, London UK, July 2024.

ABOUT THE AUTHOR

Raised on a steady diet of Star Trek and Doctor Who, Amelia Faulkner stood no chance in not becoming a grade-A geek. They have sat on the board of the British Fantasy Society, contributed fiction and fluff to various published roleplaying games, and written non-fiction for SciFiNow and SFX Magazines. For every positive there is an equal and opposite negative, and Amelia is forced to admit that they love Wild Wild West.

In their spare time they enjoy travel, photography, walking their Corgi, and trying to convince their friends to replay the Pathfinder Adventure Card Game with all the Goblins decks.

RAVENSWORDPRESS.COM